CHASING DR. BANKS

Chasing Dr. Banks

J.O. SPENGLER

Play Well 360 LLC

Contents

This book is dedicated to the memory of my father, Dr. John Robert Spengler, the greatest man I have ever known. It is a hard thing to write a novel, and it is only by his encouragement, and support of my dream, that this book exists. My undying gratitude also goes to my talented daughter and listening ear, Caroline Spengler, my supportive wife and life-partner, Mariah, and my wonderful son and voice of reason, Matthew Spengler. I am also greatly blessed with amazing friends - Allie Renee, Laura Meherg, John Strickland, Ellen McCown Schwab, and John Molesworth - to name a few - who provided valuable feedback and support throughout my journey. Also, many thanks to Bill Newton who provided important editorial advice at the outset of this project, and gave it the necessary kick-start. Very special thanks goes to my copy-editor, Brooklyn Jongeling, and cover design artist, Dallis Foshee. Brooklyn provided essential editorial support through the many iterations of the manuscript. She was an absolute pleasure to work with, and a person I would highly recommend having on your team if you are writing a book. Dallis, a highly talented artist, and designer, created the artwork for the cover. Her extraordinary artistic talent, I believe, speaks for itself.

Chapter 1

Cut and Run

HAVING MAPPED OUT an escape plan, and knowing that I would need to sleep, if that were possible, I made my way to the guest room in the back of the house. I checked to see that the window nearest my bed — the one opening to the back porch — was unlocked, and laid down on top of the covers, fully clothed and with my shoes on. As the night wore on, exhaustion overcame me, and I was carried into a fitful sleep.

Sometime later I began to dream. I was in a coffee shop with my trusted attorney and friend, Gary, talking about fishing, and with him asking about my job and plans for the semester. Suddenly, like a glitch in a film where the scene skips ahead a few frames, the serenity of the dream was shattered, replaced by something dark and surreal.

The coffee shop had become a prison, with me inside a cell and my attorney yelling to me through the prison bars something barely discernable over a symphony of loud noises. There was an urgency in his voice, and I struggled to comprehend what he was saying. Then the mist of the dream lifted somewhat, and three words echoed through my brain — "Go, Go, Go!"

A jolt of adrenaline ran through me as I lay half-awake in bed, my conscious and subconscious mind playing tug of war inside my brain. The dream continued to play out in slow motion until the image of a jail cell and his words slowly faded, replaced by — when my eyes shot open — the faint outline of my darkened room and the sound of stern voices from somewhere beyond. Where exactly it came from was impossible to tell, something that my disoriented brain couldn't quite discern.

In the next moment, I had bolted fully awake and sat up in a cold sweat with fear coursing through me and my heart pounding. I now realized, to my great dismay and utter dread, that the loud noise and hardened voices were very real and seemed to have come from the front door. My attorney had been right about the possibility that this nightmare — a SWAT team coming to arrest me — could happen sooner than later. At this thought another emotion, anger, flooded my brain to stand beside my fear. My crooked colleagues had framed me for digging too deeply into their shady affairs, and I was now paying a steep price for their vengeance.

My feet had just hit the floor when a bright light, shining through the cracks framing my door, speared through the room. I reasoned the agents had just breached the front door and were flooding the house with light before fully entering.

Someone was yelling through a bullhorn, "Dr. Banks, come out of the house with your hands above your head. Do not resist. If you do not come out immediately, we will enter by force!"

The shock and awe tactic, as I had lectured to the students in my criminal law class, was a favorite of law enforcement, and was successful in apprehending suspects with minimal resistance. They must have known the layout of my house and suspected that I would be sleeping in my bedroom near the front. What they didn't know was that I was sleeping in the guest room in the back corner of the house, chosen for its access by window to the covered back porch where my bike, and any hope of escape, was waiting.

Despite the commotion coming from beyond my door that had triggered no small amount of anxiety, I steeled myself to the task at hand. I quietly and deliberately grabbed my go-bag, then opened and slipped through the window facing the porch, silently closing it behind me. I took a deep breath of the wintry night air that still held the scent of a recent rain. It steadied my nerves.

My eyes scanned the backyard for any sign of federal agents, but thankfully there were none. Their assembled forces were concentrated on the front of the house, likely expecting the show of force to flush out a humble college professor without resistance.

There was no way I was coming out peaceably with my hands in the air. Too much was at stake and I needed time to clear my name.

Several steps across the old wooden slabs of the porch decking brought me to my bike. My hands closed around the handlebars, damp with moisture from the humid air, as I walked my bike down the short set of steps leading off the porch.

So far, so good, as they say.

Just as I was clearing the last step, I said to myself in silent satisfaction, Noah, you were smart to heed the advice of your attorney and prepare for this inevitability. You might just have a chance of escape.

As if the fates had sensed my misplaced confidence, a loud boom assaulted my senses, sending shockwaves through my mind and body. I fought to keep my balance, but lost the fight with stability and gravity, toppling sideways with my bike in tow and hitting the wet, cold ground hard. I breathed in the strong musky smell of long-dead leaves and winter earth and succumbed for a moment to the certainty of capture.

After announcing their presence and waiting long enough to see whether I would come out peacefully and voluntarily, I reasoned while lying beside my toppled bike, the FBI must have thought that I was resisting and tossed a flash bang grenade into the house. I knew this was another tactic often used by the authorities to subdue a suspect, and which was usually one-hundred percent effective. In close range, it was blinding and deafening and would incapacitate anyone who wasn't prepared to avoid the brunt of the blast. Even outside the house, it had laid me out.

As I lay on the ground considering defeat, a thought occurred to me.

If they were coming after me with this amount of force, it didn't bode well for what would happen once I was apprehended. My enemies were taking no chances and wanted me silenced in a big way.

This thought, and the extra shot of fear injected into my senses, sent a burst of adrenaline through my veins that brought me quickly upright, still clutching my bike. Knowing that panic was my greatest enemy, I took a deep breath, regained my composure, and quickly walked my bike down a narrow trail that led through a dense stand of holly bushes behind my house. Branches on either side tugged at my clothes and snapped along the side of my bike as I fought my way through and out of their grasp. Exiting the shrubbery, I entered a small clearing that ended at a 6-foot tall wooden fence marking the boundary between my house and that of my neighbor Frank, a salesperson who was seldom home.

Though it looked like a dead-end, I knew better. Frank and I were friends, often sharing a coffee or beer together, and had long ago agreed that I could pass through his property as a shortcut to the road leading to the river. This was a route that I would often take, under better circumstances, when I wanted to enjoy the freedom, physical exertion and exhilaration that comes from riding my bike. We had loosened a section of fence to allow me to access his driveway. I would slide the loose boards to the side and then replace them when I had passed through, with the fence appearing solid once again.

Never in my wildest dreams would I have suspected the opportunity this afforded me under the current circumstances. *One just never knew.*

Running for my freedom and with this small blessing set before me, I slipped through and replaced the boards. Mounting my bike, I shot down Frank's driveway, through the sleepy neighborhood, and on to the main road leading toward the river where my kayak was stashed. Racing away, I quickly checked my watch and saw that it was almost 6 a.m. It was still pitch dark this time of the morning in the dead of winter, but I knew that sunrise would be coming soon.

As I pedaled down the road in the dark that would soon give way to a gray dawn, I felt a strange sense of freedom and exhilaration, having escaped my pursuers. I had planned my escape so that they wouldn't know that I had been in the house only moments before. The bed was made, the window was shut, and I had left no trace that I had either been in that room or escaped from it. It would also take a close inspection to find the loose boards on the fence that allowed me to pass through. They would figure it out eventually, I was sure, but this hopefully bought me enough time to make it to the river and the next stage of my escape.

Once on the water, I thought to myself, *I should be home free.*

I could feel my heart beating strongly in my chest as I pedaled down the lonesome strip of black asphalt in the predawn darkness with the cold fresh air of a recent winter rain filling my lungs. The road ran mostly through empty fields and forests as it wound its way toward the river, with trees bearing branches free of leaves that appeared in the darkness of the gathering dawn like crowds of supporters cheering me on. Thankfully, I hadn't seen any real people, or even a car, on the ride to this point. Even so, I could sense the hounds at my heels as I rolled through the countryside, expecting at any moment to see flashing red and blue lights cutting through the darkness behind me.

I pedaled on until I began to see the familiar signs — an abandoned farmhouse with a painted image atop in faded red and black lettering beckoning all to "See Rock City," a huge dead oak tree with its bare branches stretched wide, and a familiar field that in the summer promised a pick-your-own harvest of fresh blueberries — that told me I was nearing the river.

Even though I could now see the first traces of daylight, visibility was still poor. Also, the road remained wet from the recent rain. Like a horse nearing the comfort and familiarity of the barn, however, I increased my speed and raced toward the safety of the river.

The final turn was coming up, and the part of my brain in charge of self-preservation warned me that I was going too fast. As an experienced cyclist, I knew as soon as I entered the curve and my center of gravity had shifted on the slick pavement that I was in trouble. Time seemed to slow to a crawl as I felt the tread of my tire slowly lose its grip on the road. It was a sickening sensation, where all that remained was the helpless inevitability of a crash that would likely leave me with an injury — a severe road rash or broken bones among the painful possibilities.

The sideways slide slowly drew me closer to the ground, moving across asphalt, loose gravel, and finally the bare earth that framed the road. Facing forward, I didn't see the boulder that would put a jarring and forceful end to my slide, while destroying my tire and causing me to be thrown through the air like a rag doll.

I recall the sensation of briefly flying with no feeling of fear, just a detached fascination. The next thing I remember is lying on a muddy patch of ground and wondering about the extent of the injuries that would surely result from such a serious crash.

The world spun for a moment or two as my mind raced to catch up with what had happened. I slowly sat up, expecting the worst, but to my great relief, all my body parts seemed to function. My hands could grip, my elbows bend, my back, shoulders, and hips were good, and my legs, ankles and feet still worked. It was truly a miracle. I wondered how I could have been uninjured in such a major crash. The rational part of my brain could not make sense of it.

I rose and stood. I still felt fine. My clothes and hair were muddy and wet, but somehow, miraculously, I was unharmed except for some minor aches and pains and a few scratches. With all the dreadful things that had happened to me recently, I took this as a good omen, knowing that from here on out, I would need all the luck I could get.

As I picked up my backpack, I noticed another bit of good luck. My computer was intact — the documents and other contents were unharmed, and even my bottle of single malt scotch had somehow survived unscathed. I thanked the heavens above, then grabbed my pack, picked up my wrecked bike and walked the last fifty yards to the river.

When I arrived at the riverbank, I decided to throw my wrecked bike into the deep, dark swirling waters of the river to eliminate the chance that anyone would happen upon my bike and put two and two together. Even though it was an older bike and now had a broken frame, cracked handlebar, and twisted front tire, it was tough to let it go. I had ridden this bike over countless miles and in all kinds of weather, and it was now like a good friend. I realized, though, that the last good thing this friend could do for me was to help me get away.

I needed to make a clean escape and not leave any breadcrumbs behind for anyone to follow.

After watching my bike sink into the dark waters, I turned and walked into the woods that lined the river. I was relieved to find my kayak where I had left it — hidden in a shallow cave behind some brush on a low rise just out of the flood zone. I pulled it down to the riverside and removed my paddle and a bag from inside one of the airtight compartments. My kayak was the sit-on-top type, perfect for deep, wide rivers and other large bodies of water given a hull design that made it both maneuverable and stable in rough waters. It also had ample storage compartments fore and aft that would hold my belongings and collapsible paddle.

I listened intently for any signs of pursuit over the thundering of the river but heard nothing out of place. Satisfied, I reached down and stashed my go-bag in a waterproof compartment. I then pulled out my paddle and assembled it and, after donning my dry-suit, eased my boat off the bank, jumped in, and paddled into the downstream current. The river was running high from the recent rain, a fortunate condition that would allow me to reach my destination, gliding across the white-capped river, with greater speed.

The darkness of dawn had now given way to the early light of day. The overcast sky drained the landscape of color, casting the scenery in a dark gray, but it was still a beautiful sight to me. The river promised freedom, and my mood lifted as I pulled hard on my paddle and felt the blade bite through the water.

The rhythm of my movements as I paddled strongly with the current provided the same sense of serenity that it always had, even as I fled for my freedom. I loved the water. The river I was on, the Arkansas River, would eventually drain into the mighty Mississippi and on to the Gulf of Mexico. The water, when clear and free of sediment, usually had a blue-green appearance. It had a steel-gray hue that dampened the colors though on this chilly winter day. Maybe it was my circumstances, and the river being my savior as it held me in its watery embrace, but it had never looked more beautiful to me.

As I worked my way downstream, I stayed close to shore and near the overhang of a rock face that gave way to a gradual sloping bank and stands of evergreens interspersed with leafless trees lining the riverbank. Outside of Delray University, and the university town of Delray, the area was mostly rural, making it a natural destination for outdoor enthusiasts. I paddled on, enjoying the solitude, occasionally dipping my hand into the icy water to feel the current and deepen the sense of connectedness to the river I so loved. I never felt more at home than on the river.

Further downstream and past the last signs of habitation of Delray, the banks became thick with trees. The cabin would not be far ahead, sitting adjacent to the Holden National Wildlife Refuge. I had to keep my eyes peeled, as the only indication that I had reached the boundary of the wildlife refuge was a small sign on the riverbank. The cabin, and my destination, was on the downstream side of the refuge, just outside, but adjacent to this natural wonder. The refuge was home to some of the State's last remaining old-growth forest, as well as all sorts of wildlife.

The paddle down river was uneventful, but I was still quite happy to see the landmarks that indicated I was nearing my destination.

There it was. Beyond a large Hickory tree that I used as a mental marker lay a small grassy patch of earth that held the faint outline of a trail. I pulled up to the spot, giving my boat an extra bit of paddle power so that it would slide partly onto the bank, climbed forward in my kayak to avoid stepping out into the cold shallow water, and jumped deftly to dry ground.

Standing on the bank and looking out upon the river, my legs began to shake as a well of emotions swirled within me. I resisted the urge to fall to my knees and let those emotions overtake me, and instead turned my back to the river and toward the path that would lead me to the secluded cabin that would act as my temporary sanctuary.

I was free for now, and quite thankful, but knew that it would take every ounce of resourcefulness, help from those I trusted, and a good bit of luck to escape my pursuers and outwit the dark forces behind it all who sought to silence me.

Chapter 2

Forbidden Territory

(One Week Prior)

LOOSE GRAVEL CRUNCHED under my tires, disturbing the stillness of the chilly January night, as I entered the deserted parking lot. Pulling into an empty parking space, I caught sight of the building in which I had spent much of my adult working life. I was on the campus of Delray University, smack dab in one of the most picturesque places on the planet, near the banks of the Arkansas River and not far from the city of Pine Bluff, Arkansas.

Delray was the second largest private university in the country, a real powerhouse among universities. Even though I had been here countless times before, to teach my classes, conduct research and perform the countless other tasks that were asked of faculty, this was the first time that I, Dr. Noah Banks, a professor, and administrator, had approached my workplace in a cold sweat.

My heart pounded and stomach churned as I thought about my reason for being here on this lonely night. It was late in the evening on the last weekend of our winter break, and the campus was eerily quiet.

An empty college campus always gave me a profound feeling of loneliness. Tonight, it also gave me a powerful sense of foreboding. My reason for coming here was wrong on many levels, but this was about self-preservation, and as the old saying goes, *desperate times call for desperate measures.*

I had pulled in next to the only other vehicle in the parking lot — a blue and white sedan with a logo of Delray University's mascot, *the River Monster*, proudly adorning the passenger door. Our college, the College of Liberal Arts and Sciences, loaned these vehicles out to faculty and staff for travel on official university business. Since faculty and staff had not yet returned from winter break, it sat empty and alone.

I turned off the engine, not wanting to draw attention to myself, should a campus cop drive past and decide to investigate. Though it was the smart move, I knew the cold of the January night would quickly fill the inside of my truck with its wintry tentacles. I sat in silence for a few long minutes, lost in thought, and considered my options as the windows slowly began to fog. I needed to move, even though what I was planning was unthinkable. I was planning to break into the business office of the Department of Sociology's venerable and well-funded Fin-Mar Research Institute.

The Institute was co-directed by Dr. Patricia Marshall and Dr. Howard Finch, two of the most powerful and influential faculty on campus. They were serious rain-makers, raking in millions of dollars in research funding every year — but also corrupt, and as vindictive as hell. Patricia was ordinary looking, with an athletic build for a woman in her fifties, and hair dyed an unnatural shade of silver that framed a face with hawkish features. It was her eyes, though, that caught your attention. They were black as coal, with the cold and menacing gaze of a viper.

Howard, by contrast, was a tall man in his early sixties with drab, dark brown hair, a bulbous nose, and large belly that seemed to hold an endless amount of fried chicken and sweet tea, his food and drink of choice. He had a brooding demeanor, and despite the earring he often sported to elude the norm, was very much the sharp and acerbic academic. He was also a major pain in the ass.

I had the *privilege* of serving as their department head and direct supervisor which made me responsible for their actions. They didn't see it that way however and made it perfectly clear that they were neither subject to my authority, nor beholden to anyone else in the college. In other words, they believed themselves to be above the law — and in many ways, maybe they were.

I opened the door to my truck and stepped out into the cold January night. My objective was the large building housing the Sociology Department that sat across the street from the parking lot. Though only a light jacket and t-shirt stood between me and the frosty winter air, I could hardly feel the humid chill of the night.

I might attribute my indifference to the cold to my single-minded purpose on this particular evening, but I was also used to some discomfort. In my mid-forties, I was a bit of an outdoor fitness freak, biking, kayaking, trail running and hiking whenever I had the chance, regardless of the weather. My active lifestyle kept me in shape, helping me avoid the middle-age spare-tire. My appearance was the opposite of the view most people had of academics — the deskbound, frumpy old professor tucked away in the ivory tower — as I was tall and athletic with chestnut brown hair that had only begun to gray, and clear, blue eyes that still held a youthful glint.

As I approached the building, the familiar surroundings calmed my nerves slightly — but only slightly. I fumbled for my keys, found them, and used them to open the door. Entering the building, the red lights from the emergency exit signs cast an ominous glow down the branching hallways. The familiarity that only moments before had soothed me, was now replaced by the irrational fear that someone was lurking behind every door and dark corner, waiting to ambush me. *A cold chill coursed down my spine.*

I picked up the pace, moving from a fast walk into a slow jog down the dark and lonely corridors of the building I knew so well. The Institute comprised a set of offices and suites at the far end of the building, beyond the individual offices occupied by department faculty and staff. It was an area where even I, as the department head and supervisor of faculty working in the Institute, was forbidden to enter. The rationale was that the Institute housed personally identifiable information and other records related to research and financials that were the property of the Institute and "best only handled by those directly responsible."

I suspected they were hiding something — and had a good idea what it was.

As my heart rate accelerated and fear threatened to overwhelm me, I considered turning around and going home. Still, my footsteps continued down the empty hallway even in the face of immense risk.

Sometimes the only way out is through.

As if drawn by some invisible force, I arrived at the front door of the Institute. The entrance felt imposing, with floor to ceiling frosted glass windows framing a large wooden door with intricate carvings etched across its surface. The adjacent wall proclaimed in large lettering that this was indeed the Fin-Mar Research Institute.

Such a self-serving title, I thought — the name derived from the last names of Finch and Marshall, two of the most selfish and egotistical faculty on campus.

These same people were staring down at me from their gilded picture frames, each placed and spaced to ensure that no-one could miss them, and to remind all who entered that they held a place above everyone else. This lit a quiet flame of anger within me, quelling any hesitation to continue my quest.

A few days earlier, I had palmed a master key while visiting the dean's secretary. It was just lying there on the far end of her desk, begging to be picked up. With the master key, I could gain access to any area of the building. It was a crime of opportunity.

Opportunity was knocking again, so I quietly opened the door and entered the sacred halls of the Institute without a sound.

Vastly different than the hard linoleum that floored the hallways of the rest of the building, here my feet were met with the luxurious feel of an expensive carpet that graced the floors of the Institute. While I was disgusted that so much money was evidently spent as a demonstration of wealth and prestige, I was thankful that it allowed me to move down the halls without a sound.

I was looking for the business office and, even though I had never been here, knew where to find it. Once, when we were coordinating office moves within the building, I was given a map with the location of offices here. I recalled the general location from my examination of the map and, with only one missed turn, found the hallway and then the entrance to the business office.

This was where I hoped to find evidence that would prove wrongdoing on the part of Howard and Patricia. Near the end of last semester, a disgruntled student and former Institute staffer had entered my office unannounced and shared a thumb drive with internal files, along with her suspicion that the Institute was involved in shady dealings — the crux of which was the setting up of a secret corporation to divert donor monies, and state and federal grant funds, to Howard and Patricia's personal accounts. Though the information contained in the files was not conclusive of wrongdoing, it *was* enough to trigger a duty to report this suspicious activity to the university. The university auditors conducted a cursory investigation that went nowhere, and which only served to put me in Finch and Patricia's crosshairs. I knew that it was only a matter of time before they engaged in some serious retaliation.

If only I could find that key piece of incriminating evidence before they made their move.

Holding my breath, I inserted the key into the business office door and turned the handle. The satisfying *click* of the lock disengaging met my ears and I stepped inside, silently closing the door behind me. The central office was spacious, with cubicles for staff and row upon row of filing cabinets.

The room was illuminated by the faint glow of night lights placed along the walls, providing enough light for me to see my way around without the need for a flashlight. This was helpful, but also disconcerting, as I would be visible to anyone passing by the window facing the hallway. I just had to hope that no-one would be crazy enough to be here on a Saturday night.

Along the far wall, just past the last row of filing cabinets, I spotted the doors of two faculty offices and immediately recognized the names on brass plates proclaiming the occupants — Dr. Patricia Marshall and Dr. Howard Finch.

As I moved further into the room and near the row of filing cabinets adjacent to the faculty offices, I heard a faint sound that I couldn't quite place. I ducked behind the row of cabinets and waited, my heart threatening to pound out of my chest.

Where had the sound come from, and what was it? It wasn't the sound of someone talking. It sounded more like a low moan. *There it was again!* It was almost rhythmic in the way it sounded.

I thought to myself, *God, if someone is in here, I am totally screwed!*

My mind told me that it was impossible that anyone would be here on a weekend night before the term started — and it didn't make sense that the sound would come from a person. It was probably just the air vent, or a portable heater or fan that someone had left on.

Regardless, I crouched low behind the row of cabinets and waited for several minutes before proceeding. I now felt a new sense of urgency. Since I didn't know where to start, and didn't know any of the computer passwords, I decided to search the closest filing cabinets.

I made short work of the flimsy lock on the nearest cabinet with my fixed-blade knife and opened drawers, using my pen light to go quickly through the files. Searching through the files, I couldn't shake a sense of foreboding and the feeling that I was not alone. A silent clock was ticking down in my head. It was probably just nerves, coupled with the strange sounds I had heard, and the fact that I was creeped out being in this empty building on this night, of all nights, when no-one in their right mind should be here. *But still —*

Pushing my anxieties aside, I continued to search and soon hit pay dirt. I had stumbled upon several files and a few loose papers that appeared to hold records of financial dealings between the Institute and other people and entities. I didn't have time to read through them, so I quickly gathered up the papers and closed the filing cabinet.

With the documents in hand, my only desire was to get the heck out of Dodge. The hairs were standing on the back of my neck, and I couldn't shake the feeling that someone was watching me. The rational part of my mind told me, though, that I was alone and there was no need to worry. I would have certainly heard footsteps or a door opening if someone else were here.

Noah, I said to myself, *get a grip.*

I was ready to bolt for the door when a thought came to me. I had a key to Dr. Marshall's office — and I might never have the opportunity again. I just couldn't pass up the opportunity to do a quick search of her office. *Who knew what I might find?*

With my mind wavering between reason and impulse, I followed the latter and quickly slid the key in the lock before I had a chance to change my mind.

When the door swung open, it became abundantly clear that I had made an *unbelievably* bad decision. Standing in the doorway — in shock and bewilderment — my mind struggled to make sense of the scene before me. On the floor lay Dr. Marshall and Associate Provost Dr. Amos Snow, who, with platinum blonde hair and porcelain-white skin, appeared as a ghostly apparition in the semi-darkness. The two were engaged in a level of intimacy that would have made a prison guard blush. It had long been rumored that Patricia and Snow were awfully close, but this brought it to a whole new level. It is said that the brain will sometimes shut out particularly stressful and traumatic experiences as a protective mechanism — and my currently overloaded brain was doing just that as I quickly looked away. It was now clear, however, that the moan that I thought I had heard earlier was *indeed* a moan – and it had come from *this* office.

As I turned to flee this nightmare, Patricia's angry voice rang out, "Stop right there!

I turned and looked back. As comprehension of who stood before her shone in her wicked eyes, she asked in her most condescending voice, "What are *you* doing here?"

Then, in a tone that was stunningly cruel, she said forcefully, "Noah Banks, your life is over!"

I gasped, with my throat empty of words, then turned and ran with all my might toward the door to the business office that led to the hallway and beyond — anywhere but this cursed place. Blinded by fear and racing through the semi-darkened room, I failed to notice the hulking figure blocking the doorway. It was Dr. Howard Finch. At six feet, two inches tall, sporting an earring and faded ballcap and, with his unshaved face and ruddy complexion no doubt the product of a night of drinking, Finch at this moment looked more like a bounty hunter than an academic. I could smell the stale odor of tobacco and whiskey on his rancid breath as my mind raced to understand why he was in the building on a weekend night.

Instead of merely blocking my escape, Finch grabbed my arms and held me tight in an iron grip. It occurred to me that although he was much older, he was extraordinarily strong for his age. I struggled against his grip but stopped as I realized that Finch had cast his gaze in the direction of the office. *We both froze.*

Patricia, having quickly donned a pair of pants, and a sweater to cover her naked torso, appeared like an evil phantom in the doorway — the force of her malignant aura drawing our attention her way.

Finch broke the spell, spewing out words on his whiskey-infused breath saying, "Look what we have here Patricia. A little mouse has lost his way," adding, "Patricia, if you would be so kind as to call the campus police, I'll keep Dr. Banks in my care until they arrive."

Sensing a slight loosening of Finch's grip and fueled by fear and adrenaline, I threw out an elbow, striking Finch hard in the jaw. Momentarily stunned, Finch released his grip. I then leaned and drove my shoulder hard into his ample belly, knocking him into a cubicle and sending him tumbling.

Spinning away, I sprinted out of the business office, dropping a few loose papers in my haste to escape. Racing first down the carpeted hallways of the Institute, and then down the halls beyond — my shoes pounding across the linoleum-tiled floors — I never slowed. As I reached the exit, I chanced a look back and saw that the darkened hallway was empty.

Pushing through the doors, I flew across the street to the parking lot and, upon reaching my truck, breathlessly jumped in and started the ignition. In the next moment, my truck was fish-tailing out of the parking lot, loose gravel spinning beneath my wheels.

Chapter 3

Taking Stock

LEAVING THE CAMPUS in my rearview mirror, I drove aimlessly along familiar backroads in an effort to calm my nerves and process all that had happened on this fateful night. There were many questions, most of which I suspected the answer — and none of the answers were good.

There was one thing I knew for sure. Given my actions tonight, I would now be considered a threat to the university — and that was *not* a good thing.

Looking down at the passenger seat beside me, I took comfort in knowing that I had at least come away with several folders stuffed full of papers that might hold important clues to the suspicious activities of my colleagues.

I couldn't do this alone, however, and right now, advice from a trusted friend would be more valuable than gold.

I knew just who to call.

Pulling to the side of the road next to an abandoned field with a low mist rising from the earth, I picked up my cellphone and hit the number for my long-time friend and Delray University colleague, Ted Hartmann. It was late on a weekend night, and I held my breath through several rings, not knowing whether he would answer.

Given the late hour, I was relieved when Ted answered. I could tell that I had disturbed him from a sound sleep, and knew that with four young children, Ted needed all the sleep he could get.

My best friend answered in a groggy voice. "Hey Noah. Is that you? It must be important for you to call this late. You know that I'm usually in bed by this time."

"I'm sorry Ted," I said, my voice laced with guilt for waking him. "I knew that you would probably be sleeping but I'm in trouble and need your help and advice."

"No problem," came the expected reply. "I'll be right over."

Wait" I said. "I could really use a beer. How about we meet at the River's Edge Bar and Grill. It shouldn't be too busy with school still out of session."

"OK," came the reply, and ten minutes later, with the documents I had taken from the Institute in tow, I was rolling into the near-empty parking lot.

The River's Edge was one of my favorite spots for a tasty lunch, or a good beer and apps at night. The place had a ton of character, having been frequented by many people over the years who had shared good times with friends and colleagues. There were dollar bills taped to the walls, many of which were signed by past patrons; a beautiful, wide mahogany bar; and tables and booths with names, hearts and some colorful language carved into them with pocketknives or kitchen utensils. The management was long past caring about this innocent vandalism, as it added character to the establishment. It was also a comfortable place, frequented more by university faculty and staff than students or the hard partying types. It made for a good place to talk.

Ted arrived as I was finishing my first beer and ordering my second. Sitting at a booth in the main room across from the entrance, I saw him enter and waved him over. Ted was easy to recognize, as he was tall and athletic, an endurance athlete who had run most of the major marathons, with a mop of reddish-brown hair and bright green eyes that held a keen intelligence. We greeted each other with a handshake, and he sat down across from me in the booth. I was lucky to have a friend like Ted. He was one of the few people whom I could completely trust.

Carol, a waitress we knew well from our prior visits, came over to our table and said in her sweet southern drawl, "It is good to see you two in here tonight. It's kind of lonely with the students and most of the faculty still out on break. Ted honey, what will it be?"

Enjoying the moment, Ted replied, "It is always good to see you too Carol. I'll have the usual double IPA on tap."

"Coming right up, hun," Carol replied, and was off to place the order with the bartender.

Now that we were alone, I could read the concern on Ted's face. We had been through a lot together and braved the university process and system, both having moved up the ranks from assistant to full professor. It was a brutal process, with success often based as much on politics as actual accomplishments in teaching, research, and service. While I was a sociology professor, Ted worked in the Political Science Department. He was a well-known and well-respected scholar in his field.

Ted waited patiently for me to get my act together and form my thoughts. I was sure that he could see the strain in my features and body language. I told him succinctly, and in a detached, academic sort of way, all that had transpired earlier.

Ted listened intently, and I knew that what would come next would be what I needed the most. He would question me like a personal injury trial lawyer who smelled a big pay day. He had a knack for getting to the point and finding the key facts and issues that would help lead to a solution.

This time, however, Ted surprised me.

He said, "Noah, you are a great friend with unquestionable ethics and a great mind, but this time I think you are in way over your head with few, if any, options. We both know that the university is the unblinking beast, and you are in the belly of the beast now. The university will now perceive you as a serious threat. When this happens, nine times out of ten, they will move to get you out. The usual path is for them to give you an option: agree to leave quietly, and take the carrot, usually an offer of paid leave, or they will play hard ball. In this case, you had an unauthorized master key, broke into a university office without permission, and took documents that don't belong to you. I think you can guess how this will play out. They may not even give you a choice."

Ted was right. I had just poked *the beast*, as he called it, with the metaphorical big, sharp stick. Even though I had the supposedly protective veil of tenure, Ted was right. I had to anticipate the worst.

Ever the optimist, I said "Ted, I know that I'm screwed, but there *must* be a way through this. I *am* holding two valuable pieces of information: the sexual act that I witnessed, and possibly some information that would implicate a lot of people in some serious wrongdoing. This *has* to be of some value."

Ted, countering my optimism, replied, "Noah, we don't know if there will be anything useful in these folders and, as far as the intimate act is concerned, they would probably just deny it. You lack any solid evidence that it ever occurred and, even if you did have evidence to go public, it would only give them ammunition to paint you as a disgruntled and vindictive professor. There is no evidence that Patricia and Snow were colluding and, if rumors about her marital relationship are true, I'm sure her husband Carl doesn't care. It all boils down to a personal issue between consenting adults."

Clinging to hope, I said, "Can you at least look at the files and see if you can find anything useful. I just can't focus right now."

Ted simply nodded as I handed him the files, feeling like I was making the hand-off to a football teammate with no time left on the clock, hoping they could pull off a miracle and score the go ahead points to win the game.

While he took his time reading through the documents, I ordered fried mozzarella sticks and settled in. Ted was meticulous and intelligent, and I knew that he would take all the time he needed to thoroughly read and analyze the information. He looked up several times from his reading, knowing that I was bursting with anticipation, and told me in a serious and analytical tone that he had not yet found anything that would directly implicate my colleagues in any wrongdoing. He went on to say, however, that the documents did at least raise some good questions about my colleague's purpose in setting up their corporate enterprise, and the flow of funds to them at least raised reasonable suspicion. He suspected that the university auditors did not have access to this information.

It made sense, I thought to myself, *that Finch and company were withholding information.*

As Ted neared the end of the folder with only about five or six documents to go, it became clear that he had found nothing of great interest or value. He looked up from the papers once again and said, "Noah, there is some good information in here, but it is like working a puzzle with only about half of the pieces. I'm afraid that it won't be all that helpful to you. Let me finish up and we can discuss the bigger picture."

As Ted went back to work reading the last of the documents, he suddenly paused with a curious expression on his face. I saw him carefully separate a piece of paper with handwriting on it from one of the pages of computer print. From where I was sitting, it appeared different in two ways: one, it looked like stationary paper, and two, the words on it were handwritten.

Could this be something important?

Ted looked inquisitively at the anomalous document for a moment, and then read the contents. He then read it again, this time letting out a low whistle.

I was bursting with anticipation.

He looked across the table at me with a smile forming on his face and said, "Well, my friend, you might want to take a look at this one."

An inkling of hope was forming.

I asked with impatience, "What is it, Ted? Let me see."

Ted handed over the document, careful to keep it free of the condensation from our drinks on the table's surface, as if it were the last remaining copy of a valuable ancient document. I took it from his hands with great care, and read the words embedded in ink on the fibers of the paper. Not believing my eyes, I read it a second, third and fourth time before handing it back with trembling hands.

The document I had read was a hand-written and signed internal memo from Dr. Finch to Dr. Marshall outlining a complex plan to divert grant and donor money illegally through a corporation formed by Finch to eventually end up in their personal bank accounts.

Bingo! I thought. If it could be proved that they had carried out the plan described in the memo, and some of the plan's missing pieces could be discovered, Finch and his cronies might be spending some time behind bars. The memo, though not stating names, also raised the implication that others were involved, potentially opening a larger can of worms. I considered the involvement of the IRS, and huge implications for Delray University; from potential civil and criminal liability to bad public relations. In my search for the truth, it seemed that I had inadvertently stumbled upon something *very* big and ugly.

All I could say was: "This is remarkable," as I placed the memo back in the file folder, hoping that this document might be enough to keep the wolves at bay.

In fact, I was practically buzzing with hope.

Ted quickly brought me back down to earth, however. With his next words, I learned why. "Some financial documents in the files appear to indicate that substantial amounts of money were moved through the corporation with large payments made to certain research consulting firms. I suspect there was a kick-back, but the trail ends there. We only know that Finch said that he and Patricia stood to make a lot of money. We have no evidence of the movement of money into and out of the various accounts or how, specifically, other university personnel were involved. That information would have likely been destroyed — or is so deeply buried that it would be irretrievable."

As my adrenaline waned along with my enthusiasm, it was replaced with a deep seated feeling of dread. "So essentially what you are saying, Ted, and what I am beginning to realize, is that all I've really managed to accomplish by taking these documents is to paint a larger target on my back."

Ted looked at me gravely, only deepening my feeling of despair, and said "Noah, my friend, while it is possible that this information could be used as leverage in some way, I think you need to consider the broader implications of your actions tonight in the context of what we have learned from the language in this memo."

I waited for Ted to continue, and when he did, his words only reinforced what I feared.

Ted, very slowly and with genuine compassion said, "Do you recall where, in the memo, Finch mentioned an "even bigger payday," and implied that Patricia knew what he meant? He also boasted that he had connections outside the university who could "plug any leaks" if anyone got too close to learning what they were doing."

My body lightly shook, and in a broken voice I responded "Yes, Ted. I remember that."

Ted looked me straight in the eyes and said "You will need to be incredibly careful, my friend, as the stakes are very high. Even though this scheme is clearly crooked, and a big deal, there may be something much more sinister going on than we know. Your colleagues are quite unscrupulous and dangerous, but their mysterious connections implied in the memo may be even more so."

I pushed my beer and plate of mozzarella sticks aside, having now completely lost my appetite, and asked the only question that made sense. "So, what do we do now?"

Ted leaned forward, took a deep breath, and replied, "We need a plan. Noah, I think that you should go home and try to get some sleep. I have a feeling that you will need it, given the challenges you will likely face over the days, weeks, and months ahead. I know you are stressed, but please maintain good situational awareness, watching to see if you are followed, and taking the necessary precautions for your personal safety."

Out of caution, I asked Ted if he would be willing to hold onto the documents and keep them safe. I feared that someone might come to my house and, either with a warrant, or by force, take them from me.

As we shook hands and parted ways, I felt more alone than I ever had in my life. The night had turned colder, and a dense fog was building. Pulling out of the parking lot onto the main road, I immediately saw flashing lights in my rearview mirror. My heart and mind raced as I built scenarios in my mind that Finch, Patricia, or Dr. Snow had called the police on me, and that I would be spending this cold, dreary night in a jail cell.

As the patrol car sped past and the flashing lights faded in the distance, I realized that I needed to stay calm. I took a deep breath and drove on, realizing that I was too caught up in my emotions to think logically.

I knew the police couldn't be coming for me yet, given that Patricia, Finch, and their associates didn't know where I was, and even if they had known, it would take some time for them to act. Universities were notoriously slow in acting on most things, and especially something of this sort. They would need to work out a strategy first, and then implement it. My colleagues were meticulous planners and it would take them at least a week to decide upon what action to take, and then another before they could get me on their calendars.

While classes didn't start for another week, administrators would be back to work on Monday, and the faculty would be expected to be in their offices preparing for the semester. It was a least a good bet that my weekend escapade would be on their minds as they began the week.

But who knew, maybe this was just the beginning of a cold war of sorts, where things played out slowly with both sides holding their cards and waiting for the other to act.

As it turned out, I could not have been more wrong.

Chapter 4

Facing the Music

AFTER A QUIET and uneventful Sunday, spent on tasks around the house designed to keep my mind off my troubles, Monday came far too early. Too scared to go back to campus, I worked from home. It was a place that usually made me feel comfortable and safe.

The familiar furnishings were mostly antiques that I had picked up at auctions and estate sales and had painstakingly refinished. My favorite was a dark mahogany coffee table sitting atop a blue-accented oriental rug that protected the Heart Pine hardwood floor. It was the centerpiece of my living room, framed by comfortable, dark leather couches. Adorning the walls in purposeful locations were my prized works of art, some of which had been gifted to me by family, and others that had taken a considerable chunk out of my paycheck. A big screen television and computer workstation where I currently sat provided a stark contrast to the rustic and cozy atmosphere of my home.

Technically, I should have been at my office, but I didn't want to run into any of my supervisors who were sure to be there — or colleagues for that matter. Most would be dutifully in their offices getting a head start on the upcoming semester.

I couldn't escape checking my email though. As department head, it was my responsibility to keep abreast of any issues that were sure to come up and do my best to put out the small fires before they became blazing infernos. This also meant that I would have to face the inevitable — an email from someone up the chain chastising me for my actions over the weekend.

Maybe they would wait or grant me a reprieve. This was my fervent hope.

I screwed up the courage to view my emails, and looked down the list. There were the expected requests from faculty for all sorts of things, a few student issues, the occasional ad that slipped through the spam filter, and then .... *There it was.*

Staring me in the face like a coiled rattlesnake ready to strike was a message from my dean, Dr. Jeremy Winston. I held my breath and clicked on it. My eyes sped across the words, fueled by the anxiety spewing across the synapses of my brain as from an open faucet.

With bile rising in my throat, I could almost hear Dean Winston speaking to me in his most condescending upper-class Bostonian accent. He wrote that he would like to meet with me tomorrow, Tuesday, and that his assistant would set up a meeting for 10 a.m. We would meet at his office. He further stated that the matter was urgent and that the meeting was mandatory.

Meetings with Dean Winston were never confrontational but always had that underlying hint of malice disguised by his calm demeanor and melodic accent. My best guess at his reason for meeting was to get a feel for what I knew — and what I planned to do about it — so that he could head me off. It was also likely that he would slowly and tortuously eviscerate me with his words.

I stood and paced for a few minutes, allowing my mind to process the dean's message. As important as the message itself was the speed by which it had been delivered. Events were unfolding much faster than I had anticipated.

Calmed by the physical act of pacing, I sat back down and sorted through the last of my emails. The mundane task helped me regain my bearings. The remainder of my emails were pure vanilla. Most just wanted a piece of me, in the form of work or time. As faculty, your time was an undervalued commodity, and you either had to delete most of the email requests or reply with a polite "no." With students, it was usually a different matter, as I rarely refused a request for a letter of recommendation or to provide advice.

The rest of the afternoon passed uneventfully, followed by a night of restless sleep. When morning finally arrived, I ran through my usual routine of a brief workout, shower, breakfast, and a check of my emails. At 9:30 a.m., I jumped in my truck and drove to the building where, only a few nights before, I had broken into my colleague's office — an act which had assuredly precipitated this meeting. I took the elevator up to the fourth floor, where I would find the dean's office suite, and made my way down the hall toward his office. When I arrived at the suite, I saw that his administrative assistant, Paula Greasy, a woman with whom I had a good collegial relationship, was out sick. *I was alone.*

I knocked on the dean's closed office door. From somewhere inside, I heard Dean Winston's muffled voice say, "If you will be so kind as to wait, I will be with you in a minute."

I took a seat in the waiting area and, after about five minutes, he opened his door and I entered his spacious office — one with an expansive view of campus. His office furnishings were of the highest quality, with plush chairs, a large mahogany desk, and bookcases and armoire made of black walnut. The room smelled of leather and Bay Rum Cologne. We shook hands, and he offered me a seat.

Dean Winston said, "So, Noah, I trust that you had an enjoyable holiday."

Wanting to move the conversation along, I simply said, "Thank you. It was enjoyable," and then made the mistake of asking, "So how was yours?"

This prompted Dean Winston to launch into a ten minute narrative about his visit to relatives back in New England, and a story about a cat named Henry that had found its way into the Christmas tree, wreaking all kinds of havoc. He laughed at his own story and I, to be polite, forced a smile.

Dean Winston, as usual, was dressed impeccably in a three-piece suit, exuding confidence, and superiority. When meetings were with faculty and students, however, he countered this formality by wearing one of his obnoxious ties with cartoon characters, or animals such as puppies or kittens adorning them. I think that he was purposeful in his choice of ties, in that they were meant to disarm people, and perhaps send the subliminal message that he was, at heart, a regular commoner and educator.

On this day, he wore a tie with cartoon characters racing around a Christmas tree.

Beyond the fancy suit and well-coiffed hair, I thought, *there was nothing classy about this man*. Beneath this thin veneer lived a man who was as shallow as they came and would sell out to the highest bidder at a moment's notice. He was certainly not one to be trusted.

Finally, after he had completed his oration, the conversation shifted to more serious topics. He started with "Noah, I heard that you ran into Dr. Finch and Dr. Marshall in the Institute offices over the break."

I thought, *yeah, we had run into each other — quite literally.*

He looked at me squarely and said in a serious tone, "I have spoken with both of them, as you may have suspected, and they provided me with some very disturbing news. It has come to my understanding that you broke into the Institute's business office last week and stole some important confidential papers."

Dean Winston paused for effect and to see my reaction before continuing.

Not wishing to give him the satisfaction of seeing my discomfort, I remained stoic.

He cleared his throat and continued, "Howard met with me privately yesterday morning and told me that he had dropped by his office last Thursday afternoon — which happens to connect to the business office — to pick up research materials so that he could work at home over the last weekend of winter break. He said that he caught you rifling through papers in one of the Institute's filing cabinets."

Wow, I thought. They were already covering their tracks, saying they had caught me on *Thursday* afternoon instead of over the weekend late at night — the actual time that I was there. This eliminated any questions that might arise as to why Dr. Finch would be in the office late on a weekend when school was out of session and make any revelations that I might potentially make about Dr. Marshall and Dr. Snow found having sex on the office floor seem like an attempt to make up some self-serving, crazy story.

It was my word against theirs, anyway, when it was all said and done.

My mind raced. I needed to say something and at least *try* to counter the lies they were telling, and provide some needed misdirection.

Thinking quickly, I said in a rush, "Dean Winston, I'll be honest with you. The reason that I was in their business office unannounced is that a student had asked me to grab a document from a filing cabinet related to some work she was doing for the Institute. She had texted me that she was concerned about going there as the area was off limits to most students, and she felt that I, as an administrator, would have access. She told me that she had to meet a deadline on an Institute project, and it could not wait."

As the words left my mouth, I realized how weak it sounded, and that I had been foolish to attempt this deception. The dean had assuredly been informed of the entire matter, and knew the when, what, and where of everything.

Dean Winston peered at me over his glasses with a disapproving look, and merely nodded. He then said in a voice as smooth as silk, sounding like the snake in *The Jungle Book,* "Noah, I am extremely disappointed in your behavior. Given that this is so unusual, I have asked for advice from our university's legal counsel on how to proceed. After I have had the opportunity to speak with them on the proper course of action, it would be wise to have both of us meet again with the appropriate university officials to discuss what is acceptable regarding other faculty's private documents. We will also need to discuss the proper course of disciplinary action."

I simply nodded, as my throat seemed to swell and sweat began to bead on my forehead. I took a sip of the bottled water that I had brought with me and asked without thinking, "Did Dr. Finch or Dr. Marshall say anything else?"

Dean Winston, with an annoyed expression, took a deep breath and responded, "Well, yes. They agreed that university legal counsel should be involved. They also suggested that it would be wise to speak with the associate provost, Dr. Amos Snow, about your behavior to make sure they were covering all their bases in case they were required by university policy to take some action. As you are aware, he oversees faculty disciplinary matters here at the university. I suppose you will hear more on this if it comes to it. For now, I suspect that an apology would be in order, and of course you will need to make sure that you don't *ever* find yourself in their offices uninvited again."

"Noah," he continued as he prepared to make his last point, "it also goes without saying that you will need to return *everything* that you have taken from them." For good measure, he then said in a more forceful tone, "Is that understood!?"

"Absolutely," I muttered.

Dr. Winston closed his notebook and picked up his pen, indicating that our meeting was over.

Before standing, however, he looked directly at me, and said in his most arrogant voice, "I almost forgot. I believe that you were wondering about whether you would be continuing in your role as department head. You may recall that I had suggested last semester that you might be better served returning to your faculty role. Well, I've given this further thought. In light of this recent incident, I have decided to return you to faculty full-time, and appoint Dr. Finch as the interim department head, effective immediately."

He then asked the rhetorical question, "I think that he will make an excellent department head, wouldn't you agree?" Without waiting for a response, he said with finality, "Please understand that this decision is not subject to debate. If you will excuse me, I have an important meeting to attend, and I do not wish to be late."

With that, Dean Winston ushered me to the door, out of the office suite, and into the hallway where I stood trying to process the implications of what he had just told me.

Things were moving extremely fast and getting worse by the minute. Patricia and Finch didn't know that I had the memo, but they would at least be suspicious about what, and how much, I knew. Now, with Finch as my direct supervisor, he had the ability to, at the very least, make my life miserable. What else he might do was anyone's guess.

Hoping to avoid my colleagues, I took the back stairwell. My mind was too occupied with processing all that was happening to make small talk with anyone, and I wanted to avoid Patricia and Finch. Winding my way down the empty stairwell, I left the building by the back door.

I fast-walked to my truck, got quickly inside and sat alone with my thoughts. My lizard brain was on high alert, knowing deep within that something even more unpleasant was coming my way. It was time to sort it out. Firing up the truck and turning on the heater, I sat alone with my thoughts.

Finch and his cohort didn't play fair, and they would be especially vindictive since — not knowing what cards I held — they would now perceive me as a threat to be eliminated. They wouldn't just attempt to slow me down or play cat and mouse. They would seek to destroy my reputation and career and bury me deep enough that I wouldn't be able to come back from it.

To make matters worse, the memo I had smuggled from the Institute suggested there might even be some dangerous folks outside the university gunning for me since I was now — thinking back to the language in Finch's memo — *a leak that needed plugging.* Finch, Patricia, and their cohort also held all the cards, especially with the upper university administration — in the person of Dr. Snow — behind them.

Boy, had I opened a can of worms!

Needing to get out ahead of them, if possible, I sorted through the possibilities of how they might attempt to take me down. They could use a female student, as they had in the past with other faculty who had crossed them, to make a false claim of sexual harassment. They could create a false narrative that I was a racist and treated students unfairly because I was biased and hateful. They could claim that I had falsified data in my research or plagiarized someone else's work. Any of these false claims would be akin to serious blows — and were horrible in their own right — but might not constitute a knockout punch.

As I travelled down the well of my colleague's depravity in my mind, one terrifying idea rose to the surface.

To truly ruin me, and destroy my credibility, they would need to make it look like I had done something *so horrible* that the public, including my friends and family, would find it utterly repulsive — so much so that it would justify my removal from the university and banish me from university work forever. Worst of all, it could land me in jail.

I had an idea but would need to speak with a colleague first. The person I had in mind had been the head of the Sociology Department for a brief time earlier in my career. Enough years had passed that I couldn't remember the details, but I recall that he had also gotten crosswise with both Finch and Patricia. We had a lot in common. His name was Bill Conrad.

I dialed up Bill on my cell phone and was fortunate to reach him. He worked from home a lot these days and flew well below the radar. He answered, and I said, "Hey Bill, it's me, Noah."

"Oh, hi Noah," Bill answered in a friendly voice. "I hear that there is a lot going on over there in the viper pit these days. Unfortunately, most of it does not appear to be good."

"No, it's not," I said, without elaborating.

"What can I do for you?" asked Bill, cutting to the chase. "I'm sure you didn't call on a workday just to shoot the breeze."

"I need to verify something. Since you keep your ear to the ground, you probably know that I'm experiencing some challenges here."

"I don't know the details," said Bill, "but suspect that the challenges you faced last semester from *certain powerful faculty* have not gone away."

"You could say that," I replied dryly. "Let me ask you something. I know that you have always been super-careful with the security of your computers. Why is that?"

"You must be referring to the fact that I take my hard drive home with me every time I leave the office, and never leave my laptop unattended. I can guess your next question. It would be, 'why?' I never told you this, but I learned a few years back that Patricia and Finch have close connections to some of the IT staff in the college. They either threaten or cajole them, but either way, they are able to have them do their bidding."

They have an insider in IT then, I said to myself.

"This is where it gets interesting," said Bill, "and one of the main reasons I am now such a paranoid old professor. Once, when I was department head, I overheard Finch talking to Patricia as I was passing by Finch's office. The door was cracked open a bit, so I stopped to listen. What I picked up from their conversation was that they had targeted one of the faculty, for one reason or another, and were scheming ways to have him terminated from his faculty position in the university. What they said next haunts me to this day."

"What did they say?" I asked, anticipating the answer that I dreaded to hear.

"Finch told Patricia that he had a guy in IT who was under his control and would do anything he asked. Finch then said, and I remember these words clearly, 'If we want to not only ensure that he is out of our hair, but is utterly destroyed, I can have my guy plant child pornography on his computer.' I then remember hearing Patricia making a cackling sound and clapping. It sounded utterly demonic and psychotic. From that point on, I knew that they would stop at nothing to destroy another person if it were in their best interest. I didn't want to be that person. That is why I'm so cautious to this day."

My body flooded with adrenaline as I listened, and I found that I couldn't speak.

Bill, sounding concerned, asked, "Noah, are you still there? Are you OK?"

Finding my voice, I replied, "Yes, and ... no, Bill. I appreciate the information. From what you have told me, I need to secure my computer ASAP. I was just informed earlier this morning that Finch, starting immediately, has replaced me as department head. He is now my boss."

"Jesus!" said Bill, "You go do that then — and the sooner the better."

"Thanks," I hastily replied, and hung up.

Chapter 5

Framed

WITH MY HEART pounding and, fueled by fear, I shut off my truck and jogged across the parking lot back to the building entrance. I entered the building and walked quickly to my office.

I needed to secure my computer.

As I entered my office, I glanced at the prints of outdoor scenes that adorned my office walls, as well as a few diplomas and awards. My bookshelves were stacked with books, some of which covered my topics of study, as well as some that were there to help me think about issues from a different angle. On my desk were items that were meaningful or practical — a lamp with a stained-glass lampshade, a golden apple from the time that I was awarded the university teaching award, some nick knacks, pens, a stapler, and memorabilia from my time as a college professor.

What was noticeably absent, I discovered to my utter dismay, was my computer. Where it once sat, there was now an empty space — occupied by dust bunnies and a few stray cords.

Filled with paranoia, I quickly dialed up Irma Tobar, who, until just this morning, had been my administrative assistant. Irma stood about five feet, three inches tall, with steel-gray hair, gray-green eyes and a no-nonsense look. Beneath a tough-as-nails exterior though, Irma was a genuinely kind person, who often went out of her way to help others. I had great appreciation and respect for Irma and trusted her completely. She had been there for me through thick and thin during my time serving as department head.

Irma answered on the second ring. "Hello Irma," I said. "I didn't want you to hear this second hand, but I was let go from my department head position today."

Always a step ahead of me, Irma said softly, "I know, Dr. Banks, and I'm so sorry. Dr. Finch came by just a short time ago and told me that he is taking your place. As you know, I was staying on because I admire you and have enjoyed working for you so much. I am going to give my notice this week and retire."

"Thanks for letting me know, Irma," I said, feeling that I had let her down. Even though it was inevitable that they would remove me from my administrative post, I still felt guilty for some reason and was sorry that it had to end this way.

"Well, you probably already know this too," I said, "but my computer is missing."

Irma, sounding troubled, said, "I am sorry, but I couldn't stop them. It was an order from Dr. Finch who is technically now my boss, even though it makes me sick to my stomach. Two guys from IT came by to pick up your computer not more than 15 minutes ago."

Alarm bells were sounding in my head. This was all happening far too quickly. The fact that my computer had just been taken, and Finch had abruptly become my supervisor, could not be a coincidence.

As if she were reading my mind, Irma said, "Given my experience with Dr. Finch, and the timing of all this, it seems quite fishy."

"My thoughts exactly, Irma," I said. "Did Dr. Finch tell you anything that might help me understand what is going on?"

"No," replied Irma. "He called and just told me that IT was coming to pick up your computer, and that if you protested, then I should let him know. He said that if you got angry or violent, then I should keep my door shut and call campus police. I was shocked when he said that. You are one of the nicest and most level-headed people I know."

"Thanks, Irma," I said, stifling a feeling of irritation. "As we know, he is very manipulative. Did the IT staff tell you anything?"

"Not much. They just said they were given orders to take the computer to perform routine upgrades and add software. They seemed somewhat confused by this. I overheard one of them ask the other why they had to take the computer to do these tasks, instead of doing it in the faculty's office as was normally the case. I couldn't make out the reply very well, but I thought I heard him say something about just following orders."

After a slight pause, Irma said, "Oh, and Noah, they said they would be returning your computer by the end of the week."

I thanked Irma, told her that I would take her to lunch sometime soon, and hung up the phone. Even though the temperature in my office was cool, I was sweating.

I was too late.

My computer was now under Finch's control. I knew him to be as conniving and nasty as they come, and now I knew from Bill that planting horrible and incriminating files on an adversary's computer was in his playbook.

If my hunch was right, and Finch, and whoever else he had in his camp, were successful in framing me, I would be found guilty of a federal crime and potentially serve at least a dozen years in a federal lock-up — never mind the disgrace, stress, and despair this would cause me.

With these thoughts quickly creating a forest fire of panic within me, I leapt from my chair, and ran down the hall toward the IT office in hopes of retrieving my computer. Halfway there, however, I stopped.

What is the use? I thought. *If I make it there out of breath and in a panic, won't it make me appear culpable? They were under orders from Finch, anyway, and wouldn't return my computer to me even if they wanted.*

I had reached a dead end. This new spike of adrenaline, coupled with a proportionate spike in my blood pressure, had left me slightly dizzy and nauseous. I needed to calm down and think this through. I walked unsteadily back to my office, but instead of going back to my desk, I had another idea.

I decided to make a call to Ted on my cell. After waiting a few seconds for him to answer, I said, "Hey Ted, it's me. Would you like to grab some lunch? There is something that I need to run by you." I hesitated to say more, never knowing who might be listening.

"Sure, Noah, the usual place I suppose. I just need to wrap up a few things and can meet you there in about 30 minutes."

"Great! See you in 30." I was looking forward to a greasy burger and some much needed advice.

When I arrived at the River's Edge Bar and Grill thirty minutes later, Ted was waiting for me at a back booth, sipping an iced tea. Taking a seat opposite Ted, I ordered a burger, fries, and a glass of Coca Cola.

Skipping any small talk, I got straight to the point. I said, "Ted, I met with Dean Winston today."

"So, how is that old insincere bag of hot air?"

"Worse than ever," I replied, and then provided him with a recap of the conversation.

Ted, listening carefully, replied, "Did he tell you to return the documents that you took?"

"Yes, that and make an apology, and to never even think about doing anything like it again. Oh, and he removed me from my department head position."

Ted said, "I know that sucks, but I guess you suspected that would happen."

"I did – and it gets better."

"How so?" replied Ted.

"He replaced me with Finch, and then Finch had my desktop taken away by IT for *upgrades*."

This comment stopped Ted in his tracks. With a look of both puzzlement and concern, he said, "You have entered some very dangerous territory, my friend."

This was the second time he had given me a dire warning, and this didn't happen often – well, ever — with Ted. I could feel the walls closing in around me.

We sat in silence for a few minutes, both of us considering the enormity of my circumstances and not seeing any scenarios where the outcome was good. Ted suspected, as I had after speaking with Bill, that they had taken my computer to plant something malicious on it. We bounced around some ideas and finally decided that we had reached a dead end.

I took a bite of my burger and a sip of Coke and sighed. "Well, at least they haven't taken my university issued laptop yet, so those jerks can't plant something on it too." I added, sarcastically and for good measure, "Thank goodness for small miracles."

Ted laughed, and then a look crossed his face that told me his sharp mind had just seized upon an idea.

Ted spoke slowly and with deliberation. "So," said Ted, "what I am about to say might offer you some hope, but I wouldn't bet the farm on how it might turn out."

"OK, tell me what you're thinking."

"Well," said Ted. "It may be time to play a little offense, while they think you are only playing defense. Do you remember that friend of mine from college — the computer genius I told you about?"

"Yeah, I think his name was Joe or something."

Ted said, "His name is Josh, and he *really is* a computer genius. He has one of those build-it-yourself computers at his apartment that he could probably use to hack the Pentagon. It has a water-cooling system inside to keep it cool enough to handle the processing power and subsequent heat that it generates. It is quite amazing. Anyway, he has killer programming and coding skills. We keep in touch and do some online gaming together. He is a good friend and someone who I could absolutely trust with anything that I wanted to keep confidential."

"He sounds like he knows his way around computers," I said, not sure where this was heading.

Ted went on to say, "What you said earlier about your laptop made me think. If Finch has incriminating files planted on your desktop as we suspect, I don't think he'll be content to stop there. I suspect that he will want to go for the homerun and do the same to your laptop. I think that we should think a few moves ahead and outsmart him."

"How can we do that?" I asked, pleased with where this was heading.

"My idea is to see if Josh can work some magic on your laptop's hard drive. If Finch and company plant malicious files on your computer, they have to associate fictitious times and dates to the files."

"To make it look like it happened *before* they took possession of it," I added. While not technology-minded, I at least grasped this simple idea.

"Exactly," Ted responded, with the patience of a teacher explaining introductory material to a class of freshmen. "This is how we can catch them. If we put a hidden program on your laptop computer — think 'friendly virus' — that can identify malicious files and when they were *actually* installed, then we would have proof that the files meant to incriminate you were planted *after* you handed over your laptop.

"And I could catch them with their hand in the cookie jar," I said with a smile. "That would be awesome! The hunter will finally become the hunted."

Ted said, "We just let them do their dirty deed, and then take it from there. After that, I think it would be wise to have your lawyer handle things."

Grateful for his help, I offered, "Lunch is on me. And if this works out as planned, I will owe you lunch for a year."

"Sounds good to me," said my good friend with a broad smile on his face as he stood to leave. "I'll call Josh and we can work out a time for him to come by your house to install the program."

As I watched him head toward the door, I took a few final sips of my soda and processed what we had just discussed.

I had to admit that it was a long shot. Maybe I was just being paranoid, and IT *had* only taken my desktop computer for upgrades. And even if they *were* up to no good, they may be satisfied with planting something on my desktop and not bother with my laptop. Regardless, it was worth a try. *What did I have to lose?*

I drove home feeling like I was entering the gathering winds of an approaching category five hurricane. I would have to try and stay afloat long enough to save my reputation and academic career, or in a worst case scenario.... No, it was better that I not think about worst case scenarios.

The first thing I did when I got home, after throwing my coat on a chair and pouring myself a glass of water, was to pull up a chair next to my laptop and open my email. Sorting through them, one email immediately caught my attention. It was a mass email from Dean Winston to everyone in the college officially notifying us that, in addition to appointing Dr.

Finch as the new head of my department, he was appointing Dr. Marshall as senior associate dean.

This was clearly planned with me in mind, I thought. The university was covering all their bases and ensuring that I would have no-one to turn to up the chain of command. Any official channels go through the department head, and then to the dean - who then reports to the associate provost, who at Delray, deals with all faculty matters. In my case, even if I could bypass the department head and dean, I would hit a serious roadblock at the level of Dr. Snow, the associate provost, given his *relationship* with Patricia.

This left me with only one remaining option, one that is available to every U.S. citizen. I could contact a lawyer. Given the legal implications of what was occurring, I needed the best legal advice and representation that I could get. I knew who to call but decided to wait and see how things played out. As it turned out, I didn't have to wait long.

I spent all day Wednesday and most of Thursday performing routine tasks, such as preparing for class and working on a paper that I hoped to have published in an upcoming edition of a journal. I worked from home on my university laptop and kept my mind focused on the tasks at hand to keep the ever-present fear of what might lie ahead from invading my thoughts.

Still, it was impossible to keep out the thoughts of what might come next, and on Thursday afternoon at approximately 5:00 p.m., my worst fears were realized as I opened an email that would turn my life upside-down.

If the email earlier in the week from Dean Winston ensuring that I was completely powerless and under the control of some unbelievably bad people was a nail in my coffin, this one was akin to someone slamming the coffin lid and applying super glue to it. It was short and to the point, but the implications were enormous, and frightening.

The email was from Dr. Finch, my new department head, and immediate boss. It was written in block paragraph form, laced with malice and insincerity. He was in his element, and I knew he was loving every ounce of pain he was inflicting upon me.

He first apologized for the delay in having not yet returned my desktop computer. He said that my computer had been sent to IT for routine updates and software patches and it had taken a few days for them to get to it given how busy they were at the start of the semester.

Then came the kicker.

The next line of text said that while they were working on my computer, they happened to come across some files that were *overly concerning*. He said that IT immediately contacted him and told him in detail what they had found. Out of respect for me, and compassion, he said that he was going to keep an open mind and wanted to speak with me in person about this before doing anything more. Then, like in a demented good-cop, bad-cop routine, added that likely both the university and law enforcement would be involved at some point.

Compassion?! You must be kidding! I thought. *That man has never felt a sliver of compassion for anyone in his entire life.* I took a deep breath, let my anger subside and continued reading.

He next said that he would do everything in his power to help me through this.

Yeah, right, I thought, as my anger surfaced once again.

He went on to say that I would receive a meeting invitation for 9 a.m. tomorrow morning, and that the meeting was mandatory. If I were to miss the meeting, there would be dire consequences, and any assistance from my *superiors* at that point forward would be withdrawn.

What assistance? I thought, realizing that this was just another manipulative trick to get me to come to the meeting.

He concluded the message by informing me that Dr. Marshall and Dean Winston would be in attendance and that I would need to bring my laptop so that IT could run diagnostics on it as well. For good measure, he added a warning that I was not to delete any existing files or tamper with my computer in any way — as they would be able to tell.

Even though I knew he would attempt to frame me, it still hit me hard. They really had decided to play hardball. They were also timing this – with this email sent at 5:00 p.m. — so that I wouldn't have an opportunity to meet with my attorney prior to the meeting, or to bring him to the meeting to provide advice and representation.

It was time to cover my bases, and there was no time to spare.

Chapter 6

Setting the Trap

IT WAS LATE in the day, and I had to move quickly. There were two calls I had to make: the first, to Ted; the second, to my attorney Gary Easterling. I had known Gary for quite some time now, having heeded his advice on various legal matters over the past few years.

Ted answered my first call, and I told him about the email from Finch and the next morning's meeting. Without hesitating, he said he would be over in 30 minutes with Josh, his tech friend who, as luck would have it, was over at his house. He also said he was bringing the files.

My second call, to Gary, was less fruitful. His assistant, Gayle, answered and told me that Gary was in a late deposition and wouldn't be back in the office until tomorrow morning. I left a message, providing him with the 411 on my situation, and that I needed his help. I also told him that it was urgent. Gary was highly competent and, as a former university attorney, knew just about everything that a person could know about the good, the bad, and the ugly of Delray University.

Thirty minutes later, as promised, Ted showed up with his tech friend, Josh. After brief introductions, Josh went straight to my laptop with his screwdriver and a determined look.

He found the hard drive, unscrewed it from its compartment underneath my laptop, and pulled it out. He then connected it to some fancy device that was then connected to his laptop. I gave him my username and password, and he entered the inner workings of my computer. After typing furiously for several minutes, he sat back with a satisfied look on his face.

"What just happened, Josh?" I asked out of curiosity. I was fascinated with technology, but honestly didn't know much more than a few key tech words and phrases, and how to operate some basic word processing and database programs.

Josh replied, "Well dude, I think you'll like this. I was able to access your hard drive and insert a program that is undetectable to anyone without some serious skills and super powerful equipment. I'm certain that the university folks don't have the know-how to find the program. They most likely wouldn't even think to look for it. What I put on your machine is like a virus, but a friendly one, that will tag the time and date of anything added to your computer, or any changes made, from this point forward."

"That sounds perfect, Josh. I'm just thinking out loud, but if they do plant something, and then accuse me of it, the next step would be to work with my lawyer to retain the computer as evidence. Then, we could access the program to provide proof that the malicious material was added *after* I had turned in my laptop."

"That sounds about right," Ted chimed in.

"Josh," I asked, "Would you be willing to provide testimony should it become necessary?"

"Sure, dude," replied Josh. "After learning what those jerks have done to you, I would be more than happy to help. I'm also not concerned about pissing off the university since my business isn't affected by them."

"Great," I said, and boy did I mean it. It was still David versus Goliath, but at least I now had something with which to counter their nasty tricks.

After re-inserting my hard drive and putting things back together, Josh asked "Do you have anything that you want to back up or delete?"

"No, I'm good," I replied. I had saved and backed up all the files that I needed earlier.

"Thanks again, Josh," I said as he headed toward the door and on to his next job. "I'll keep you posted on what happens and whether we need your help again. I'll buy you a beer once all of this craziness is over."

"Sounds good, dude," said Josh, and he was out the door.

"It looks like your computer is good to go," said Ted. "Josh did a fantastic job as usual. When you have your meeting, just give them the computer, and act a little bothered by it, which I'm sure won't be too hard. You don't want them to have even the slightest suspicion that you are turning the tables on them. Also, Noah, I don't want to be a 'Debbie Downer,' but don't think that this will be the end game, like in the movies, where you catch them in the act, they all go to jail, and you ride off into the sunset. Remember that the university has tremendous resources and can spin just about anything in their favor. This is just one small battle in a larger war that will likely wage on for a while."

"I know," I replied, as Ted's words of wisdom tempered my excitement and brought me back to the sobering reality of my situation. "I told you that I have a meeting coming up, but what I didn't tell you is that it is early tomorrow morning. The whole cast of characters, Patricia, Finch, and Dean Winston, will be there."

"By calling the meeting so soon," replied Ted, "they must want to make sure that you don't have time to lawyer-up beforehand."

"My thoughts exactly. I called Gary but he is in a deposition and can't meet until tomorrow — after my meeting, and *after* I turn in my laptop."

"Does he know that we were going to plant the hidden program on your laptop?" asked Ted.

"Not yet. I just left a message that I wanted to speak with him. I realize that the timing on all of this isn't ideal, but it is what it is."

"I wouldn't worry about that," replied Ted. "All you can do is take one step at a time given the opportunities and constraints that are presented to you."

I appreciated Ted's wisdom and intelligent advice. It did little, however, to quell the anxiety building within me, and the urge to run as far away from this mess as humanly possible. I told myself that, if and when I needed to run, I would be ready.

The serious tone of Ted's voice brought me back to the present.

Ted said, "Listen to me. I know that what you are going through isn't pleasant and it is bound to get much worse. When you meet with them tomorrow, say as little as possible and just try to listen to their BS without getting emotional. You must think about the long game. They *want* you to lose your temper and say something incriminating. It will only help them build their case against you."

Ted then handed me what looked like an ordinary pen.

"OK," I said, feeling perplexed. "Why are you giving me a pen? I appreciate it, but I already have too many."

"This is no ordinary pen. It actually works, but its main purpose is to record conversations without anyone knowing. As you know, my dad is a personal injury attorney, and sometimes he has the need to keep track of things that are said. I don't ask whether his use of it is legit, and he doesn't say. Anyway, it might come in handy for you. I'm sure that, as seasoned administrators, they most likely wouldn't say anything tomorrow that would incriminate them in any way, but it couldn't hurt to record the conversation anyway."

Ted went on to say, "Just turn it on before the meeting and it will record for several hours. When you are finished recording, you can play it back, or copy the recording to your phone or computer." Ted pulled a windows compatible USB device and earphones from his pocket and handed them to me.

"Thanks, Ted," I said. "I really mean it — and I want you to know that if things get hairy, I have an escape plan and will be heading to a place that is off the grid."

"Good," said Ted. "You don't need to tell me more. In fact, it's better if you don't. That way I can claim ignorance. Of course, knowing you so well, I could easily guess."

Ted, pulling some files out of his bag, said, "I guess you will need these. These files include both a photocopy and an original of the documents you took from the Institute. I made copies so you have backup. Although you are under an obligation to return the originals, they don't know *exactly* what you took. I took the liberty of putting the originals of most of the financials and uninteresting documents — those that are public record anyway — in a folder that you can hand over to your supervisors when you meet tomorrow."

Ted handed me a file.

"Of course," he said with a wink, "I didn't include Finch's memo or some of the more sensitive documents in this file. I thought it wise that they didn't know that you had anything incriminating in the least in your possession. You have enough trouble without getting them even more worked up. If they knew you had the memo, who knows what they would do. Remember what Finch said about people he knew who could 'plug leaks.'"

Ted handed me a second file. "What I'm handing you in this file are the originals that may be important in offering evidence of wrongdoing, along with Finch's memo. These documents would be better kept with you. I would guard them with your life."

"Thanks," I said.

Ted handed me a third file. "This one contains photocopies of everything. I ran out of ink at one point but think that everything is in there. I thought you would want to keep this one in the care of your attorney, Mr. Easterling."

"I do," I said. "But I'm concerned that Gary will be hesitant to accept photocopies of documents that have been taken without permission. He may incur liability or receive an ethics violation for holding this material."

"Well then," replied Ted. "Why don't we seal this in an envelope and mark it in care of Mr. Easterling with a note that says the envelope is only to be opened with your consent."

"That is perfect," I said.

"In that case," replied Ted, "I'll run it by his office first thing in the morning and leave it with his assistant with a message to that effect."

"Thanks, Ted. I'll be in touch soon, one way or another, and will definitely fill you in on my meeting tomorrow."

The rest of the day passed quickly and was followed by a night of restless and intermittent sleep, imagining the many ways that these vampires could use words to drain the life from me at the meeting tomorrow, and the many ways I could imagine responding — everything from no response and blank stares to snarky responses or acts of aggression.

As I lay in bed, my mind went to the extremes, thinking back to my visit to London's Clink Prison Museum several years ago and imagining my colleagues confined to that hideous place back in the 1400s. After a few minutes, I snapped out of my reverie, and away from that horrid place and time, knowing that I would need to keep my cool tomorrow.

Shifting my thoughts to the meeting, I knew that it would be pre-scripted. It didn't matter what I said since the ending,

in their minds, was already written. From my perspective, however, the ending didn't belong solely to them — and I had a
pen in my hand that might help me write my own.

Chapter 7

Consequences

I HAD SET my alarm for 6 a.m., but it didn't matter. I had been lying awake with my eyes closed in a futile attempt to get back to sleep since around 2 a.m., nearly four hours ago. My alarm sounded dutifully at 6 a.m. regardless, just as it was programmed to do. I took that as my cue to get up and start my routine — a welcome thought, as it would help distract me from the daytime nightmare that would surely ensue.

I ate a light breakfast of oatmeal and banana bread and washed it down with fresh roasted coffee from Nicaragua, one of my favorites, while playing a game on my phone. The mindless computer game always helped to calm me and free my subconscious mind from the mental clutter that seemed ever-present. After breakfast, I did the next thing that calmed me; I changed and walked to the living room to perform my 30-minute exercise routine of light weights and aerobics. I did this 3 or 4 times a week, and it did wonders for my mental and emotional health.

Past the age where I was concerned about six pack abs and a perfect body. I just wanted to maintain enough strength and endurance for everyday life and the outdoor activities that I loved. I was an avid cyclist and enjoyed going for rides to the river where I kept my kayak stashed. On some weekends, I would ride to the river, jump on my kayak, go for a strenuous paddle, and then bike back to my house. I lived alone and had no pets since my dog, *Loki*, had died a year earlier.

After a good workout and a long shower, I packed up my computer, stuck the pen with the hidden microphone into my shirt pocket, jumped in my truck, and headed over to the university and the meeting that I dreaded. As I thought about it, the words of an old lawyer friend came to mind. When talking about being in depositions or meeting with the opposition, he would say, "It was a great meeting. I was among friends; I just wasn't one of them." I would soon be among friends, and it was certain that I wouldn't be one of them.

I drove the 15 minutes to campus with the radio off in silence, letting my mind freely wander and emotionally prepare. It didn't help much. My nerves were on edge, and I was a bit jittery. Arriving on the main campus of Delray University, I found the lot to my building – one I knew by heart — and parked. Feeling slightly out of breath from nerves, I walked across the lot and adjacent street, entered the building, and took the stairs to the fourth-floor conference room in the Dean's suite, eliciting unpleasant memories of my visit there earlier in the week.

Arriving at the suite five minutes early, I walked through the door to find Paula, positioned at her desk outside the conference room, with a welcoming smile on her face. I had known Paula for a long time, and we typically greeted each other with playful banter. Today, however, I wasn't in the mood.

"Hey, Paula," I said in the most cheerful voice I could muster. "How are you today?"

She looked straight through me, knowing that the cheerful voice was just an act, and said, in a just as cheerful, but far more convincing voice, "I'm fine, Noah. It looks like it is turning out to be a beautiful day. Since you are a few minutes early, can I get you a cup of coffee or something?"

"No thanks, Paula," I said. "I think I'll just have a seat and wait." I didn't have it in me to continue the small talk, and Paula sensed it.

She also knew, as a seasoned administrative assistant, that my meeting would be unpleasant, so she simply said, "I wish you luck, Noah. They should all be ready shortly."

Left to wait until 10 minutes past the hour, Dean Winston stepped out of the conference room, walked over to where I was sitting, and invited me in.

So, I realized to my annoyance, *they were in there all along – making me wait.*

Dean Winston was uncharacteristically brusque, with a hardness to his eyes that I hadn't seen before. I would have mistaken the look and attitude for anger if I didn't suspect that it had more to do with fear. He was juggling metaphorical hand grenades and was likely quite worried that it might scar his precious career. As I stood and prepared to follow the dean into the conference room, I remembered the recording device that sat in my shirt pocket. In a seemingly innocuous move, with the dean's back to me, I raised my hand to my shirt pocket and clicked on the pen's recording device.

The dean, in a nervous gesture, glanced back at me as my hand fell to my side, and ushered me into the dimly lit conference room. The room smelled of stale coffee and the sweat and lingering breath of the dozen or so faculty who had earlier occupied the cramped space. The wall was adorned with pictures of former administrators, all older white males, and all portraying an air of authority and competence, regardless of whether it was deserved.

Dean Winston told me to have a seat across from Dr. Finch and Dr. Marshall. They both had mixed looks of satisfaction, triumph, and something akin to meanness.

Once I was seated, Dean Winston looked my way and said, "Let's get straight to the point, shall we? I have brought Howard and Patricia here to act as witnesses to this conversation, provide input and insight where needed, and chime in on anything that I might have missed."

"First, though," he said with an air of self-importance, "I see that you have brought your laptop computer. Very good. Please give this to Howard so that he can keep it safe. He will provide it to our IT department so that they can analyze the device. We need to make sure that we can either identify or rule out any concerns with this computer, given what we found on your desktop."

The dean, pausing for effect, continued, "Before we discuss the issues surrounding your computer, I wanted to let you know that both Dr. Marshall and Dr. Finch will be bringing formal complaints against you through university channels for your trespass to their offices and the property that you took from them. Along with these complaints is the requirement that you return any documents that you took from them. I trust that you have brought them with you as well so that we can get that matter out of the way."

"Yes, I brought them," I said matter-of-factly.

"We all realize that this was an immature act on your part and one that we were originally willing to overlook. However, considering what was found on your computer, your colleagues and I feel that your behavior has risen to a level beyond immaturity to something far more serious."

"Dean Winston," I said as my insides felt like they had twisted into something that couldn't be untwisted, "perhaps I should have a lawyer present."

Dean Winston had now fully gained his composure and said in his most charming and condescending Brahmin accent, "You don't need to worry about incriminating yourself Noah. This isn't an interrogation, and we really only want what is best for you. This meeting is mainly just to let you know what avenues your colleagues and the university will be pursuing, and the reasons for it. Howard and Patricia mean you no harm, but you must admit that you would do the same thing if the shoe were on the other foot."

No harm, I thought, and almost laughed out loud. *They meant me no harm the way a lion means a gazelle no harm.*

The dean continued, "Now let me speak to the computer issue."

Computer issue, I again thought to myself, *that smug Bastard is calling it a computer issue. This has literally life and death consequences for me, with an end to my life as I know it hanging in the balance.* I resisted the urge to jump across the conference table and choke the life out of him, and just listened.

He said, "So, as I believe Howard told you earlier, we had sent your desktop computer to IT to perform routine software updates and diagnostics. While performing these tasks, they came across several picture files, as well as some video files that were, well, disturbing to say the least. It would be best described as 'child pornography.'"

Even though Finch's email had implied that they had found incriminating files on my computer, the dean's words gave it a sense of finality. This had the potential to not only end my career but see me end up in jail. I knew that if a criminal conviction came to pass, I wouldn't be the first innocent person to land in jail. Fear began to consume me as I sat anchored to my seat while adrenaline pumped through my veins. My heart raced, and I began to sweat.

The dean, sticking to the script, said, "I have been informed that these files are dated, and time stamped, which happens when you load them, and the dates and times indicated they were put on your computer beginning about a year and a half ago, with videos and images added at intervals from that time to the most recent, which was about a month ago. It seems that you have been quite busy with — well, let's call them 'extracurricular activities' on your work computer."

A cold silence fell over the room. Patricia looked over at me with a look of concern on her face that belied the look of triumph in her eyes. They had just stuck a metaphorical dagger through my heart and couldn't be happier.

She said, so convincingly that I almost started to believe her, "Noah, although I was deeply disturbed by your actions, I feel that what you really need is help. Please know that I am here for you if you need to talk. I can also provide advice on local mental health services that might be able to help you."

Man, now I really wanted to throttle her too. *What a load of crap*, I thought to myself, remembering Ted's advice to say as little as possible.

Finch remained mute and just stared blankly at me from across the table. I could just make out the faintest glimmer of amusement in his eyes though.

I bit my lip and remained silent.

"Well," Dean Winston said, breaking the tension, "This is what will happen from here. You will receive notice from the university of termination for cause. You will, of course, have the opportunity to present your case and defend yourself."

As if in a dream, I scanned the room and saw blank looks on the faces of Finch and Patricia. It must have taken a herculean effort for them not to show outward signs of gloating.

The dean then went for the kill when he said, "Noah, you also must know that we have notified the FBI and have an obligation to turn your computers over to them. They have taken possession of your desktop, and we have agreed to turn your laptop over to them once we have run diagnostics on it. Dr.

Finch will be working closely with university IT staff to ensure that your laptop remains secure and that diagnostics are run according to university protocol."

That is the fox guarding the henhouse, I thought to myself.

Dean Winston continued, "The FBI has jurisdiction over this issue, as they have authority to handle cases of child exploitation."

My breathing accelerated and I could feel a pulse throbbing in my temple. *The FBI? Child exploitation? Can this really be happening?* I thought.

"We are, of course, cooperating fully with the authorities," he went on to say. "Based on our conversations with them, I would encourage you to stay close at hand until we know where this is headed. I'm sure that the authorities will want to speak with you at some point soon."

I looked quickly back at Finch and saw the faintest of a smile — or perhaps it was a smirk — cross his face. He was really enjoying this.

Without skipping a beat, the dean continued, "We really wish that we could do more to help, but I'm afraid that the evidence is piling up against you. We sincerely want what is best for you Noah so please feel free to call if you need anything. Now, I have another important meeting that I must run off to — so if you would please let yourself out."

And with that, the meeting was over, and I was left with the very real prospect of losing my job, as well as spending some time in a holding cell, prior to a longer term of confinement in a federal penitentiary.

My anger and fear had now given way to a feeling of detachment, and a lightheadedness that left me unbalanced. I thought that I might faint but didn't care.

I walked blindly out of the conference room and didn't even respond when Paula gave me a look of genuine concern and said gently, "Goodbye, Noah, please take care."

The small part of my brain that was still functioning in the moment hoped that she didn't believe that I was a pedophile. She was a good person, and I cared about how she perceived me.

I then walked, without feeling, down the stairs and out to the parking lot to my truck. Before I reached it, I heard, as if from a distance, a woman's voice telling me to hold on a second.

I turned to see Patricia Marshall heading toward me. To my utter surprise, she gave me a full body hug. If it was because she felt some guilt, or it was all just part of her act, I couldn't know. I cringed — an involuntary response to someone I found to be utterly repulsive. Patricia pulled back a few feet, perhaps sensing my loathing for her, and met my eye.

She then asked, in what sounded like her best Wicked Witch of the West voice, "Have we now learned that it is unwise to mess with us? You have now become the perfect example to keep all the sheep at bay and discourage anyone else from being foolish enough to investigate our affairs."

My mind suddenly took a sharp U-turn, remembering the recording pen that sat in my shirt pocket. It was still recording, a fact which changed my mind-set from one of the hunted to the hunter. It was a welcome feeling, and one that sharpened my focus. As my mind raced, my first thought was that maybe I could use this opportunity to build a case for retaliation. To do this, I needed evidence that the punitive actions taken against me were based on acts that I had made in good faith in an official capacity — such as initiating the investigation into Finch's corporate activities last semester. Retaliation was a legal claim that I might be able to use to help clear my name and, if successful, be rewarded with a nice payday as well.

As she was enjoying this opportunity to gloat, and perceived my hesitation as weakness, I saw my opportunity and asked, portraying my best expression of indignation, "What did I ever do to you or Howard, outside of the other night? I have always been cordial, and even supportive in the past when I served as department head. Why would you do this to me? Why would you work so hard to have me terminated from my job, and ruin my life?"

Patricia looked at me with an air of extreme arrogance and replied, as if speaking to a scolded child, "It was because you didn't treat me with the respect that I deserve, and you had Howard investigated by the university about the corporation. This could have set us back. We were able to fill our bank accounts by moving money from certain accounts that were, shall we say, off limits — through the corporation, as you have undoubtedly figured out. Howard had worked extremely hard to create this brilliant scheme which..."

Patricia hesitated, unsure of how much she should say, but then continued. "This is much bigger than you would ever know, Noah. You didn't know to leave well enough alone, did you? You were more of an annoyance, than anything, at least until you had Howard and his activities related to the corporation investigated by the university. And then you had to go and break into our offices. What a mistake. I want you to know that it isn't personal. Please remember that. It all comes down to you getting into our business. For that, you will pay dearly I'm afraid. When will you ever learn that it doesn't pay to be ethical? I'm sure you will have time enough to think about this, though, while you are in prison."

With that, she turned on her heel and walked away, her head up and back straight, and with an air of utter conceit.

It was time for me to go home, but I had a few stops to make first.

Chapter 8

Preparations

MY FIRST STOP was to see my attorney, Gary Easterling, at the boutique firm of Easterling Law Offices. The firm employed eight attorneys, with practices focusing on employment, contract, and tort law. Gary specialized in employment law, and tort law, an area of law that addressed physical and emotional injury, as well as damage to a person's reputation. The firm was considered the best firm in town when one was harmed by the university in some manner, and Gary, a former university attorney, was the lawyer that every university administrator both feared and respected the most.

While Gary had served officially as my attorney, he was also a friend — not the type where you hang out all the time, but more of an arms-length friend. He had to be since he was my attorney. We had fished together a few times and grabbed a beer or coffee on occasion. He knew me well enough to know that I had a high ethical code and integrity in my dealings with both colleagues and students. In fact, he half-jokingly warned me once that my *Boy Scout mindset* would get me into trouble one day.

I walked through the door of the plush office building to the smell of coffee brewing. I don't think they ever turned the coffee machine off, as it was such important fuel for the legal machine. The front office was designed to induce a relaxing mood in visitors, with overstuffed couches and chairs, original oil paintings of pastoral scenes on the walls, and even a tropical fish tank in the corner.

I greeted his assistant Gayle with a smile and warm *hello.* She looked up and said, "It is good to see you again, Noah. Gary has been expecting you. He is between meetings but said that he would have a few minutes to meet. I understand that it is urgent. I hope things are OK with you."

I grinned and said, "Nothing that a good attorney can't fix." Not wanting to say more, I thanked Gayle and walked down the hallway to Gary's office.

Standing in the doorway to his office, Gary sensed my presence and looked up from his computer. He immediately got up and walked over to shake my hand saying, "Noah, it is great to see you, my friend. Let's talk in the conference room across the hall where we will have more room. Gayle likely told you that I'm between meetings, but I'll make what time you need, given that you said it was urgent."

When we were comfortably seated at the conference table, I said, "Gary, this *is* urgent. I'm afraid that I finally got myself into some serious trouble."

"I suppose that it has something to do with the university then," said Gary, knowing that I was a professor at Delray.

I took a sip of the rich, black coffee that Gary had brought from his office and, as concisely as possible, shared my recent experiences. I told him about breaking into the Institute and seeing Dr. Marshall and Associate Provost Snow engaged in a sexual encounter on the office floor, the documents that I had taken, including an important memo, and my encounter with Dr. Finch. I then gave Gary a synopsis of my meetings with the dean and my unsavory colleagues, and the changes in administrative roles.

Gary sat quietly and listened intently. When I next told him about the incriminating files they had planted on my desktop, the involvement of the FBI, and their intent to bring proceedings for termination for cause, Gary's look of concerned interest changed to one of razor-sharp focus. I knew that my problems had just landed squarely in his wheelhouse.

Gary said, "Please stop there for a moment, Noah. Have you said or done anything since they made the accusations related to the use of your computer?"

"Well, when I met with them this morning, I did turn in my laptop as they had requested."

"I wish you had waited," said Gary. "We might have been able to keep it out of Finch's hands through some legal maneuvering."

"For the first and probably only time in my life, I was able to say, "I think that I am a step of ahead of you Gary. Since I knew they would confiscate my laptop, my colleague Ted, who you know, connected me with a knowledgeable and trustworthy computer tech who put a hidden program on my computer that will reveal the *actual* time and date that any malicious files are planted on it. That way, if they plant anything on my laptop now, we can catch them red-handed."

"Well," said Gary, "that is a smart move. Let's hope it works."

"There is another thing that I need to tell you," I said. "I secretly recorded our meeting this morning, as well as an unanticipated conversation with Dr. Marshall who caught up with me in the parking lot after the meeting. She said things that might be incriminating to both her and Finch."

"It will be important, at some point," said Gary, "to listen to the recording and read the documents. I assume that copies of the documents you mention are in the packet that Ted left with Gayle."

"They are," I said.

"It is better that I leave them unread," said Gary, "for reasons I'm sure you know, as I saw your request to wait. It may be necessary to open the envelope and read the documents at some point, but I'll leave it sealed for now."

"OK," I said. "I certainly understand that. Also, as I mentioned, the dean told me that the FBI would be involved. He explained that this would happen since they had jurisdiction over child exploitation matters." Just saying this caused my pulse to quicken, a stress response that I couldn't control.

I forged on. "The dean also said that they had turned my desktop over to the FBI but would run diagnostics on my laptop before they turned that over to them as well. Dr. Fitch is overseeing that. Also, Dean Winston said that he had spoken with the FBI and understood that they would want to speak with me soon, and that I should stay close by."

Gary shook his head and said, "You weren't kidding when you said that you got yourself into some serious trouble. I was wondering what was going on when Ted dropped off the sealed envelope, followed by your request for an urgent meeting."

Then, as if he were a fortune teller with knowledge of the future, Gary told me exactly what he thought would happen next.

He said, "Noah, I believe that law enforcement will be coming to *apprehend* you — not *speak* with you. They will likely show up at your door with a show of force — most likely a SWAT team — by Monday at the latest. There is no way to know for sure, but I am certain that they will act as soon as they have procured the proper warrants and have a plan in place with a team ready to execute the plan."

"But I am just a college professor," I said, feeling like I would pass out, "not a hardened criminal with a cache of automatic weapons."

"It doesn't matter," said Gary. "This is a serious crime, and the university will probably want to make a statement, with news coverage of a SWAT team taking you down, and images of you in handcuffs. They will probably leak it to the media so I would expect the press to be there soon after the agents arrive. From what you have told me, it sounds like certain powerful people want to bury you deep. I don't know why, but I believe that you unwittingly uncovered something darker and more disturbing than you thought possible."

My gut churned, and I felt as though I might get sick.

Gary, sensing my unease, kept on pace. "I can't advise you to run, but I know that you have a place where you can hide and get off the grid. If you left before they came for you, and they later ask why you were not at home, you can claim that you were just taking some time away, while still in the vicinity — close-by as the dean requested — to clear your head or whatever they might believe. You can only stay gone for a few days though. I would say five days, tops. Be aware though, that if they come to apprehend you, and cannot find you, they could still put out a BOLO, and even offer a reward for your capture."

Offer a reward for my capture? When would I wake from this nightmare?

I couldn't help but blurt out, "So now I'm a common criminal with a bounty on my head? My reputation will be destroyed! I'm innocent!"

In a calm and professional voice, Gary said, "We will have to repair your reputation later. Once we get you out from under these false accusations, we can go on the attack and file civil lawsuits for retaliation and defamation. We will have to go where the evidence leads, though, and it will be a tough fight. Be sure to get a good copy of the recording you made and send it to me. Right now, the only evidence that I have is in the sealed envelope.

Even though it felt like only throwing a thimble-full of water on a burning building, I said, "Gary, you can rest easy knowing that there is some useful information in that envelope."

What Gary said next brought me back face-to-face with my predicament. He said patiently, "Anyway, for now, just know that if you choose to stay, they have enough evidence to put you in a prison cell until things are worked out. If the bail is set for a high dollar amount, you may be stuck there. There will also be the inevitable delays that the university will employ through legal maneuvering to keep you there. So, you may be in there awhile, and trust me, it is not the type of place you would want to have an extended stay, particularly given the particular allegations they are bringing."

I was thinking that I couldn't agree more.

"What we *can* control at this point is to ensure that your desktop is secure and can't be tampered with further. I know it is with the authorities, but as an important piece of evidence in any subsequent criminal proceedings it must be treated as such. I'll start the paperwork right away on that but will give your colleague's IT person a little time to work on your laptop. I'm sure they'll use the weekend to plant something on it, if that is what they choose to do. Who knows? They may be doing their bad deed even as we speak. From what you told me, the trap set by your tech friend sounds like a good one. Hopefully, it will work. I will have an order issued by the court to secure your laptop sometime next week."

Gary then lowered his voice and said in a near whisper, "Remember what I said, Noah, the Feds *will* be coming for you. Make your preparations now for a quick getaway and have everything you will need at the ready just in case they move up their timeline. They may wait until after the weekend, but I wouldn't count on it, and would certainly advise leaving no later than Monday. I sense that you have a long and difficult road ahead of you."

Gary got up from his chair and walked me to the front. He told Gayle to cancel his remaining meetings for the day. He needed some time to think this matter through and start planning for the events that he, given his many years of experience litigating matters with the university, might reasonably anticipate.

He simply said, "Good luck, Noah. I'll do my best to help you through this."

We shook hands, and I left. It felt good, knowing that I had honest and competent people in my court. Gary's words of warning were ringing loudly in my ears. It was time to run, and there was a growing feeling in my gut that I had better move fast. I didn't want my future self to be sleeping on a steel shelf with a dirty mattress and becoming intimate with cell mates who thought I was a pedophile.

On the drive home, a cold steel rain fell from a blanket of clouds above, portending the gloom and trouble that was certainly to come. My only salvation, at least a temporary one, lay across rural backroads by bike, and downriver by kayak to a secluded cabin tucked a hundred yards into the forest beside the Arkansas River.

The cabin was not mine, but instead owned by my former girlfriend who could have been — and should have been — my lifelong partner, Amanda Strauss. We had been in love but had chosen to pursue careers instead of our relationship. Despite this fact, we remained good friends. She had moved to Pine Bluff to work at a large accounting firm while I chose to follow my career as a college professor. She let me keep the key to her cabin though knowing that I would take good care of the place, one that she rarely visited. We never visited the cabin at the same time, most likely because neither of us wanted to be alone together and risk opening an old wound — or perhaps face our true feelings for one another.

It was a cozy place, and I kept it well stocked with all the comforts of home. One could stay there for at least a month without needing to buy provisions. The best thing about it though, at least for my current purpose, was that it was completely off the grid.

On my way home, I stopped by a drug store and picked up two burner phones and a few supplies. Luckily, the store was empty and the cashier, blinded by boredom, paid me little attention as she rung up my order. My second stop was to an ATM where I withdrew as much money as the machine would allow. This would supplement what I had stashed away in the safe at the cabin. Who knew what I would need in the coming days, weeks, or months?

I made it home about half past noon and, after making lunch, set about preparing for a quick getaway. My home was a comfortable one-story, two-bedroom structure that sat on a half-acre of land just outside of town and an easy drive to the university. Given that my mode of transportation for the first stage of my escape plan was my bike, I needed to make sure that it was in good working order. So, later that afternoon, I made some repairs. My bike had suffered minor damage from an earlier ride, when a not-so-friendly local in an oversized truck ran me off the road and into a stand of saplings. Both my bike and I took a bit of a beating.

I finished fixing my bike just as it began to grow dark. It seemed like the rain had ended just as the weather app had predicted — and I hoped it was right. I leaned my now fully functional bike against the wall just outside the window to the guest room where I would be staying tonight and hung my helmet from the handlebars.

I knew that the clock was ticking, and I was more than ready to make a run for it. I didn't want to risk, though, riding in the dark and paddling down river on a cold, rainy night. It was better, I reasoned, to have a nice meal and a glass of wine and try to get a little sleep. Maybe it would be another day or two before the authorities would show up at my door. It was all just too much to wrap my mind around and I hoped that this would all just go away. But the words that my father had drilled into me could not be ignored.

Hope for the best. Prepare for the worst.

I knew there was wisdom in these words, so tonight I would sleep with my clothes on, and with my escape plan at the ready.

Chapter 9

Den of Thieves

IN AN UPSCALE neighborhood, far above the pay grade of most faculty, the Institute's major players met at Dr. Marshall's house for a clandestine meeting.

Dr. Marshall was wealthy, though she lacked taste and class. This was reflected in her home, which had not a smidgen of architectural style or grace, nor the least feeling of warmth. The house and grounds were sterile and lacked any of the usual signs that would indicate a cheerful home. There were no flowers around her house that blossomed in the Spring and Summer, nor trees to provide shade, or a perch for songbirds. No children played outside. In fact, from the outside, the only sign of life was the occasional cold ray of light coming from somewhere inside what could best be described as an "ice palace."

Patricia and her husband Carl had amassed a fortune. Carl was the mirror image of Patricia. As the owner of a local car dealership, he was known to be unscrupulous — and like Patricia, his greed knew no bounds. Patricia had many female staff who worked for her, the most vulnerable of which she would *introduce* to Carl. It was rumored that he would take certain *liberties* with these students, having yet to be held accountable given certain well-placed threats from both himself and Patricia. It was sickening to hear. They were monsters.

Patricia was given full autonomy at Delray. The university tended to look the other way when she crossed the line — which was often — given the large amount of grant money she reeled in, and academic recognitions she had received. Delray University was primarily focused on two things: money and rankings, with money coming primarily from donors and large federal grants, and rankings determined, in part, by the number of prestigious honors or awards granted to faculty. Faculty who could check these boxes often became quite wealthy and powerful, as was the case with Patricia, and some of her colleagues seated around the table tonight. The problem, however, was that these particular faculty lacked a moral compass.

The interior of the house, while well-appointed with expensive appliances and furnishings, was just as cold and impersonal as the exterior. Though lacking warmth, the interior was made somewhat less sterile by the artifacts and souvenirs brought back from trips abroad adorning every nook and cranny. There were carvings from sub-Saharan Africa, paintings from Chile, artifacts from the aboriginal people of Australia, jade statues from China, and more — all intended to portray both wealth and a sophisticated lifestyle.

Arriving earlier, and seated around a large, circular oak table in the open kitchen and den area, were six people. In addition to Howard, Patricia, and her husband Carl, were colleagues and fellow faculty, Dr. Larry Pickering, and Dr. Anansi Jackson, as well as Patricia's right-hand woman, Dixie Borders.

Dixie was Patricia's assistant and an Institute staff-member who was trusted to keep Institute business and financial matters that skirted the law — or fell beyond — away from prying eyes. She was in her early thirties, with a plump pimply face and flabby body, made that way by sitting all day, binge drinking soft drinks and eating fast food by the truckload. She was also selfish to an unhealthy degree. She would do anything to please Patricia, whether through active and knowing involvement in sketchy dealings, or by just looking the other way.

Larry and Anansi were close colleagues and fellow Institute members who lacked even a hint of ethics or integrity between them. Larry, a tall, lanky man in his late fifties, wore earrings in both ears, and pulled his jet-black hair back into a braided ponytail. His appearance was maintained presumably to demonstrate that he was above caring about trivial matters, or just anything that didn't please his selfish nature. His aggressive and mean-spirited behavior was often overlooked given his many academic achievements, and especially his substantial grant funding. Larry was a big-time grant-getter, having been the architect behind the large grants and funding that fed the machine of the Institute, and which saw a substantial chunk of money from these grants find its way into the pockets of those seated around the table.

Anansi, in her late 40s, with eyes as black as pitch and hair to match, was an imposing figure, standing nearly six feet, three inches tall. Anansi, which means "spider trickster" in African folklore, was aptly named, given her cunning, wit, and use of deception. She outwardly portrayed both humility and reason, which belied an ambition and selfishness that knew no bounds. While appearing to be the most honest of the bunch in terms of her outward appearance as a soccer mom, devoted mother and spouse, and advocate for social equity and helping the underserved, she was at least as conniving as the rest. She had not an ounce of integrity or concern for ethics and would literally say or do anything to climb over people and up the ladder of what those meeting that night would consider *success*. She was the poster child for the type of person who would smile to your face while stabbing you in the back.

The gathering on this night was a den of thieves. None of the bunch, even Carl and Patricia who were spouses, were close in the sense of being friendly or intimate with one another. They were only bound together by the fact that they were all complicit in their unethical and illegal activities and shared one common attribute: greed.

Patricia had gathered them all together to discuss the circumstances pertinent to Noah Banks and their nefarious dealings, and to ensure that everyone was on the same page. Her power was also on display to keep anyone from falling out of line.

Patricia began the informal meeting with a loud cackle — uttered as an expression of cruelty – that might have passed as a laugh in another context or setting. Hearing it was enough for even her husband Carl to recoil a bit, given how purely malevolent it sounded, and given the accompanying expression of spitefulness that played on Patricia's face.

Patricia had brought out a bottle of fine wine from the cellar, a Chateau Margaux of reasonable age, though certainly not of the most expensive variety, and poured each at the table a small portion.

"Now," she stated with a look of triumph, "I will make a toast." "This toast," she said, her voice dripping with sarcasm, "is to our *wonderful* colleague, Noah Banks. May he now understand, to his great regret, that he should never, *ever* stand in our way or meddle in our affairs."

A smattering of applause from those around the table ensued.

She continued, her grin baring teeth as would a feral dog, "May he be appointed a roommate who is large and mean, hates child molesters, and who will show him the attention that he deserves over the many years he will spend in prison." She followed this with a big swig of wine, and then another cackle, this one louder and more forceful than the first.

Another smattering of applause, this time accompanied by nervous laughter, followed among the group.

When the room returned to silence, Howard said, in a voice as smooth as honey, "We will definitely be better off with that *little problem* out of the way." Howard was particularly good at keeping his emotions in check and staying focused on the business angle. He had worked in industry prior to entering academia, finding his current occupation to be much more lucrative, if played correctly and without the encumbrance of ethics.

Howard continued, "With no-one meddling in our business, we have better opportunity to look for ways to expand our enterprise and increase both our collective and personal revenue. He did take some documents from us that he has now returned — though that little punk probably didn't give us *everything* back. But it is of little consequence since we don't keep any incriminating evidence in our filing cabinets. Dixie can follow up, but I don't think that we have anything to be worried about"

He then added, in his best attempt at portraying sympathy, "I must also say that I am terribly disappointed in Noah. Finding those files on his computer was a real shock. I believe that he will be punished for his evil ways both here on earth and in front of his maker. I take no pleasure in this, I assure you."

His colleagues around the room looked at him with bewilderment and trepidation. They knew that Howard could lie with impunity, and they knew that he despised Noah. They had speculated among themselves that Howard actually believed that the lies and deception he crafted were true — the sign of a true sociopath.

"Dixie," Howard said, "You would probably know better than anyone what was in the files that Dr. Banks stole, given that you were responsible for organizing the files contained in the cabinet he took them from."

Dixie, beaming with confidence and reveling in the attention, said in reply, "I know *for a fact* that there weren't any documents in the cabinet he took the files from that could incriminate us. He dropped some papers the night he was there, so we know the exact filing cabinet that they came from. It held some notes, tax returns and financial information relevant to the Institute that we wouldn't necessarily want to broadcast, but they are technically in the public domain. We were intentional in ensuring that our written records would not provide enough pieces to the proverbial puzzle for anyone to see the whole picture and implicate us in any wrongdoing. We also must remember that we have the university behind us — at least *certain* influential university administrators."

Anansi, ever the diplomat, stole a glance at Patricia and, in her most charming voice, quickly interjected, "We know how much the university has graciously supported our important grant work to build the science and help the people and communities who need it most. We have a wonderful associate provost, the charming and intelligent Dr. Amos Snow, who fully supports our efforts. I'm sure that I join all of you in expressing how much we appreciate his support."

Anansi always spoke as if the room she occupied were bugged, and her words would be played back on television and the websites of the major news outlets. She, as with many faculty and administrators who lacked a moral compass, was a charmer, with a ruthlessness just under this thin veneer. Exceptions to the rule were Larry Pickering, who lacked any social grace, and Dixie who had yet to thoroughly develop the art of subtlety. They were often at risk of saying the wrong thing — or at least saying it the wrong way.

Anansi concluded by saying, "We will work to further our *relationships* with individuals both within and outside the university so that we will have the resources to support our Institute and continue doing our good work."

Patricia slightly and subconsciously blushed at Anansi's veiled reference to her relationship with Amos Snow — a relationship that her husband Carl could care less about. Anansi, ever attempting to score points with powerful faculty to strengthen her alliances, knew that she had just added a few points to her ledger.

Larry, a heavy drinker with the manners of a Labrador/Pitbull mix that had yet to be neutered, had finished his glass, and poured himself another, this time filling it to the brim. This earned a disapproving look from Patricia. Even though she was quite wealthy, she was known to pinch pennies and didn't wish to waste a bottle of good wine on her colleagues, much less be forced to open another. Larry didn't seem to notice or care.

"Hell," said Larry, "I won't sugar coat it like Anansi did. I'm glad that Son of a Bitch is going to prison. I hope they shank him quick so that I can dance on his grave."

This elicited a few gasps from those present — with a wide-eyed stare from Patricia, and a disapproving nod from Howard.

Heedless to the reaction of his colleagues, Larry continued, "I'd like to toast our IT guy for his ingenuity in planting the kiddy porn on Dr. Banks' computer so that it framed him perfectly. We have too much at stake here to let that little piss-ant tell his story, even if the university has our back, as Dixie points out. We will need to remain vigilant, though. If he is able to slip the hook somehow, we may need to resort to more *extreme* measures. As we all know, we have friends who can help."

Larry snickered and said, in a sing-song voice, "We know some dudes in some mighty looowww places.

Patricia, with a look of annoyance, quickly called the meeting to an end, pulled her chair back with a loud scrape, stood, and said, "Larry, I don't think that will be necessary. I have it on good authority that Dr. Banks will have no chance of slipping the hook, as you say."

With that, she ushered everyone out the door, pleased with herself that she was not forced to waste another bottle of good wine on her colleagues. When everyone had left, and Carl had gone upstairs to the study, she uncorked a bottle of 1990 Latour that she had saved for special occasions and poured herself a healthy portion. She sat down in her favorite chair and smiled to herself as she sipped the delicious Bordeaux.

Patricia held a secret — one shared by her lover, Amos, and one that she had kept from the group. Amos, whose position as associate provost allowed him access to information held by only a select few, had learned the time and place that the FBI would seek to apprehend Noah. He had shared this information with Patricia, who now knew that things would move faster than anticipated — and that made her incredibly happy.

She was going to sleep very well tonight — very well indeed.

Chapter 10

The Cabin

PATRICIA HAD UNDOUBTEDLY slept well last night. The same could not be said for me. At least my preparation, coupled with a lot of luck and a speedy escape by bike and boat, had bought my freedom from the authorities for the moment and, when she soon learned of my escape as I knew she would, likely ruined the taste of Patricia's morning soy caramel macchiato.

Once on dry land, I grabbed the bow handle on my boat and headed up the trail toward the cabin. Dragging my boat up the path for about twenty yards, I stopped at an old wooden shelter where I would store it. I removed my dry suit and placed it in the aft compartment along with my paddle, grabbed my go-bag, and covered my kayak with an old tarp to hide it from prying eyes. Satisfied that all was in order, I slung my pack over a shoulder for the remaining walk to the cabin.

As I walked up the trail, I felt a profound sense of freedom. Regardless of what happened from here, this day was mine. I would build a fire, eat, drink, and just let my mind wander into the contemplative zone. I walked the final distance to the cabin where everything was undisturbed and in order, entered the clean and comfortable place, and did just that.

The first order of business was to build a fire. I found the shelter beside the cabin where the firewood I had chopped and stacked last Fall was stored, and carried it inside. I built a roaring fire in the fireplace, and then took a much needed shower. The hot water washed over me, removing the dirt and grime from my body, along with a fair share of stress and anxiety. Donning a fresh, clean set of clothes, I pulled out my sleeping bag and pillow from the bedroom closet and laid in front of the fire on a thick, plush rug that I had bought for the cabin.

Feeling safe for the first time in what seemed like forever, I fell sound asleep.

I awoke some eight hours later around 5 o'clock with no other sound than the crackling of the fire. I grabbed some cheese spread from the fridge that I paired with crackers and poured a glass of scotch over ice. I sipped the rich and peaty single malt and let it slide down my throat to warm me from within, while the crackling fire did the same from without. The warmth and comfort of the moment allowed my mind to roam freely over the state of higher education as I recalled the more sordid details of my experience behind the curtain of academia. Someday, I mused, I'll write a tell-all book about my experiences. I only hoped that it wouldn't be from a jail cell.

After resting all day Sunday, I woke on Monday to one of those winter days that, after a storm had passed, promised to bring achingly clear blue skies and air as pure as water from a deep well. After breakfast and a cup of Ethiopian coffee, with the deeply rich taste that reminded me of the many mornings spent on my porch at home mentally preparing for my day as faculty at Delray, I decided to go for a walk through the forest.

The forest floor was damp, silencing my footfalls as I walked the narrow game trail that would guide me through the forest and along the river until it crossed the trail leading back to the cabin. Along the way, I passed through a pine forest and inhaled the sweet aroma. At one point, as I walked along the river, I sat on a log and tossed pebbles into the deep waters along the riverbank. The pebbles hit the water, sending small ripples outward for a short distance before they quickly sank and tumbled into the depths. Watching them hit the water, I contemplated my own life and how the ripples might represent the impact that my life had on others, while my ability to continue making a positive impact in this world seemed to be sinking into the deep waters of fear and despair.

I had been provided the opportunity to make a positive impact on the lives of my students and some of my faculty colleagues. My work also had a larger societal impact, given my research and service.

But what will happen to me from this point forward? I thought to myself. Will I sink and tumble into the depths like those stones, or do I have an obligation to fight for the opportunity to continue making a positive contribution through my life and work?

It was a small thing, throwing those pebbles into the river, but it somehow gave me hope, and something more — a desire to keep fighting for what was right, even in the face of immense odds.

Feeling a renewed sense of purpose and resolve, I rose from my perch and continued walking along the river until I met the trail that would lead me back to the cabin. Along the way, I stopped and checked to make sure that my kayak was secure. I found everything to be just as I had left it and made my way back.

Returning to the cabin, an uneasy feeling began to take hold. I didn't know what had triggered this feeling — call it a sixth sense or some form of intuition — but I knew better than to ignore it. Pulling the door closed and locking it behind me, I walked to far end of the main room and grabbed a burner phone out of my backpack. I dialed Gary's direct line.

He answered on the first ring, and said in a rush, "Man, you really are a popular guy."

"What do you mean?" I asked with growing alarm.

"It seems you have half the world looking for you, and most of them mean business. There are federal agents, state and local police, and a whole pack of journalists. Dean Winston has put out a request through the media for you to turn yourself in. He said that he and your colleagues are concerned for your safety and will do everything they can to help, if you decide to make the right decision and come back in. Of course, this is just an attempt to lure you back so they can put you in a holding cell."

For some reason, my mind had fixated on the word media. Stunned, I asked, "What form of media? Television, internet? Were there interviews?" even though I already knew the answers before asking the questions. There was no way that news like this involving a college professor and former administrator at a major university hadn't gone viral.

Gary, confirming my worst fears, said, "Dean Winston, Dr. Marshall and Dr. Finch, the only ones allowed to speak on the matter, provided scripted television interviews that were picked up by the media and shared via the internet."

My heart sank.

In a trembling voice, I asked, "Gary, what did they say?"

Gary responded, "I know this is hard, Noah, but hang with me. We will get through this, OK?"

"OK," I replied, feeling less hopeful than Gary.

"They said that they expressed deep disappointment in your behavior and that your actions took them totally by surprise. They also said that the rigors of academia were just too much for you to bear, as it was for some of the weaker-minded people in the profession, and they felt great sympathy for you. They also said they believed that after accepting the consequences of your actions, you would feel better and could eventually go on to leading a normal life after a period of rehabilitation."

They couldn't help it, I thought. They had to kick me while I was at my lowest with the "weak-minded" comment. They were shameless.

"Is there more?" I asked, as if this whole surreal experience was about another person, and not about me.

Gary quickly continued. "The university, for its part, sent out a formal statement on the matter as well."

My head was swimming now and I felt like my mind had left my body. With fear and anger rising in me, one word came unbidden to my lips.

"Assholes!" I practically yelled into the phone.

Gary said, matter-of-factly, "I think that just about sums it up."

"Listen," I said as I worked hard to bring my emotions back in check, "I've downloaded the recording from my meeting last week, and the conversation with Dr. Marshall in the parking lot and can play it back if you are in a secure location."

Gary replied, "Thanks, I was just going to ask you about that. I'm in my office with the door closed. Let me do this old-school and pull out my tape recorder. I'll put the phone on speaker and record it as you play it over the phone."

After the recording had played, Gary said, "I'm not sure that it would be admissible in court, but it sure is nice to have. I think that we can possibly use this in several ways. Now would also be a suitable time to tell me what those documents you have in the folder contain.

I told him that it was mostly financials, but the essential information could be summed up in one memo, and read the words that Finch had written verbatim.

"Wow," said Gary when I had finished. "And I thought I had seen it all." Pausing for a moment, Gary said, "Can you hold on a sec? I just received a text from my wife. OK, it says that she needs me to pick up our daughter from school. She is not feeling well. I'll need to hang up and call you back from the car."

A few minutes later, my phone rang, and Gary said, "I'm in the car now and you're on speaker. I have been mentally processing the information you shared with me and had been wondering why certain people within the university have gone to such extreme measures to ruin your reputation. It gives them too much exposure to liability. They usually take the high road."

"I was wondering the same thing," I concurred.

"I think it is possible that the dean, and those in the chain of command above Dr. Snow, including the university president, provost, and general counsel are being played by Dr. Snow and your colleagues."

"You mean that all of this could be compartmentalized, with Finch and his colleagues feeding false information to the dean, who then informs those up the chain? That is a very dangerous game," I said, with the realization dawning.

"Yes, it is," said Gary. "And it implies that the stakes are quite high. If we can discover your colleagues' 'end game,' then it should tell us why all of this is happening to you."

"And what does Associate Provost Snow have to do with all of this?

I wish we knew. I have deposed Dr. Snow several times in lawsuits against the university and can tell you that he is one of the most conniving and treacherous people that I have encountered in higher education. The provost mainly avoids him, and the university president rarely has any interaction with him other than through formal university functions. Even the university lawyer, Jim Sanford, avoids Snow like the plague."

"That was my impression of him as well from the few times we met," I said. "So, Gary, what does this all mean?"

"I really don't know with certainty. I do still believe that we will get through this, though. Please listen close and take my advice. Given what we know, and the danger you are in, do not, under any circumstances, reveal your location to anyone.

"It goes without saying, and I could be disbarred for even suggesting this, but do not turn yourself in. Those connections on the outside that Dr. Finch implies in his memo probably have connections on the inside as well — by inside, I mean, the jails. I can't put too fine a point on this Noah. If you want to live, you need to stay hidden."

"I can do that," I replied.

"I will handle things on my end. We have secured your desktop, and I'm sure that if your colleagues plan to put any-thing malicious on your laptop computer, they will up their time frame. I believe they will want to sustain the momentum they have established, keeping university officials sufficiently stirred up and wanting to put this matter — and you — behind them quickly to avoid any further bad publicity.

"I'll make a request to secure your laptop when we get off the phone and will push hard to have it locked up so that we can ensure that they won't have time to run diagnostics and find the program that you planted. I want to catch them in the act as it is the only way to clear your name — and hopefully turn the tables."

"That makes perfect sense," I muttered, my head spinning.

"Call me back tomorrow at noon sharp, Noah, and I'll fill you in. Please remember to take my advice and lay low."

Before I could even say thank you or goodbye, Gary had hung up. As I sat there alone in the cabin, the enormity of it all hit me. What would my parents think? I had kept them completely out of it, but by now I was quite sure that report-ers and the authorities had swarmed them, asking all kinds of questions about my whereabouts, motivations, past behaviors, and the like.

Fortunately, I thought, my parents didn't know that I was staying at the cabin. It was also fortunate, but made me feel terrible to the core, that they had no prior knowledge of any of this, or how much trouble — and danger — I was in. My parents were tough as nails and from a generation that had seen their share of difficulty, so I felt certain they could handle it. They also knew me better than anyone and would know that the accusations made against me were unfounded. I took some comfort in this knowledge.

Both of my parents were teachers, my father having worked as a lecturer at a small liberal arts college, so they both knew the games that were played in academia. Also, since I often vented about my colleagues, they knew their sinister nature. Nothing, however, could have prepared any of us for this level of cruelty and deception.

I would take Gary's advice and remain hidden. It wouldn't be long, at any rate, before I would learn more about how this would all play out. At this point, there really wasn't much more for me to do until I spoke with Gary again tomorrow, so I went about doing the things that one usually does to pass the time: eating, exercising, reading, sleeping, and just waiting.

Unknown to me was that not long after my call had ended with Gary, another would be made that would set in motion events that would again change the course of my life. It would be wise to trust my intuition.

I wasn't safe here.

Chapter 11

Sinister Forces

AT A SECRET location near Delray, Leroy Jones answered his phone on a secure line. Leroy knew who called his private number so there was no need for introductions.

Before the voice on the other end of the line could speak, Leroy said, "Hey Cuz, what can I do you for?"

The voice said, "We have a problem, Leroy. It's Banks."

"What the hell," said Leroy, his voice dripping with cruelty, "I thought we had that problem resolved. Isn't he heading to prison? I told my boys in the pen that he was coming, and they were already anticipating a date night for him that was guaranteed to not end well. Sometimes date night ends with a shanking."

"Yeah, yeah," the voice said. "Tell them to find another date and listen up. We've just learned some information that calls for a change of plans."

"What did you find out," replied Leroy.

The voice said, "You didn't know this, but we had groomed — through the usual methods — a custodial staff in Dr. Bank's college to do some spying for us. We had secretly, through our connections, helped him get a side job cleaning the East-erling Law Offices. As you know, that spineless snake, Gary

Easterling, is Bank's attorney. We had him plant some bugs in both Easterling's office and his paralegal's office."

"I like your style," said Leroy.

"Yeah, well, Banks called him a few hours ago. We learned by listening to their conversation that Banks has a secret recording, and a memo that he stole from the Institute that is incriminating enough to bring unwanted attention to ourselves. We can't let that see the light of day."

"Did he make copies of that memo?" asked Leroy, seeing the implications.

"We can't be sure but we don't think so. He read the memo to Easterling over the phone, and neither mentioned having any copies. The Feds no doubt went through Banks' house with a fine tooth comb after those bumbling fools failed to catch him. No reports came back to us through our contacts that they found anything. I think it's a sure bet that he has the only copy, and he is holding it close to the vest. I'll have to give that boy some credit. He is smart."

Leroy chuckled, "You getting soft on me Cuz? He's still just an annoying little problem — like a flea on a dog's ass, if you ask me."

The voice began again, a little more firmly now, "The stakes are just too high now to allow him to tell his story. From the conversation with his attorney, we have learned that he knows a lot more than we had suspected. He also has a secret recording of a conversation he had with a colleague from the Institute that is incriminating. If he and his attorney use this information to their advantage, which we're sure they will, either in a lawsuit or a leak to the media, all of our hard work and planning will go up in smoke. We need to eliminate Banks. With him gone, his attorney will no longer have a client, or the evidence, and we can continue our enterprise free of interference. We need to take drastic measures. This is where your expertise is needed."

"You're speaking my language, Cuz," replied Leroy.

"Fortunately," said the voice on the other end of the line, Easterling's paralegal talks to herself a lot while she works — and, from the bug placed under her workstation, we have heard everything she says. From what we could gather, she had taken it upon herself to find out where Banks had gone to ground. We're not sure why — out of curiosity maybe. It doesn't matter. What does matter is that she hasn't told Easterling yet — and we think we now know where Banks is holed up."

"I'm all ears Cuz."

"From our surveillance, we were able to discern the nature of her search. She discovered that our boy has an ex-girlfriend with a cabin not far from here — right on the eastern border of the Holden Wildlife Refuge. I pulled up Google maps and found a cabin where I think he is hiding. It is the only one located near the eastern border. I know that some of your boys hunt illegally around there from time to time. See if they have ever run across a cabin in that area."

"That should be easy. What then?" asked Leroy, his voice dripping with murderous anticipation. It was the voice of a true psychopath.

The voice said simply, "Take some of your boys and eliminate him."

"Now we're talking," said Leroy.

"Make it look like it was just some ignorant rednecks out seeking some vigilante justice. That shouldn't be hard for you to do."

"Very funny," replied Leroy.

In a more serious tone, the voice said, "Let's keep the real reason for doing this between you and me and your inner circle. The boys who go with you should believe that it's about vigilante justice. I know it won't be a hard sell, eliminating a scumbag pedophile."

"Sure Cuz, no problem. We'll hold him down inside the cabin with a hail of gunfire, set fire to the place, and burn him alive inside. That way we can eliminate him, the memo, the recording, and anything else he has up his sleeve all at once. It gets me all excited just thinking about it."

With urgency, the voice said, "Also Leroy, we need this done quick, and don't leave any evidence like shell casings behind."

Leroy, who could turn violent in an instant, said, "Cuz, if you don't stop talking, I'm gonna get angry. You know how careful I am about things like that, and I've trained my boys well.

"Sorry, Leroy," said the voice. "I understand. I'm just a little nervous."

"No need to worry, Cuz. We'll do it right. The boys and I will make sure there isn't much left of the place to search through. We don't have to worry about our work and planning going up in smoke. The only thing that will go up in smoke will be Banks and the cards he's been holding."

"I have no doubt," said the voice, and I appreciate your personal involvement in making sure this is done right."

"You well know, Cuz, that I keep a very low profile and don't usually get involved in the dirty work. Not because I don't want to, but because I'm too important to 'The Cause' to risk being captured. I'm just doing it as a personal favor, and it will feel good to do some wet-work for a change and bar-b-que that pretty-boy Son of a Bitch."

"Thanks Leroy," said the voice, "I'll be back in touch tomorrow early evening, by which time I would expect the deed to have been done."

"OK, Cuz, I'll take care of it and will take great pleasure in sharing the details."

With that, the call ended.

Chapter 12

Under Siege

AT NOON SHARP the following day, I called Gary. He picked up without hesitation and, in an animated voice, said, "They took the bait!" Buoyed with hope, I asked, "So what happened?"

"Well, earlier this morning, I made the request to procure and safeguard your laptop computer. University legal counsel said that they would comply once IT had finished their analysis of the computer's contents. I feigned a threatening legal posture to not arouse suspicion since I wanted to give them enough time to do their dirty work — and they did just that.

"Just a half-hour ago, the university made an announcement — this time saying that another of your work computers, your *laptop*, also had incriminating video and image files on it. They also announced they had found other files — ones that made you appear unhinged — and shared it all with the media."

Finch really doesn't know when to leave well enough alone, does he? I thought to myself.

"Hang on," said Gary, sensing my eagerness to ask questions. "There is another important development. Shortly after the university's announcement came out, I received a call from Jim Sanford, the university attorney, saying that the FBI would now be securing your laptop. We will need to work with the FBI, and through the proper channels before our tech people can have at it, but it shouldn't take long. I know someone who used to work for the university but is now doing independent consulting. He is one of the best. A bit pricey, but I'll front the cost for you until we get further along. I'm betting that we can succeed in a civil lawsuit once this settles out, so I'll get my payment then. How does this sound to you?"

"Wow," I said, "That sounds great. What should I do?"

"Officially, I am asking you to turn yourself in to the authorities. Unofficially, follow my advice from yesterday."

"Look," said Gary, "It will be difficult for a while, I won't sugar coat it, but in the end we will prevail. Just keep the faith and trust me on this."

"*Thank you*, I said, my words feeling hollow. There was no way that I could adequately express my gratitude. I hung up first this time and sat motionless with the phone in my hand for what seemed like many minutes.

Once I had snapped out of it, and came to grips with my emotions, I allowed my mental discipline to kick in and sort out what I knew. They had taken the bait and now it would be in the hands of our tech experts to reveal the truth about the planted files. My career and reputation was still greatly at risk though, and the FBI was still after me. Who knew how long it would take to clear my name — and if that would even happen given the power wielded by the university. I was still on the hook, regardless, for breaking into the Fin-Mar Research Institute and taking the documents. *I was still a man on the run.*

The thought also occurred to me that Amanda didn't know anything about what I was enduring, or that it had all been manufactured by some very corrupt people to destroy my life and reputation. In all honesty, however, I was more concerned about her wellbeing than what she might think about me.

How long would it take for someone to look back into my history and find her? Was I putting her at risk?

Fueling my gut instinct that it was no longer safe to stay at the cabin, was a literal concern. If someone learned of our prior relationship, and she were tricked or coerced into telling them about the cabin, they would be coming for me.

It was time to leave. But first, I would leave a message for Amanda should she ever return here. The thought then occurred to me that I should also leave one for my parents.

Knowing that the cabin, sitting isolated and vacant for long stretches, could be broken into, we had installed a hidden safe for storing money and valuables.

It was perfect for what I needed to do.

I wrote a three page note, intended for Amanda and my parents, explaining what had happened to me and why. I also explained why I was innocent of the charges and accusations, along with my sincere apologies for not letting them know sooner. I knew that Amanda, if she were to find the note, would share it with my parents.

Walking to the rock chimney and standing on the lower portion of the fireplace, I reached up and pulled lightly on an edge of a rock slightly protruding from the face of the chimney. The rock — or more accurately, a thin veneer of it — swung outward on cleverly concealed hinges, revealing a small fireproof safe.

I removed a large wad of cash that I had stashed there a few months ago, and replaced it with the handwritten note and, beneath it, an envelope containing the pen and documents labeled simply "evidence." I then closed and locked the safe and moved the faux rock covering back to conceal the safe. I reasoned that the evidence would be safer here than in my boat and wherever I was headed on the river. I could always come back for it.

I had to admit that it was a longshot that Amanda would come back to the cabin and check the safe, but long shots were all I had.

I didn't know how long I would be gone, but I reasoned that it would be best to leave first thing in the morning and start heading downstream. The silent alarm in my brain was providing a compelling warning. This time no-one, not even Gary, would know where I was. Heck, even I didn't know exactly where I would be tomorrow night. On this night, I wouldn't stay in the cabin, but would instead take the added precaution of camping at a secluded spot far into the woods.

I prepared eggs and bacon, along with a thermos of coffee, for the following morning and packed as many provisions as I felt my boat could safely carry. Well prepared for the journey ahead, I locked the door and headed off into the woods to spend the rest of the day and evening. I planned to leave before sunrise tomorrow.

I walked through open woods and down a nearly invisible game trail to a spot in a small clearing that I used for camping whenever I wanted to sleep under the stars, or just be alone with nature. In the clearing, there was a bed of dry pine needles spread across the forest floor. A log, which I had carved out to provide a comfortable seat, sat beside a small fire pit ringed with river rock. Luckily, it had turned unseasonably warm, with high temperatures in the mid-sixties and lows at night only dipping into the low-forties.

An experienced wilderness camper, I had all the gear that I needed for the night and however many nights lay ahead of me while on the run. My gear was lightweight, including my tent, which was durable, wind/waterproof, and comfortable.

As the day wore on, I took a short nap and then built a small fire, intentionally creating one that would give off little smoke. I cooked a hot dog and heated up some baked beans over the fire. I always loved eating food cooked outside over a fire, because it really didn't matter what you were cooking, it always just seemed to taste good. I washed it down with a Coke and made mental preparations for what was to come.

As I sat and mentally mapped out my first few nights and camping spots downstream, I was suddenly distracted by the faint smell of smoke and the staccato sound of gunfire in the distance.

Dousing the campfire, and quickly packing and arranging my gear, laying it against the trunk of a tall evergreen, I set off in the direction of the gunfire to investigate what was happening. It sounded like it was coming from the direction of the cabin.

I made my way slowly and quietly through the woods toward the cabin, and the source of an ever-growing cloud of smoke. As I drew near, I could hear human voices and the sound of sporadic gunfire from automatic rifles. I knelt behind the hollowed-out trunk of a long-dead oak tree, wondering, *Had the authorities found me? Why then would they have set fire to the cabin? And who was shooting and who were they shooting at?* I was sure that wasn't part of the FBI's protocol.

The voices soon revealed that they were not the authorities. One said, in a thick, surly drawl, "Burn, you sick Son of a Bitch. This will teach you fancy college boy what we do to sick Bastards like you. We care about our kids and don't cotton to the likes of you. We know you're in there and you can either come out or burn, just like you will in hell."

I could hear more of the group, it was impossible to say how many, laugh and yell obscenities in response as they continued to take random shots at the cabin.

I crawled from my hiding space, then rose to my feet and, crouching low, walked quickly and cautiously away. Once confident that I was well out of sight, I broke into a full run through the woods back to my campsite, leaving the ruined cabin and sound of scattered gunfire in my wake. Back at the clearing, I quickly stamped out any possible remnants of the fire, gathered my belongings and warily made my way through the woods toward the shelter where my boat was hidden, stopping occasionally to listen for any sign of immediate danger. It was possible they had positioned someone at the riverbank to prevent my escape. I could only hope that their bravado and overconfidence would keep their focus on the cabin, as they watched it burn to the ground.

Nearing the shelter where my boat was hidden, I slowed and crept quietly forward, keeping to the back side of the old wooden structure. The sound of gunfire had subsided to the occasional *pop, pop*, in the direction of the cabin, indicating they were winding down and their focus might soon shift. I didn't want to be anywhere near this place if it shifted in the direction of the river. Thankfully, at least for now, I was alone. I breathed a sigh of relief before removing the tarp that covered my boat and quickly storing my gear. I pulled my boat out of the shelter and onto the trail, grasping the bow handle. With the clock ticking down in my head, I practically ran down the path toward the river dragging the fully-laden boat behind me, my leg muscles aching under the strain.

Fortune smiled upon me when I reached the riverbank and found it vacant. Breathing heavily from the exertion, I opened the forward compartment and, leaving the dry suit, retrieved and assembled my paddle. Remembering the burner phone in my pocket, I pulled it out and chucked it into the river, not knowing whether it was this device that had led those Bastards to the cabin.

As I pushed off into the relative safety of the river with black smoke billowing up behind me through the woods, two things were clear: one, I needed to go completely off the grid and, two, I owed Amanda bigtime.

LATER THAT DAY, Leroy was back in his secret compound enjoying a cigar and glass of whiskey, neat. He heard the distinctive ring that told him who was calling and picked up the phone.

The voice that called sounded hard and tense. It said, "Give me a situation report."

Leroy, countering the serious tone with an equally contrary casual one said, "No need to get all serious on me, Cuz. We handled the situation."

The voice asked, "Are you sure that you eliminated our *problem*?"

Leroy, his voice a bit slurred from the drink, said, "We never had eyes on him if that's what you mean. My boys did a quick search of the woods near the cabin though and didn't see hide nor hair of him. One of the boys did find signs that someone had been going in and out recently though, and checked the door and found it locked, so it would stand to reason that he was inside. With the cabin burning, and the fire department on its way, we didn't have time to hang around and look for him. Besides, the fire burned so hot that the devil himself couldn't have gone near that cabin."

The man behind the voice was not happy. He had no way of knowing for certain whether Noah was still alive and out there somewhere. If he had escaped, with the area encompassing many miles of wilderness, he could stay hidden indefinitely.

All he could say was, "Thanks Leroy. We think that his attorney has a few tricks up his sleeve, but without a client, it doesn't matter anymore. We still have Easterling's offices bugged, so if we have any indication that he is still alive, and where he could be going next, we'll let you know."

"Sure, Cuz," replied Leroy. "I think we got him, but it always pays to cover all your bases. I wouldn't have made it to where I am by being stupid. If you ever find out that Banks *cat* has nine lives, and somehow escaped, I want to be the first to know. I'll take some of my best boys and we'll go hunting for him. If it comes to that, he will need more than luck to survive."

Chapter 13

Lawyer Advocate

GARY EASTERLING WAS in a good mood. The trap had been sprung, and he could now prove his client's innocence — at least for the charges related to the incriminating files that had been planted on Noah's laptop computer.

It had all happened very fast.

Yesterday, after speaking with Noah, he had demanded that his client's laptop be secured and, after seeking and obtaining the necessary conditional approvals from the FBI, his request had been granted. A call to Judge Harry Nusbaum, his friend from his law school days, had resulted in the acquisition of the appropriate paperwork and greatly helped to expedite matters.

Once the laptop was secured and in his possession, he called in his IT expert to inspect the computer — of course, under the watchful eye of an FBI computer forensics expert.

After two hours of examining code and running full diagnostics on the computer, his expert leaned back, took a deep breath, and said, "Mr. Easterling, without a doubt, these files have been doctored to reflect an inaccurate time and date." He then spent the next fifteen minutes explaining how he reached this conclusion. The only other person in the room who could understand it all was the FBI computer tech who was monitoring the situation. He simply nodded and quickly left the room to make a call, presumably to his superiors.

Gary smiled. He had them over the barrel now. He even had a signed affidavit from his computer expert stating that the malicious information had been placed on Dr. Bank's computer after it had left his possession, with a list of times and dates when each file was planted on the computer.

The real times and dates of when the incriminating files were planted were all very close together, occurring over a three hour time span last Friday afternoon – the same day that Noah had handed over his laptop, and not long before the FBI had raided his home. They had moved very quickly.

Given the speed by which things were moving, he needed to put the brakes on it.

Enough was enough.

His client had clearly been framed and should no longer be on the run from the authorities. Even though he knew that the FBI computer tech would have alerted his supervisors, he didn't trust that the wheels of justice would move fast enough on their own.

To give those wheels a boost, Gary decided to email a copy of his computer expert's affidavit to his longtime nemesis, Jim Sanford, the head attorney for Delray University. He knew that he wouldn't have to wait long for a reply — and he wasn't disappointed.

Less than ten minutes had passed when Gary's phone lit up with a message from Gayle, telling him that a Mr. Jim Sanford was on line two. Gary waited a minute before punching the button on his phone. When the call connected, the booming and cocksure voice of Jim Sanford said in greeting, "Hey there Gary, it's me, Jim. How's it going? Still telling those fishing stories about the big one that got away?"

Gary decided to play along. "Sure Jim, you should have seen the size of that monster. I could probably guess why you're calling."

"You've always been a *smart* one," said Jim in his best southern drawl. "Let me tell you, I sure hated to hear about your client. Dr. Noah Banks, is it? Seems like he's had a rough time of it. Let me make this short and sweet. To show good faith, and that the university cares about its faculty, we are going to drop all charges against Dr. Banks."

"That sure is kind of you," replied Gary sarcastically, relishing the opportunity to stick it to his nemesis. "Especially since my client is innocent and the university framed him."

"*Come on*, Gary," replied Jim. "There is no reason to get all worked up. There were some mistakes made here, and I assure you that we will get to the bottom of it. If you would show the good sense to keep this under your hat until the university can do some checking on who was behind it, I would be most appreciative. Once we find the rascal responsible for this, we will be releasing a prepared statement that should help to improve matters for your client."

His voice dripping with sarcasm, Gary said, "Thank you Jim. I hope that you realize that the 'mistakes' that were made by *your* university were both unconscionable and have resulted in my client experiencing extreme emotional distress and substantial pain and suffering. I look forward with great anticipation to the next time we meet. It will be on ground familiar to both of us. Have a great day."

With that, and before Jim could reply, Gary hung up. He rarely had to reign in his temper, but Jim's arrogance was just about more than he could take. Gary had lived long enough and fought enough legal battles to know that this was far from over. Still, this was good news, and could portend success in a civil suit, as well as good publicity for himself and his firm.

He knew that he was getting ahead of himself and was sure that Jim had something up his sleeve. When you boiled everything out of the conversation, all that was left was Jim's request — akin to begging, coming from him — that Gary hold off on making any announcements until the university had made theirs.

Gary rocked back in his office chair and thought, *How would the university spin this?* He had worked for them in the past and knew their tactics. They could come clean and throw Finch under the bus, but this would open them up to liability and be devastating to public relations efforts and donor relationships. This was off the table as an option.

There was one good option for them, Gary thought. It was to shift the blame. If he were a betting man, he would bet that their next move would be to prepare a statement that would place the blame on some poor junior IT staff member and quietly ruin their life, just as they had attempted to do with Noah. The bad actors in the college, and everyone else in administration up the chain, would then be off the hook.

Gary picked up the phone and called Rob Ross, a journalist with a modicum of integrity, who was with a news agency that knew how to milk a story for all it was worth. Gary knew he had a major story, and it wouldn't take much to persuade Rob to run with it. He was pleased when Rob answered.

"Hi Rob, this is Gary, your attorney friend. Boy, do I have a story for you. I'm sure it will make your day and score you some serious points with your boss."

Rob, not one for small talk, replied matter-of-factly, "That sounds great Gary, do you mind if I record our conversation?"

"No problem, go right ahead. My client, Dr. Noah Banks, a professor of sociology at Delray University, has been seriously mistreated. The manner in which the university and his direct supervisors have treated him is unconscionable. And Rob, pay attention because this is where it gets really interesting. My client was accused of placing graphic pornographic images and videos of children on his work computers."

"Wow," replied Rob. "*That* Dr. Noah Banks? He has been all over the news. I had even considered running that story down myself. I'm sorry. Please continue."

"No problem. After this came to my attention, we had both his desktop and laptop computers secured so that our tech people could look at them. We called in the very best computer expert to run diagnostics on his laptop computer, and he found that the incriminating files had been planted, the proof being that the files had been added *after* Dr. Banks had turned his computer into the university. We suspect we will find that malicious files were planted on Dr. Bank's desktop as well, once our computer experts have a look at it."

"No kidding," said Rob, amazed at his good fortune for getting the scoop on this story before any of his blood-thirsty colleagues. He would indeed score some serious points with his boss.

Gary continued. "Off the record, they will probably spin this to frame some poor junior IT staffer and claim that university administration was *unaware* the files had been planted— which, granted, at least for the most part, they probably were. I fear for my client's safety given the false and extremely harmful accusations the university and his supervisors have made against him. This has the feel of retaliation, and the accusations they have made against him are both false and defamatory. We will get to the bottom of this, you can be assured."

"So let me get this straight," said Rob, his sharp journalistic mind processing what he had heard, "someone working for Delray University framed Dr. Banks. Do we know who the *actual* person might be? You also said that those in university administration were 'probably' unaware. Is there anyone you can think of who *was* aware?"

"We don't know who exactly, but we do know that his department head, Dr. Howard Finch, took custody of his computers. His laptop was acquired during a meeting with, and in the presence of, Dr. Finch, an associate dean named Dr. Patricia Marshall, and the dean, Dr. Jeremy Winston. We also know that Finch suspected him of filing an anonymous ethics complaint against him. It would have to be proved but this could be a form of retaliation. As for who in the chain of command might have been aware, the suspects are few and I don't want to speculate."

"Fair enough, said Rob, while typing furiously. "It also seems extreme."

"Yes, it does. Before we lost touch with him, he confided in me that he suspected there was something more sinister at play that might even involve people outside the university."

This keeps getting better and better, thought Rob, as visions of a Pulitzer were beginning to form in his mind.

"Thanks," said Rob, this will give me several leads to run down. Any idea where he might be hiding?

"Nope," lied Gary, although he had a pretty good idea.

Pivoting, Gary said, "Listen Rob, we now know that someone set him up — planting files on his laptop to ruin him and, as I alluded to earlier, we feel confident that we'll discover that they did the same with his desktop. Once we have verified that, I'll let you know."

Rob, knowing that this was a *huge* story, and one that would likely get better the more he learned, said, "I'm sure more questions will pop up as I conduct research for the story. Can I loop back with you?"

"Certainly, said Gary, confident that he had set the hook. I am more than happy to help."

After ending the call, Gary leaned back in his chair with a feeling of immense satisfaction. He had done well by his client. He had taken a step toward repairing Noah's image in the public eye, and perhaps more importantly, planted the seeds to benefit the defamation and retaliations lawsuits he planned to bring, knowing that Rob's story would reach a large potential jury pool.

Gary was jolted from these thoughts when his desk phone rang. It was his paralegal Brittany, a third-year law student and one of the brightest minds he had known, asking whether he had a few minutes.

Gary sat up, sensing that she might have something important to share. "Sure Brittany, I'll be right over." He walked the short distance down the hall to her office and, stopping in the doorway, could see Brittany sitting at her desk peering intently at her computer.

Noticing his presence, she looked up and said, "Hi Gary, I found something of interest and wanted to share it with you."

Gary said, "Sure, Brittany, what is it? I was working on the Banks matter when you called."

"That would be good timing then. I made discoveries pertinent to Dr. Banks that might be of immediate interest. I took it upon myself to do some research. I hope you don't mind."

"Not at all, Brittany," replied Gary. "Please proceed."

"I think I know where Noah is hiding. First, let me give you some background. Digging into Noah's past, I came across, through a Google search, a reference to Noah and a young woman named Amanda Strauss who had run a 5k together. There was even a picture of the two standing side by side. They looked like the typical happy couple. I also found a few other references and several pictures of them attending other events together.

"After following a few possible leads to a dead end, I looked up Amanda Strauss and learned more about her. She is now

36 years old. I also discovered that she is a former graduate student in accounting at a liberal arts university in Pine Bluff, only 65 miles from Delray. I assume that they must have met while Noah was a junior professor at Delray University, and while she was in school there. After graduate school, Amanda got a job at a large accounting firm in Little Rock, where, by all accounts, she has been quite successful. I then began a search..."

"Hold on Brittany," said Gary in a voice that was more impatient than he intended. "I already know that Gary was close to a woman named Amanda in the past, and that she has a cabin by the river — *and* that is where he is probably staying. I even know the approximate location. No-one else knows this so please keep this in confidence."

"OK," said Brittany, un-phased by her boss's revelation. "What you probably don't know is that Amanda has a brother, John Strauss, who is mysteriously absent on the internet. I had to dig deep in our databases to find him. He has a home just north of Baton Rouge, Louisiana. Noah obviously isn't hiding in Baton Rouge, but as you taught me, you never know when certain information might come in handy."

"Good work Brittany," said Gary as he turned to leave.

"There is more," said Brittany, halting Gary in tracks. "Hot off the press — I found where the university has come out with a prepared statement about the laptop incident."

"Wow," said Gary his interest now piqued. "That was fast. I just got off the phone with Jim Sanford. They must have had it prepared before we talked and hit the send button literally right after I ended the call. What does it say?"

Brittany, summarizing the announcement said, "It is basically a very dry statement saying that computer security was of the upmost importance to the university and that everyone should take it very seriously. It goes on to say that there was an incident involving a breach of computer system protocols that resulted in the unfortunate misperception that one of our university faculty had been involved in criminal and unethical behavior. It further states that there is an ongoing and active investigation into the nature and circumstances leading to the incident. They stress that all faculty, staff, and students be cognizant of security measures, and provided a link to university policies on password protection and other security measures that could be taken to protect yourself."

Gary was good at reading between the lines when it came to university announcements. He said, "Can you read back what they said about a breach of computer system protocols?"

Brittany read it back.

Gary rubbed his chin and said, "This further supports my suspicion that they will place the blame on some powerless junior IT staffer. It is a small thing to admit that university protocols were breached and that a lower-level employee took advantage. It is a much bigger issue if they have to admit that the university — which would include Finch as department head — were complicit in it."

"Do you think that Noah will ever be able to clear his name?" asked Brittany. "My impression of him is that he is a good person."

"I think that he has a long road ahead of him." replied Gary. "It bothers me that the university didn't make an attempt to clear his name. It is likely because they still view him as a threat and don't want to bolster his reputation and credibility. There are some crazy and violent people in this world who would never believe that Noah was innocent, unless it was spelled out in black and white. The university would need to be completely transparent and honest, which they would never do, for Noah to even have a chance at saving his reputation. Fortunately, there is a legal system with juries of our peers who can help people like Noah find justice and right the wrongs that have been committed against him. It is one reason we become lawyers, Brittany."

Brittany smiled and said, "That is *exactly* the reason I went to law school, and why I want to be a lawyer."

Then, as she looked back at her computer and started to speak, Gary noticed that a troubled look had crossed her face.

She said, "Oh no. Something just came up on my news feed and it doesn't look good."

Gary walked around behind her to get a better look at her screen as she summarized what was written.

"This is a news report about a fire that had burned a cabin on the border of the Holden National Wildlife Refuge to the ground."

"That is where..." Gary and Brittany said in unison. Brittany completed the sentence. "Where Amanda's cabin is located."

"What else does it say?" said Gary, with genuine concern in his voice.

"It looks like it happened yesterday afternoon. There isn't much information, but it says the authorities suspect foul play. They didn't say why. Also, the reporter was able to interview a fireman who said that, given the intensity of the blaze, it would be unlikely that we would ever know whether anyone had been inside. All that was left of the structure was a rock chimney and the remains of melted and charred appliances."

"We'll need to notify the FBI," Gary said quietly.

"But we can't do that," argued Amanda. They can't know that you knew or suspected where he was hiding."

"I won't let them know that. I'll tell them your research uncovered this information just today." They need to know, Brittany, and it is our duty to tell them now. Besides, if there is something to find, their forensics team will find it. We need to know whether Noah was in that cabin when it burned to the ground."

"I shudder to think that he was," said Brittany. "So, the million dollar questions are: who committed the act, and how did they know he was staying there?"

"*You* found out, didn't you?" questioned Gary.

"I swear," said Brittany, I've told no-one except you about any of this. I do talk to myself a lot while I'm working at my desk, but I usually have my door shut. It helps me problem-solve."

Brittany glanced over at Gary and noticed that his demeanor had suddenly changed. Without saying a word, he pulled out a piece of paper, wrote something on it, and handed it to her. She understood and merely nodded.

Written on the paper were the words, "Keep quiet. I think we have been bugged. Look under your desk."

Brittany nodded and leaned down to look. *There, stuck to the underside of her desk was a small listening device.* Sitting back up, she gave Gary the thumbs up sign.

Thinking quickly, Gary said, "Brittany, you have done great work. Why don't you take the rest of the day off?"

"That sounds great. Thanks Boss," replied Brittany in her most convincing voice.

A moment later, Gary was gone. He walked down the hall and out of the building to make a call on his cell phone. His call was to a private investigator he had on retainer who could sweep his offices for bugs, and have diagnostics run on his computers and office phones to see if they were clean.

He knew that he had been careless and kicked himself for it. He had recently hired a part-time custodian, Jake, whose primary job was in the College of Liberal Arts and Sciences at Delray University — the same college where Noah worked. He didn't believe in coincidences. He was Gary's prime suspect in planting the listening devices — likely done under threat from those who meant to harm Noah. He decided not to confront

Jake, but instead tell him they were cutting expenses and wouldn't need him anymore.

Gary then brought his thoughts back to Noah. He hoped beyond hope that he was safe. He knew that Noah was smart and had a sixth sense when it came to recognizing danger. The odds were good that Noah had escaped, but he couldn't know with certainty.

He also couldn't know whether Noah, had he survived the attack, would have had the opportunity to take the recording and memo with him. These were two critical pieces of evidence that he would need for negotiations in lawsuits against the university.

The dual emotions of concern for Noah and anger at those responsible boiled up inside him. There was nothing more he could do here, so he decided to head home and go for a five mile run to clear his mind and reduce his anxiety.

Ever the optimist, he was convinced that justice would somehow prevail, in whatever form it took. For that to happen, however, Noah would need to survive.

Chapter 14

Down River

AFTER PULLING OUT and into the safety of the river, I paddled hard downstream until my arms ached, and I lacked the strength to keep up the grueling pace that was set in my haste to escape. Needing a rest, and far enough downstream to be out of immediate danger, I placed my paddle across my lap and drifted.

The sky was clear, and the temperature mild. If I hadn't been running for my life, it would have been a very enjoyable trip down river. I had passed two or three river otters playing along the bank, the typical geese and ducks flying low over the water, and a few deer grazing along the riverbank. This was truly a beautiful part of the country, with the nearby White River known for spectacular trout fishing, and this part of the state spotted with beautiful natural protected areas that were perfect for outdoor recreation.

Lost in my reverie, I almost missed the landmark, a large boulder next to the riverbank that marked the place I had mentally mapped out yesterday — before all hell broke loose — as my first stopping point downriver. It was a site I had visited before, during better times, for it's natural beauty, but now, with the prospect that people were out there looking for me, there was a more practical reason for stopping here. The area by the riverbank showed no sign of human presence, with no discernable trail — and further in, there was a dense grove of evergreens that would conceal my passage.

I pulled up to the bank, hopped out, and dragged my boat to a spot where it would be well hidden. I grabbed my tent and gear, put it in my backpack and walked along a narrow, overgrown trail that led into the dark woods. Thirty minutes later, leaving the woods to the bright light of day, I soon found the camping spot I was seeking. It was located on a high bluff overlooking the river, protected from view by anyone below. It provided an excellent view of the sunset that would occur about an hour from now, had a low rock ledge to sit on, and level ground covered in soft needles on which to pitch my tent. It was perfect.

After setting up camp, and with nothing else to do, I settled back to enjoy the sunset — reminded that all we really needed in life had been given to us for free – we just had to recognize it. In that comfortable spot, I allowed my mind to wander back once again to my situation and the paradox of being persecuted for doing the right thing. It then drifted to thoughts of Amanda, turning abruptly to the envelope that I had left for her in the safe at the cabin.

Learning that her cabin had burned down would surely bring her back to see what remained. Would she remember the safe and find the envelope I had stashed there? *I had to know.* When I had put it there, I could not have fathomed that the cabin would have been torched, leaving me running for my life. You must play the hand you've been dealt, I guess.

On the morning of the fifth day, having waited long enough to feel that the coast was clear, I decided to set off for my return to the cabin. After a breakfast cooked over the campfire,

I packed up my gear and hiked back to the kayak. The weather had turned cooler, but the sky was still clear. It was time to go.

I was anxious about returning to the cabin but, steeling myself to it, loaded my kayak, pushed off from the bank and turned upriver for the strenuous journey against the current. The goal was to assess the damage, and retrieve the recording device, and documents and memo, from the safe — if these items had survived the fire.

What took me an hour to reach my camping spot downstream took me nearly twice as long paddling upstream against the current. When I was near, I took a first pass on the opposite bank, paddling upstream to look for any signs of people or activity near the bank. When satisfied that the area was clear, I crossed the river and drifted close to the bank and the place where I would normally land my boat. It was quiet and peaceful, and I didn't see or sense the presence of another human.

Fearing the main trail from the river might be under surveillance, I turned and paddled back upstream and landed my boat on the bank where the narrow game trail passed close to the river. I pulled my kayak onto the bank and dragged it only a short distance this time, into the woods and away from the trail. Not knowing what lay ahead, I planned to make my approach through a dense area of forest.

Satisfied that my boat was well hidden, I walked quietly toward the cabin, stopping every so often to listen to the sounds of the forest for any sign of human intrusion. I passed familiar landmarks and the small clearing where I had planned to camp before my world imploded only a few days ago. It was just as I had left it, and I neither sensed nor saw anything that would signal trouble. *All seemed fine.*

As I approached the area where the cabin once stood, I crept closer while concealing my approach. When the husk of the burned-out cabin was in sight, it became clear why no-one was here. The crime-scene folks must have completed their work and left — the only evidence of their presence being a section of crime scene tape still tied to the charred remains of a tree. *There is no reason for anyone to remain at a burned-out cabin in the woods*, I thought.

What I saw were the blackened ruins of what little was left of the cabin, along with the chimney stack and the remnants of a few appliances. The acrid smell of burnt wood and the cabin's former contents still hung in the air. There was also a large boulder that had once added a sense of charm to the cabin that had been situated adjacent to the front porch. It seemed to stand sentinel to the senseless violence that had occurred here.

I moved toward the burned-out husk of the cabin with only one goal in mind — to see if the contents of the safe were still there, and if they had survived a fire so intense that it burned everything else beyond recognition. Looking around, I realized that the fire crews had arrived in time to save the surrounding forest from burning. That at least brought me some comfort.

I approached the area where the cabin once stood and walked through the ashes up to the chimney. It was amazing how the chimney had remained mostly undisturbed after such a violent fire. It was charred in a few places but otherwise seemed untouched. *Well*, I thought, *it was a fireplace after all*.

I reached up to the hiding place in the chimney and pulled on the rock that concealed the hidden safe. It looked as though it had been left untouched.

Thank goodness for small miracles.

Also, to my immense relief, beyond the rock façade was the face of the safe, looking clean and undisturbed. Holding my breath, I turned the lock according to the numbers imprinted in my mind and opened the safe. I let out an audible gasp.

The safe was empty!

I reached my hand in anyway, in what I was certain would be a futile attempt to find anything — reminding me of how I would often check my empty mailbox at home, feeling along the bottom, in the false hope that I had missed a letter that had lain flat.

Feeling along the smooth floor of the safe, I found, to my immense surprise and relief, that the safe hadn't been completely empty after all. Pulling my hand out, what I found in my fingers was a small slip of paper. I looked at it closely and found that it had a series of letters and numbers written on it. I straightened the slip of paper and took a closer look. It read "AS5512MC2WKS." Hope filled me as I pocketed the paper, closed the safe, and headed back to my boat and the river.

It seemed like more miracles were heading my way. Amanda and I had a secret coding system that we had developed when we wanted to leave notes for each other while she was in graduate school. Her friends were nosey, and the student mailboxes were more or less public, so she and I would leave coded messages when we wanted our communications to stay confidential. It was incredibly simple, but difficult to break if you didn't know what to look for.

I recalled the note that she had left in the safe, and deciphered it in my mind. I knew that AS stood for Amanda Strauss. She was letting me know that it was she who had removed the contents from the safe and left the slip of paper. The 5512 MC stood for an address on Magnolia Court in Baton Rouge, Louisiana that I knew about. Her brother had attended graduate school at LSU, and her parents had bought a small house for him while he was there. He had gone on to work for one of the alphabet agencies – FBI, CIA, NSA.... Even Amanda wouldn't — or couldn't — tell me which one, or what exactly he did for them. I did recall, however, that Amanda once told me that his house sat empty most of the year except when he was using it, or on the rare occasion it was used by close family or friends.

Amanda must have been planning to be there and wanted me to meet her there in two weeks — the notation "2WKS" — about the amount of time it would take me to paddle with the current downstream from my current location. We had once considered paddling down the Arkansas River to its confluence with the Mississippi and on to New Orleans, and calculated how long it would reasonably take us given the river current, average paddling speed, hours paddled per day, and rest breaks. It gave us a good estimate.

After she visited the cabin and found the envelope, she would have gone to the shed and noticed that my boat was missing, and likely seen the marks I had left from dragging my boat. She knew that I was alive, and for some reason that brought me a huge sense of relief. It was also quite comforting to know that, if she wanted to see me, she clearly didn't think that I was a monster — or blame me for the loss of her cabin.

For the first time in what seemed like forever, I felt a sense of joy and hope. I now had a firm destination in mind.

I pushed off from the bank and spent the next two weeks paddling and drifting downriver, only stopping to camp, rest and eat.

After entering the Mississippi River, I stayed close to the riverbank and avoided the shipping channels. The river was notorious for its swift and unpredictable currents, but my sturdy boat and years of experience paddling rivers proved to be of value.

Most of my camping experiences along the way were un-eventful, some serene and beautiful, and others uncomfortable due to cold and rainy weather. It was similar to the ups and downs that one experiences in life — the twists and turns of the river mirroring the course of my life.

The flow of the river and peace that accompanied the journey had given me time to think not only about my circumstances, but also those in higher education. I really did fear for the future of Delray University, a place that I loved.

At Delray, I had seen firsthand – and was experiencing firsthand – the way that greed destroyed lives and, if left unchecked, could erode the foundation of a great university. I had always believed that accountability should be more than a buzzword and apply to all levels of the university hierarchy. I hoped, if those responsible for framing me were brought to justice, that it would serve as an example for other universities, and perhaps even lead to a change in culture that reflected honesty, fairness, and integrity in higher education.

Mighty idealistic thoughts, I mused, *for a man on the run.*

When thoughts of the injustice done to me and others became too much, I would paddle as hard as I could until my arms burned and muscles ached, and then resume my steady pace.

Once or twice during my journey, I met up with some wild hogs that were more curious than hostile, and other wildlife that viewed me as some strange creature gliding across the river. A few times, when I was near civilization, I hid my boat and stayed at a mom-and-pop motel, paying cash to keep my anonymity, and avoid both the authorities and anyone else who might be looking for me.

I also came off the river occasionally to grab a hamburger and other provisions to make life more enjoyable, as well as pick up everyday essentials. I led a simple, frugal life on the river, and saved a good supply of cash. I felt that it would prob-ably be needed at some point in the future — if for no other reason than to get back to my hometown — since I clearly wouldn't be paddling back upstream. The river provided only a one-way trip.

At long last, I arrived on the river upstream from the city of Baton Rouge, about half a mile from my destination — the house on Magnolia Court. I paddled my boat up to the riverbank and, finding a good eddy and flat riverbank, pulled my boat onto it, removed my gear, and put it into my backpack. I left my tent but took my backpack, packed with my clothes and some essentials.

I then pulled my boat further up the bank and into some thick brush where it was well-hidden. This was not a likely place for people to visit, but I wanted to exercise as much caution as possible since I had grown extremely attached to this boat. *Who knows, with my luck, I might also need it for another river escape*, I thought half-jokingly to myself.

I walked up the shrub-covered bank to the highway and, looking like someone who could scare small children, began the trek toward Magnolia Court where I hoped to find the house with Amanda waiting inside.

A half hour later I neared the address for the house and, I hoped, a new and better chapter in my life.

I was strangely nervous and uncomfortable with my appearance. We had not been together for some time now, so there was no reason for me to feel this way. Maybe it was just nerves from the larger ordeal that I was experiencing, or fatigue from the past two weeks of paddling and camping along the river.

When I reached the house, I found that it was small but very well kept, with a neatly manicured lawn and two small magnolia trees in the front yard that bracketed the sidewalk leading to the front door. It provided me with a feeling I had almost forgotten — one of comfort and warmth.

Chapter 15

Reunion

LEROY HAD ARRIVED in Baton Rouge about two weeks prior with a select group from his inner circle, all with combat experience, having served in various branches of the military. Each had been dishonorably discharged, most for over-aggressive behavior and assaults on civilians while on leave from various assignments.

He and a select group of *his boys* had left Arkansas to scout the location shortly after his contact — whose identity was well-guarded — had provided him with the location of where Noah would come next. He had been told that it was a home listed as belonging to Amanda Strauss' brother.

Amanda, as he knew, was Noah's ex-girlfriend. He imagined that she and Noah must still be close for her to take him in and put herself at risk. *Once Noah is out of the way*, he thought to himself, *me and my boys will be sure to spend some 'quality' time with her.*

He was sure that they could finish the job easily and have a little fun in the process. Neither seemed like they could put up much of a fight or had the ability to escape from them when the time came. With the boys he had brought down here, he was certain they would not get away. *It will be like shooting fish in a barrel*, he told himself with pleasure.

Just three days ago, growing bored and restless after waiting nearly two weeks for Noah to show his face, he had taken a chance and decided to impersonate a roof repair representative so that he could get a closer look at the house. Wearing a baseball cap and sunglasses, and keeping his head down in case the house had hidden security cameras, he had walked up to the front door and knocked.

The *girl*, Amanda, to his surprise, opened the door a crack. He had resisted the urge to push through the door, subdue and hold her captive, and wait for Noah while he and the boys kept her company. It would have been more fun that way, but there were just too many unknowns to take that risk. His blood boiled as he remembered how she looked at him, with confidence and arrogance, and how she told him firmly but politely to leave. It had only made him more determined to see that both she and Noah met a painful and brutal end to their lives.

As he was lost in these thoughts, his beeper sounded. It beeped three times, the code he had been waiting two weeks to hear. The text came next with a few details, all written in a code that only his group could understand. He learned that his lookout had spotted Noah. He had arrived by foot carrying a backpack. This meant that he had most likely walked from the river. After they eliminated Noah, they would find his boat and dispose of it. They might even find a way to make it look like a boating accident.

This was going to be fun, he thought.

I WALKED UP to the front door, removed my pack, and knocked. There was no answer. I thought to myself, *Oh no, what am I going to do now?* I knocked again, this time a bit louder, and waited.

Another few minutes passed, and my nervousness was turning to grave concern. *Had something happened to...?* As my hand reached the door for one last attempt to knock, the door opened, and a friendly face with beautiful green eyes framed by wet hair and a big smile greeted me.

In the next instant, she was in my arms, and time and space seemed to do all sorts of crazy things. I had no idea how long we held each other, or whether I had blurted out something stupid. I just remember what seemed like entering another realm of existence, one with a pure bright, blinding light. When we separated, we both just looked at each other with a kind of detached numb feeling that was quite wonderful.

Amanda was the first to speak. She broke into an even larger smile when she said, "Well, well, don't we smell a little fishy. One would think that you had been without a bath for a while. Why don't you go back and take a shower and then we can get you something to eat. There are some clothes in my brother Jake's room that you can use. You two are about the same size so they should fit you well enough."

The hot shower felt like heaven, the clothes did in fact fit quite well, and the house smelled like a house, or more accurately, a home, should smell. Amanda, in a sweet and comforting voice said, "Noah, I cooked some stir fry chicken last night that I've heated up for you. Have a seat and I'll bring you a glass of sweet tea to go with it."

I had forgotten what a great cook Amanda had been, and it seemed she hadn't lost her touch. When we dated, we would share the cooking responsibilities, and enjoyed a friendly competition as to who could prepare the best meals.

Sitting there, feeling so good that it hurt, I wondered how I could have ever let her get away. Was there any chance now that I could win her back? One never knew.

I had finished the meal when Amanda came over offering a hot tea with Manuka honey and milk that she had prepared.

She sat across from me at the round oak table, opening and turning on her laptop and peering over the screen while we talked and sipped our tea.

She was anxious to hear about my experiences. I started at the beginning with my evening exploits at the Institute and ended with my frantic escape from the cabin and trip down river. I then apologized for being the reason that her cabin had been destroyed, and how I hoped that I had not put her in harm's way.

I said, "You should know that you are currently harboring a fugitive."

Looking at me with a slight smile forming at the corners of her mouth, she said, "Noah, although I find fugitives to be very sexy, I'm happy to report that you are no longer a fugitive."

Her comment floored me. *Did she just say that I was sexy?* I asked myself. *What did that mean?* My mind also went into overdrive hearing her say that I was no longer a fugitive.

I didn't need to ask why or even follow up on that comment, though, as I had complete trust in her and knew that she wouldn't joke around about something that serious. I just sat back, with the feeling that a thousand-pound weight had been removed from my shoulders, and let her continue.

"I wanted to get that out first to ease your mind. You made big news after the university announcement that they had found, well, dreadful things on your university-issued desktop computer."

This made me inwardly cringe. I could only imagine what my parents thought when they saw it.

I said, "I know all about that, Amanda. I called Gary after the news went public, and he filled me in on what was said. If I recall correctly, they made the announcement not too long before I spoke with Gary. It makes me sick to think about it."

"I'm sure it did," said Amanda in a gentle and sympathetic voice.

Her mood brightening, she said, "what you didn't know while you were running for your life is that the university admitted that a mistake had been made. They didn't mention you by name, but the implication was that you were exonerated."

Amanda brought up the announcement on her laptop and showed it to me.

It was dated Wednesday, January 28. I said, "Wow, that was the day after I last spoke to Gary. It was also a day after those murderous jerks burned down the cabin."

"You *would* have to remind me," said Amanda with a look of mock anger that turned into a smile.

"We had secretly planted a program on my computer," I said, "that would show if anyone tampered with it after I had turned it in."

She nodded, and then showed me an article written by a journalist named Rob Ross. It had been picked up by most of the major media outlets. There were also a slew of related articles following the university storyline. I seemed to recall Gary mentioning Rob to me at some point. It was likely that Gary had spoken with Rob and planted the seeds of a story.

The story, to my great satisfaction, placed me in a favorable light, with a conspiratorial angle that implicated the university in wrongdoing. It spoke of how the university had done severe harm to its bread and butter, a member of the university faculty. Rob suggested, by implication, that I had been framed, and now that the university had been caught, it had to create a new spin.

He noted that the university had claimed that a rogue IT staff member, who had not officially been named, had planted the files on my computer, and then questioned why a member of the university IT staff would do something like that on their own. To my delight, Rob had the courage to raise the prospect that it was more likely that a university administrator had directed someone to put the falsely dated malicious files on my computer.

"That should make Finch flinch," I said with a smile. Amanda just grinned and shook her head.

Some investigative journalism on Rob's part had discovered that a young IT staff member who worked in my college, Ronald Turpin, had recently been fired from his position. In a conspiratorial tone, Rob questioned how a young IT staff member who was still learning the ropes could pull off such an ambitious act of deception.

"Rob makes some particularly good points," I told Amanda. "I hope that enough people read *this* story instead of the garbage that the university has been spinning. It angers me that they would throw this poor kid under the bus to cover up their misdeeds. He will likely never find another job as a computer technician unless he goes into private consulting work."

"There are some bad people behind this," said Amanda. "With the enormity of the story, I'm sure you can imagine the feeding frenzy this has caused among journalists. Searching for any angle they could find, the press must have done some research and found out that we had dated before. They started hounding me some, but I was able to plead ignorance — which was mostly true — and hold them off."

"I'm glad," I said, "And I'm terribly sorry that you had to be put through this."

"It really wasn't much of a problem Noah. My biggest concern was when I saw a breaking news story that a cabin — that I discovered to be *my* cabin — had been torched."

Gazing directly at me with serious, intelligent eyes that held a deep well of compassion, she said what I needed to hear the most. "But I wasn't concerned about the cabin, Noah. I was concerned about *you*. I wasn't certain how you would have known to leave the house before they came to kill you, but finding the note, and seeing that your boat was gone, gave me reason to believe that you had escaped."

"The thing is, Amanda," I said. "I didn't know that I needed to leave the cabin. At least not for sure. It was just a feeling, mainly."

"I'm glad you followed your instincts, then."

"Me too," I agreed.

"Since, knowing you, I was certain that you had escaped by kayak, I estimated the amount of time it would take you to make it here by boat, and then came down to Baton Rouge to wait for your arrival."

"You did all this for me? I asked.

"It was not that big a deal. I had accrued a good amount of vacation time from work and decided that it was a suitable time to take it — and this is a nice place to stay. The house is owned by my older brother. I think you know that he does undercover work. It's all very 'hush, hush.' His cover is that his job is delivering plastic products throughout the southern region. He travels a lot and is rarely here."

"That sounds very *Jason Bourne-ish*," I said.

"If you only knew," said Amanda. "He has shown me a few of the tricks he keeps up his sleeve. If we have time, I'll show you around and you can see for yourself."

"Do you think we are safe here?" I asked.

Amanda replied, "I would think so. I imagine there is probably a trail that someone could follow to find me, but so far no-one has seemed to figure it out. I have good situational awareness and there hasn't been anything too far out of the ordinary except for some idiot who came by the other day saying that I needed to have my roof repaired and his company could do it. The roof had just been replaced last year. I told him to get lost, in a polite way of course."

"I've had that happen before," I said. "It's just another scam."

"I know," said Amanda. "It was just that he gave me the creeps, with his dirty gray beard, dark sunglasses and hat pulled low in front. He also looked at me strangely and seemed to take just a bit too much interest in me and my house," said Amanda.

Dirty gray beard, I thought. *The guy at the cabin who seemed to be the leader had a gray beard. Was it possible...?*

Keeping these thoughts to myself given the long odds that this could be the same person, I just said, "OK, let me know if you see him around here again. I've had a lot of time to think, and I still haven't figured out how those jerks who tried to kill me found out about the cabin."

"They could have discovered our connection and my ownership of the cabin, though it would take someone with some smarts," said Amanda.

"Those guys appeared to have just fallen off the turnip truck, and likely had less than ten years of education between the lot of them. I don't see them figuring it out," I said.

"I guess there is the old saying about the blind pig finding the nut, but I don't see it either, Noah." At the exact same time, we both said "Maybe..."

I deferred to Amanda, who said, "Maybe there is a level of sophistication here that we may have underestimated."

"That is what I was thinking as well," I said. "Tell me what you're thinking."

As Amanda talked, her thoughts mirrored my own. My lizard brain was sending off warnings about how success, and even survival, often depended on not underestimating *anyone*. For some reason, even though it made sense, I feared that the people we were calling dumb rednecks and idiots were actually more intelligent and sophisticated than we thought. Amanda and I were of the same mind.

"What if," I said, "There is some connection between the people who burned down your cabin, and my crooked colleagues?"

Amanda, looking thoughtful said, "That's an angle we will definitely have to keep in mind. We don't have enough pieces of the puzzle to know yet, but once we start to see the bigger picture, I'm sure we'll find the answer.

"Oh, I almost forgot," said Amanda. "You are probably wondering about the fate of the envelope that you left in the safe."

With all that was happening, I had somehow forgotten. "Of course," I said.

"I opened it," said Amanda, "to check on the contents and found a fancy recording device that any spy would have been proud of. I respect your privacy and want you to know that I only opened it to make sure the contents had not been damaged."

She handed me the envelope. I opened it and found the contents I had placed there tucked safely within. The fire, as she suggested, had not appeared to cause them any harm.

"You know what Amanda," I said with all sincerity. "You are amazing. Thank you."

She smiled again, in a way that melted all the stress and worry from me. I got up and hugged her, and found to my surprise that tears were flowing from my eyes.

At that moment, I knew how much I had missed her, and wondered again what might have been had we decided not to go our separate ways. There would be time to think more about that later though. For now, we needed a strategy. It would clearly involve Gary, but we would need to have a few tricks up our sleeves to ensure that the slippery vipers behind all of this were held accountable.

Chapter 16

Time to Fly

OBLIVIOUS TO THE dangers lurking in the shadows, I told Amanda that it was time to call Gary.

"That sounds like a smart idea. He is probably worried sick about you. I'm sure he will also have some valuable information to share," she replied knowingly.

Given that the last time we spoke was right before the cabin was torched, I thought to myself, *he probably doesn't know whether I survived the fire.*

"I agree," I said, pushing these thoughts aside. "It is a bit of a risk, given that the bad guys always seem to be one step ahead of us, but it is too important *not* to call him."

"If we need to leave and go into hiding at our favorite hotel in New Orleans," said Amanda with a smile on her face, "It wouldn't be too much of a burden." I remembered the place from back when we were dating and was in complete agreement.

I picked up the phone and called Gary's office. Gayle answered and said "Oh my! Noah is that you? I am so glad to hear that you are alive and well."

"Thanks, Gayle, I'm fine," I replied, "and I *do* apologize for keeping you all in the dark for so long."

"We certainly understand, and this turned out to be for the best. We had a major security breach here that we are still sorting out. Gary can tell you more. Until we get this completely cleared up, he is only taking calls on his cell phone. He also changed his number."

Gayle gave me his new number and said, "Here it is in case you need it. If you provide me with your number, he will call you back."

Knowing that I would ditch this, my second burner phone, soon after the call, I obliged.

After waiting only a few minutes, my phone rang. It was Gary. He said, "Noah, my God it is good to hear your voice. Are you OK?"

I told him that I was fine and filled him in on what had happened since we last talked. Also, because I knew it would be important to him, I told him that the recording and documents were safe.

Gary, sounding relieved, simply said, "Good." I picked up on something else in his voice that I couldn't place. He also sounded concerned.

Switching gears, he asked, "Are you in Baton Rouge?"

"Yes," I replied. "I'm going to put you on speaker phone so Amanda can listen. How did you know? And is something wrong?"

"Noah, you may be in danger. We believe that the people who tried to kill you at the cabin found you through us. They may also know that you are staying in Baton Rouge."

"How?" I asked, hoping to find the answer to the million dollar question.

"We found hidden listening devices in several of our offices. I had one in mine, and Brittany, my paralegal, had one in hers. We didn't find one in the conference room so our conversation there, we believe, was secure. Brittany had done some research and learned about your past relationship with Amanda Strauss.

This led her to find out about the cabin. It was short work to determine its location. We believe they found out about the cabin by listening remotely to our conversations. Brittany also admitted that sometimes she talks to herself when she is problem solving, so they probably picked up on that."

"What else do you think they overheard," I asked, trying to sort out what I had told Gary by phone and when.

"I shut everything down and brought in my Private Investigator when I suspected that we had been bugged. That was the day after we had talked, and the cabin had burned. With no way of tracking you, they probably felt like their best bet was to spy on me.

"They probably overheard you reading the memo to me and playing the recording, since I had you on speaker phone in my office — which was bugged. They now have some information that we had hoped to keep secret from them, and that is clearly making them *extremely* nervous. I'm sorry Noah, I let my guard down, thinking that my office was secure."

"Don't blame yourself Gary, there is no way you could have known."

"Regardless, it was my carelessness that led them to you. We think that there is a connection between your colleagues — perhaps other unknown persons within the university — and the people who tried to murder you. The custodian who cleaned our offices also worked for your college. We think he planted the bugs"

"That is some coincidence," I said, absently.

"It would be," replied Gary, "but I don't believe in coincidences. Whatever it is they are into, it must be big, and involve some serious money — more than what they pilfered through their corporation. They may even use the money laundered through their corporation to fund this bigger enterprise. Whatever it is you stumbled upon, the stakes are extremely high. They have gone from threatening your job and reputation —

to attempting to take your very life. You will need to remain quite vigilant."

"I will, Gary. For now, I believe that we are safe here in Baton Rouge. They may know that I'm in the city, but I'm in a secure location with Amanda."

Gary, sounding somewhat sheepish, said, "Actually, Noah, you may not be all that safe there. Brittany, with access to records through our databases, was also able to find the house that Amanda's brother owns in Baton Rouge."

"On Magnolia Court?" I asked, as my heartrate amped up a few notches.

"Yes," replied Gary.

Amanda, who had been listening intently to our conversation, tapped a few keys on her computer and looked sharply at the screen.

She looked at me over the monitor and mouthed, "Get your stuff. We have to leave."

I quickly said, "Gary, I've got to go," and hung up.

The serious look and hard glint to her eyes told me, without words, to sweep up the papers and recorder and put them back in the envelope. I leapt from my chair and ran to the hallway where my backpack, with most of its contents still inside, was leaning against the wall. I picked it up and headed back toward the kitchen.

It was then that I heard voices, and soon thereafter, a hard knock on the door. A voice said, "Ma'am this is the Postal Service. I have a package for you that you'll need to sign for."

Amanda had a go-bag that seemed to appear out of thin air. She motioned for me to come over and look at her laptop. Her brother must have had hidden cameras placed at strategic locations around the house, because her screen lit up with real time footage in six separate quadrants on her computer with images of the area surrounding the house.

What I saw made my blood run cold.

There were five of them, including the one at the front door disguised as a postal employee. All were heavy-set and wearing camo tactical gear. If that wasn't worrisome enough, they were all armed with what looked like AR-15 assault rifles and assorted other items that were meant to cause harm. They were moving toward the house from all directions in a classic pincer movement.

I'm sure that the look on my face was one of raw fear. I knew that there was no way that we could fight our way out of this or escape. Looking at Amanda, however, I saw confidence and resolve — and something more. Could it be she had a few tricks up her sleeve?

She said, "We need to leave, *now!*"

I slung my backpack, with the envelope stowed safely inside, over my shoulder and waited, not knowing how in the world we could leave or go anywhere. We were in a house surrounded by heavily armed men. Amanda slammed her laptop together and threw it into her go-bag.

Whether they knew we were on to them, or they were just impatient, we would never know. When they kicked in the front door, however, Amanda's words were reinforced. We needed to go.

Time had run out.

Chapter 17

Diversion

AMANDA TOOK MY hand, leading me through the kitchen and straight to the pantry door. We hurried inside the pantry closet, and had just closed the door behind us when the sound of breaking glass and the pounding boots of intruders reached our ears. They were entering the house from all corners. We stood in the semi-darkness of the pantry closet, with light streaming through the door frame — with me wondering what the hell was happening, and why we were hiding in the pantry, of all places.

Sensing my concern and the questions surely running through my mind, Amanda whispered simply, "Noah, trust me."

The next thing she did answered my immediate questions but raised quite a few more. She gently moved me aside and grabbed a pantry shelf. She pulled, and it began to rotate outward on well-oiled hinges revealing a dark space beyond. My fascination with what I was witnessing was tempered by the sound of voices and a commotion that had now reached the kitchen.

I heard one of the intruders say, "Where did they go? We've searched the entire house and..." The voice stopped abruptly, right outside the pantry door. It would only be seconds before they either shot through the door, or they flung it open to reveal our defenseless position. We had not a moment to lose.

Looking more closely, I could see that the hidden space behind the false pantry shelving revealed a set of stairs. Amanda literally pushed me through the opening while simultaneously pulling the shelves closed behind us. I heard it close with an audible *click*, probably a failsafe locking system to hinder anyone from following.

In my attempt to navigate the narrow staircase in the dark, I lost my footing and began to fall, only to be grabbed from behind by my backpack and held in place. "Thanks," I whispered to the woman who was saving me.

At that moment, we heard a loud crash that signaled the destruction of the pantry door, followed by loud cursing and the obvious questions that followed. We didn't know whether they would discover our secret escape route, but if they did, this would at least buy us some time.

We made it quickly to the bottom of the stairs to find a secret tunnel leading away from the house. *Wow,* I thought, *her brother was covering all the bases with a secret escape tunnel that he could access through the pantry closet. Who was this guy?*

There wasn't time to stop and contemplate any of this. We had to keep moving. Amanda turned on her phone's flashlight app and led the way. With nothing to say, we both ran, hunched over, through the tunnel and to wherever it would eventually lead us. Our pace slackened as we raced further down the tunnel, where we eventually slowed to a walk.

"It's not much further now," said Amanda.

I estimated that we had traveled about twenty yards from the house. This would likely put us near the property line. We had to be nearing the end of the tunnel.

As if reading my thoughts, Amanda stopped and turned to me, saying, "We are here Noah. End of the line."

I looked up and saw a metal trap door with a handle, and a short set of stairs leading up to it. Amanda climbed up first and twisted the handle, then pushed upward on the hatch. She lowered her head as dirt and bits of grass rained down upon us. She then opened the hatch a few more inches, allowing sunlight to pour through, and waited. We were vulnerable.

Amanda pushed upward a bit more, just enough to peer through the opening, and peeked outside. Satisfied that we were in a safe place, and that our position was concealed from our pursuers, she pushed the hatch all the way open and climbed out. I quickly followed.

We had emerged on the far side of a juniper hedge near the property line, in a place not visible from the house. Amanda quickly dialed 911, told them there had been a breaking and entering, and gave them the address. She then hung up.

Amanda looked at me and whispered, "Get to the river, I'll meet you in New Orleans at our favorite hotel back in the day. I'll act as a decoy and draw their attention away from you."

Before I could respond and try to dissuade her, she was moving — and fast.

Knowing that chasing after her would only slow her down and disrupt her plan, I thought better of it and followed her advice; I headed toward the river. I ran the first few hundred yards, staying mostly concealed behind wooden backyard fences and trees. Once I was a safe distance from the house, I stopped briefly and put on my cap and a pair of sunglasses.

Praying that Amanda had made it away safely, and with this meager disguise, I made my way along back roads and across empty lots in a circuitous route back to the river.

WHILE I WAS running toward the relative safety of the river and my boat, Amanda was also running — but in another direction. She had climbed the neighbor's chain-link fence knowing that she would be spotted but, acting as a diversion to help me escape, bet that she could outrun the fat Bastards. Amanda had been a track athlete in college, competing in the 100 and 200 meter individual, and 4 X 100 meter relay events. She kept in shape these days by working out at the gym and running, though mostly at slower speeds and distances.

Just as expected, nearing the top of the fence, she looked back to see that she had caught their attention. There were three of them, the other two likely still inside the house. They looked to her like those survivalist militia types. The biggest of the three saw her and yelled to his partners, "Hey boys, looks like we got ourselves a runner. Go get her!"

With that encouragement, they started to give chase. Two of them continued, while the one who had barked the orders, seeming to consider a better option, ran back toward their vehicle, a large white pickup truck.

As she topped the fence, Amanda risked a look back. The two goons were faster than she had anticipated — or maybe she was slower. The realization that they might close on her induced a burst of adrenaline, bringing back some of the speed she thought was gone with age.

She landed on the far side of the fence and bolted forward, knowing that the chase and the attention on her would buy Noah precious time to escape. If they had only brought one vehicle, she thought with gratification, they wouldn't be using it to look for him yet. Her plan was working.

She looked back and saw her pursuers clear the fence. They were gaining on her. She estimated that her destination was only 100 yards further, the length of a football field.

It was time to fly.

She kicked it into another gear, one long forgotten since her college days, running full-out down the street, through a neighbor's yard, and a short distance later, into an old industrial park. She looked back and saw that they were still in pursuit, but also that they were obviously not runners. They looked to be losing steam, and with a few turns through a maze of roads within the industrial complex, she seemed to have lost them.

She realized, however, that misfortune had caught up with her when she saw the hood of a large white truck turning in her direction. She dove behind an old dumpster, just as the truck rolled slowly past. Risking a peek as it was moving away, she memorized the license plate number.

When certain the truck was gone, she left her hiding place and moved quickly along the side of an old, dilapidated ware-house to the door of a garage next to it. It was rusted and looked exactly like the rest of the building. Hidden behind a piece of rusted metal casing on the side of the building, how-ever, was a high-tech keypad. She entered the numbers from memory that her brother had shared with her and heard the comforting click of the door unlocking.

The steel reinforced door opened on well-oiled hinges, and she ducked inside, closing the door behind her. Flipping a switch on the wall next to the door, bright fluorescent lights set high in the ceiling flickered on, revealing a gleaming and spotless garage. It was as if she had entered another world. The air was cool and clean. It felt like she was in the finest of auto-mobile showrooms, with only a single car on display. Before her, in pristine condition, was an agate metallic-grey Porsche 718 Cayman GT4, known and respected by automobile enthu-siasts for its incredible power and handling. Her brother was a bit of a perfectionist, she had to admit.

Well, she thought, *he just might have to lighten up a bit, given the train wreck his house has become.* She hoped to at least keep his pride and joy, this wonderful car, in perfect con-dition. She slid into the seat, finding the keys in the ignition, and located the button for the garage door remote.

She started the car, hearing the roar of the engine, sounding, and feeling like a large cat preparing to pounce, then opened the automatic garage door and sped out. She had driven this car several times before, and was familiar with its acceleration and handling capabilities. She had also taken defensive driving courses and was well versed in various maneuvers that would help her avoid — or escape — trouble. Not wanting to be trapped in the maze of narrow roads within the industrial park, she was anxious to make her way out.

Leaving the safety of the garage, Amanda turned left, and then right, the Porsche's wheels spinning on the asphalt. It was just after the second turn that she saw them.

The two goons were standing next to the white truck and talking to their partner through the open driver's side window. It may have been the squealing tires or the roar of the engine, but they immediately stopped what they were doing and turned to look her way.

The next thing they did, almost simultaneously, as their lips began to curl into rictus grins, was to pull and level their weapons.

Amanda was about 20 yards away and heading in their direction when she saw them. Her mind raced to determine the best course of action. Fortunately, this small stretch of road was wider than most within the complex, which made her decision easy.

As the murderous pair began to raise their weapons and position themselves to open fire, Amanda hit the brakes and came to a screeching halt. She then did several things so close together that it seemed to happen at once. She slammed the pedal to the floor, reversing aggressively, counted to two in her head, took her foot off the gas, turned the wheel 180-degrees, and then engaged the forward gear, executing the perfect reverse J turn. Now facing away from the guys with their fingers on their triggers, temporarily mesmerized by the well-performed maneuver, she hit the gas and the car leapt forward, seeming to outrun the bullets that would soon travel in her direction.

A quick turn down a side street and behind a row of warehouses and she was gone. There were few cars on the road that could catch her, notably, not including the truck with her pursuers. She was happy to be away from them, but her main concern had been to avoid any damage to this beautiful piece of machinery. Fortunately, she had been successful on both counts.

She risked taking side roads that would put her near the house, and heard, to her satisfaction, the sirens of police cars arriving on the scene. There would be a mess to clean up, both literally and figuratively, with evidence of their presence clearly easy to find.

For now, though, she needed to keep her focus and get to New Orleans and their predetermined meeting place. She was worried for Noah's safety, but knew that he was strong and smart, and would hold the advantage over anyone when he was on the water.

She said a quick prayer and sped away.

Chapter 18

Trouble on the River

WHEN I FINALLY arrived at the riverbank, I found to my great relief that my boat was still where I had left it. There was no plan B for mode of transportation, and I wasn't in the mood for a swim.

I quickly pulled my boat out of the brush and slid it down to the riverbank, where I secured my belongings, put together my paddle, pushed off into the current and headed downstream. I had a long way to go, but hoped that by paddling until dark, and then making my way downstream, hugging the riverbank with my headlamp to guide me, I could be in New Orleans by tomorrow afternoon. I would probably sleep for a few hours on my boat somewhere if I could tie up along the riverbank. It wasn't ideal, but then again, these weren't ideal times.

My thoughts went to Amanda and my hope that she had escaped and was safe. Her willingness to risk her life to help save mine was almost more than my mind could grasp. I asked myself for what seemed like the thousandth time, *How could I have ever let her get away?* I guessed that there was a time and place for everything, and fate meant for us to reconnect at some point. She was intelligent, courageous, athletic, beautiful and had a great outlook on life. She was perfect.

My musings were interrupted by what I saw on the riverbank to my left. I must have caught sight of it with my peripheral vision. It was a large white truck driving slowly along a dirt road above me.

Suddenly, someone in the truck pointed excitedly in my direction. I knew in that instant they had found me. The Bastards must have had someone watching the house and realized that I had come by boat, given that I had arrived at the house on foot, without a car and carrying a backpack. The rest was easy to figure out. Just look for the most direct path to the river and follow it downstream from that point.

Alarm bells were ringing in my head as my arms tensed and I firmly planted my feet. Then, the worst case scenario happened. What looked like a rifle emerged from the back seat passenger side of the truck.

There were no other cars or people in sight on this deserted stretch of dirt road, giving them the privacy needed to fire off rounds without anyone noticing. I knew they would have to act quickly, though, before this stretch of dirt road ended at a swampy area of land up ahead.

As if reading my thoughts, the man in the backseat — dressed in camo with a full gray beard — began firing in my direction. The small angry splashes next to my boat quickly registered the dire situation in which I found myself. I didn't have a weapon, and my boat offered no protection.

I dared to look back up the hill and noticed that this dangerous lunatic in camo was taking aim and lining up the kill shot. Without time to think, I dug my paddle hard into the water, sending my boat lurching forward just as a bullet ricocheted off the plastic upper molding mere inches behind my seat. Fortunately, before he could line up his sights for another shot, I had approached a rock overhang along the riverbank.

Pulling beneath it, I reached out to stop my progress, scraping my hands in the process. It hurt like hell, but a lot less than a bullet in my side. Hiding out of sight, and hoping they would give up the chase, I waited. To my great dismay, the sound of voices soon reached my ears. I figured they must have parked the truck, and may have headed down the bank to investigate. As I waited and listened, the voices grew in volume, confirming my fear that some of the goons from the truck, I couldn't know how many, were working their way down the bank to the rock overhang above me.

One voice rose above the rest.

I had heard that voice before. It was the lunatic who had burned down Amanda's cabin, and the leader of whatever group was coming after me. *It's likely some type of backwoods militia group*, I thought to myself. From what I had experienced during our escape from the house, I would suspect they had some form of formal military training and had since trained and worked together.

The man, whose voice I recognized and suspected as belonging to the leader said, "You boys get back on up to the truck. I don't want a random police car or security detail to come driving by and see a bunch of us standing down here. It looks suspicious. Get back in the car and if anyone stops and asks you any questions, just tell them that you were out scouting for a good place to fish and sent your buddy down here to check it out."

Fishing? In this part of the river? I thought to myself. *These guys really aren't all that smart.*

As I hid under the overhang listening to their conversation, I noticed a large round opening in the bank ahead of me. Looking more closely, I could see that it was the opening to a large drainage pipe, ten to twelve feet in diameter. It was likely a storm water drainage pipe that fed runoff from rainwater into the river.

It must have rained a lot recently as a good bit of water was flowing out. As I drew nearer to the opening, I had to brace myself against the rock so that I wouldn't be pushed back out into the main part of the river. It looked deep enough to paddle into but would take some effort given the substantial amount of water flowing out.

Having reached the opening, I looked back and caught, out of the corner of my eye, one of the militia group, or whatever he was, leaning over the rock overhang and looking at me.

He said, "Hey there, professor, looks like we finally have you where we want you. Not sure how you escaped back at the house, and upriver at that cabin, but your nine lives are up. Your girlfriend is slippery, but we'll keep searching until we find her. When we do, I might just convince her to be *my* girlfriend." He followed this comment with a demonic laugh, bearing brown and yellow-stained teeth framed by a dirty gray beard. The comment, coupled with the hideous laugh, frightened me some, but pissed me off more.

With that, he pulled back from the ledge and out of view. I had now met the man who was dead-set on killing me and would do harm to Amanda, should he catch her. My concern for her sent a course of adrenaline running through my veins that was enough to power *ten* people. I had to survive this and get back to Amanda. Together, I knew that we could eliminate the threat that this man and his group posed and bring all the guilty parties to justice.

I took the opportunity, knowing that I had only seconds before he would reappear with something designed to hurt or kill me, and paddled like hell into the tunnel. Paddling furiously against the current, I worked my way about 15 yards up the tunnel to a point where the water had slowed, and I could find a handhold on an old piece of rebar protruding from the side. I felt that this far in, he wouldn't be able to see me well or, more importantly, get a good bead on me as it was dark this far back, and I was backed by even more darkness.

I had just stopped when his booming voice rang through the tunnel. He said, "Boy, you shouldn't leave the party so soon. I have a little present for you. I know you haven't gone too far, so I'm sure you'll enjoy it."

My mind raced and quickly came to one conclusion. He had a grenade of some sort. I reasoned — and hoped — that it was only a flash-bang, given that he wouldn't want to blow half the bank off and draw attention to himself, or get caught in the blast. I also reasoned that he would be satisfied with stunning me to the point where I would drift out of the pipe and be helpless to avoid the fate that he and his *boys* had waiting for me.

I had only a few seconds to act. He would need to make sure he was in an advantageous position. Then he would remove the pin and release the lever, time the throw, and heave it as far down the tunnel in my direction as possible.

With no time to spare, I quickly tied my boat to the piece of rebar fastened to the side of the tunnel, then rolled off and into the icy water, grabbing my boat by the gunwale, and flipping it as I went. I planted my feet on the bottom of the tunnel, where I thankfully found a good purchase, and turned my boat over and on top of me hoping that it would offer some protection from the concussive force of the grenade.

I had just managed to do this, finding a small air pocket in which to breath, while bracing my elbows and shoulders on the inner walls of the kayak to both hold the kayak in place and free my hands to plug my ears, when I heard the grenade clang against a side wall of the tunnel, followed by what seemed like the end of the world. Even with my eyes squeezed shut, my fingers in my ears, and with the relative protection of my boat, the intensity of the light and sound rocked my world more than I ever would have imagined.

Thankfully, the kayak had saved me from the brunt of the blast and, though slightly stunned, my senses were intact enough to get my kayak turned back upright and my body quickly back on top of it. Fueled by adrenaline and fear, I untied my boat and paddled harder than I ever had in my life. I was soon far up the tunnel and into the darker reaches.

Just as I began to feel confident that I was far enough up the tunnel to be affected much by another flash bang, I heard the report of a handgun and ringing of bullets ricocheting off the walls somewhere behind me.

Not wanting to be hit by an errant shot, I paddled deeper into the tunnel and reached a point of absolute darkness. The water had calmed as I continued paddling my way forward. I didn't know where I was going, but knew that going back was not an option. Feeling that it was now safe to do so, I turned on my headlamp — an accessory that I kept in a small compartment next to my seat — and continued paddling.

I am not usually prone to claustrophobia but being in an enclosed space without a clue as to where I was headed was beyond frightening. Just as I started to think that the only way out was the way I had come — a path that was not an option — my boat caught a current that pulled it slightly to the right. Although I couldn't see well enough to read the currents, I could clearly see a fork in the tunnel with another path leading, as the current would indicate, back to the river.

I worked my boat around the fork in the tunnel — narrowly making the turn — and was swept into the current, with no choice now but to follow this new branch. I hoped that it would dump me back into the river far enough downstream that I wouldn't be spotted — a hope that helped maintain my composure. This branch was much longer than the last one, and I followed for a while, like most things in my life these days, by faith the path set before me.

After travelling a fair distance, the light at the end of the tunnel became visible. The current picked up and swept me along, giving me no choice but to continue forward, regardless of where it spit me out. The water in this branch moved faster as I neared the end of the tunnel and, in what seemed like the blink of an eye, I was jetting back out into the river. It would have been a fun ride under other circumstances, but at the moment, I was too concerned with survival.

Upon exiting the tunnel and entering the river, I turned and looked all around. I didn't recognize my surroundings. This brought a great feeling of comfort, as it meant that I was spit out of the tunnel somewhere beyond sight of where I had entered — and the goons who were after me.

Re-entering the main course of the river, I paddled hard to put distance behind me and, when I was a bit further downstream, crossed to the other side of the river as a precaution, should they attempt to follow me. For a little extra insurance, I followed along the far side of a barge heading south with the current, undoubtedly heading for New Orleans — my destination as well.

Hopefully, I thought to myself, *those idiots will be staying by the entrance to the drainage pipe, not knowing that there was another way out, and expecting me to make a run for it before I froze to death. That should keep them busy for a while.*

Once I was far enough downstream and out of danger, I hugged the shore and stayed well clear of the shipping lanes, paddling and drifting downstream toward New Orleans, and closer to Amanda. We had come to New Orleans back when we were dating and always stayed at the W Hotel, situated in the heart of the famed French Quarter. It was our predetermined place to meet, and I couldn't wait to get there.

Chapter 19

The Big Easy

IT HAD BEEN a long night, and yesterday was a day that I would rather forget. I was dog-tired. Seeing the city of New Orleans ahead seemed to energize me though, and as I paddled along the river with the city in view, I looked for landmarks that would put me in a good position to pull off the river near the hotel. I didn't mind the walk, but at this point, I felt that the sooner I made it there, the better.

I found a dock with a large sign advertising steamboat rides, intended to capture the business of some of the many tourists that visited New Orleans, and paddled up to a section with a metal ladder leading to the water. I tied my boat to it and removed my backpack from the storage compartment, heaving it up and onto the dock.

Next came the hard part. Knowing that this would be my last port of call, I untied my boat, pushed it out into the current, and watched it float away down the Mississippi. This was not an easy thing for me to do — ditching my boat like this — but with recent events revealing the magnitude of danger we were in, I didn't want to take even the remote chance that my boat would be discovered and linked to me.

I climbed the metal ladder and came up and onto the dock. A group of tourists, waiting for the steamboat to return and take them on their adventure, eyed me with the same kind of fascination and unease that they would an alligator who had just crawled out of the swamp. Not able to see my boat from their vantage point on the high dock, it must have appeared to them that I had emerged from the river — wet and disheveled — like some beast from a movie. I bowed, tipped my hat, and gave a short wave before quickly moving past them and on down the dock toward dry land.

A few blocks later, as I neared the hotel, my confidence grew. I felt that the dangerous and brazen men that we had just escaped from would have difficulty finding us in the big city. They, and perhaps whoever was behind them, were cunning enough to bug my attorney's offices to find our location, but I didn't think that either had the smarts or ability to find us through credit card charges, or other electronic transactions. I felt certain we would be safe here, even though I anticipated a short stay. I wanted to get back home and face my troubles head on. With Amanda's help — if she were willing — we should be able to set the stage for our return with some forward thinking.

The guy with the dirty gray beard and rotten teeth who tried to kill me — the apparent leader — had said that Amanda was "slippery." This wasn't a term I would use to describe Amanda. I thought that the words *clever*, *intelligent*, and *courageous* fit her better. Even though I was concerned for her safety, I knew that she could handle herself just fine. My instincts told me that I would find her alive and well at the hotel.

I soon found myself in the lobby of the W Hotel. My appearance drew a few stares, but at this point, I really didn't care. I just wanted to get to the room. I recalled that Amanda had a thing for upgraded rooms, so I was sure that we would not be suffering in the least. After the front desk placed a call to her room, and Amanda had provided the number, I headed up the elevator to the top floor and found our room at the end of the hallway near the stairs. It was private and quiet.

I knocked on the door, showing my face in front of the key-hole. In the blink of an eye, Amanda had swung the door open and was standing in front of me. Then, with tears of joy and relief running down her cheeks, she pulled me into the room and hugged me so hard that I couldn't breathe. After a long embrace, we let go and stood back from one another.

She looked at me so intently that I thought something was wrong with my appearance, and said, "Noah, I have never been more worried. I thought that I would never see you again. After my escape, which I'll tell you about later, I made my way here. Once I had checked in, and made it to the room, I immediately pulled out my laptop and checked for any breaking news in Baton Rouge. I found a story where someone had reported a disturbance along the riverfront. They said they had heard a loud boom and what sounded like gunshots. The police investigated but found nothing."

I raised my arms and said, "Guilty. That disturbance *did* involve me — and the witness *did* hear gunshots. For good measure, the loud boom they heard was a flash-bang grenade that almost made my head explode."

I told her the whole story, from being shot at from the truck to my escape through the tunnel. When I was finished, we both laughed and cried like babies, the fatigue, stress, and feelings of relief breaking a dam of emotions within both of us. We then held each other, more gently this time, and for how long I couldn't tell. I don't think that either of us wanted to let go.

When we did, I took notice of the room. Amanda had out-done herself. The large room had a separate seating area and a breathtaking view of the French Quarter and the Mississippi River. Holding hands, we walked over and sat down at a table by the window and filled each other in on the details of our individual escapes and travels to New Orleans.

I *really* wanted to know exactly what type of undercover work her brother Jake was involved in, what with the advanced security system, secret tunnel, and Porsche stashed nearby in the secret garage. I didn't ask though, since she would tell me if she was comfortable with it. If not, it was better that it remain a mystery.

Interrupting my thoughts, Amanda said, "I called my brother as soon as I was able after my escape. To my amazement, he already knew about the incident at the house and was concerned for my safety. He told me that the local authorities were being called off the investigation, and that the Feds would be taking over."

"The Feds," I asked. "Would this be the FBI?"

"Most likely," said Amanda.

My head was spinning, and the fatigue I was experiencing from my recent ordeals certainly didn't help.

Amanda, sensing my weariness and disquiet, in a gentle voice said, "I know you have a lot of questions. I'm sorry but all I can tell you is that he works for the government. Jake has always been on the side of good, which means that he has some serious bad guys that he must contend with in his job. I'm sure that what happened back at the house has all been assessed by some people in the higher levels of certain government agencies. This will be helpful in several ways. First, the local authorities have likely been called off the case, so we won't be identified and called in for questioning."

"Wait," I interrupted, "Won't the Feds then want to interview us?"

"They might," said Amanda. "I'll need to call him and find out what they plan to do."

"What about," I said, "my escape from the FBI SWAT team? Do you think they will want to prosecute me for evading arrest?"

"Noah," said Amanda in a calm and even voice, "I'm sure that is water under the bridge by now, and besides, they have bigger fish to fry."

Thinking about the guys who looked like militia types, and their leader who was both lethal and crazy, I said, "It's more likely they have fish to *catch* — and I would most likely be the bait."

With infinite patience, Amanda said, "I know that you have been through a lot, but let's not get ahead of ourselves. I'll know much more after I call my brother, but I think that if the authorities need our help, and I say *our* help because I'm in this fairly deep as well, it will be a collaborative effort. My brother, given his connections up the chain of command, can help see to that. I think that all that has been going on with you has just risen to another level. I also think that, with the support that I anticipate, it is now time to move from defense to offense. Are you ready?"

Feeling more confident with her support, I said, "Amanda, I am more than ready!"

"That's what I like to hear. If you will be so kind as to go downstairs and get us some drinks and hors d'oeuvres, I'll call my brother to see what he may want us to do from here."

Trusting Amanda completely, and understanding her need for privacy when talking to her brother, I made a quick change of clothes, left the room, and headed downstairs to pick up a bottle of wine and some New Orleans culinary delights.

When I arrived back at the room about 30 minutes later, Amanda greeted me at the door and helped set up the table while I opened the bottle of Pinot Noir that I had purchased, a nice wine to go with the Cajun-seasoned boiled shrimp, Creole fried oysters, Boudin balls, and cheese toast.

Amanda asked, "Noah, would you like to take a shower before we eat and talk? It might make you feel better?"

Boy, did I need a shower. "You read my mind Amanda."

I took a quick hot shower, changed into a fresh set of clothes, and was back at the table within 15 minutes. It really didn't take me long to freshen up, especially when we were hungry and there was good food waiting.

After toasting to our successful escape, and sampling the delicious food, Amanda said, "I spoke with my brother and have some interesting information to share."

I was all ears, my hunger for information exceeding even that of my hunger for food.

"What did he say?" I asked, leaning forward with antici-pation.

"Well, he first told me that he knew about what had hap-pened at the house, given that sensors went off and alerted him on his mobile phone when the intruders had broken in. He then accessed the hidden cameras and was able to watch it all."

Amanda continued, "He saw what played out on the outside of the house in view of the cameras and would have known that we were inside. He said that he was worried and immedi-ately called his agency connections to get to the house ASAP. I had also called 911 — so the cavalry was on the way. We clearly didn't have time to wait for them though. He said that he had the garage where his car was kept under surveillance, so he knew that I had used his Porsche to make my getaway. I assured him that there wasn't a scratch on it."

"So where does this leave us?" I asked.

"Well," said Amanda, "this is where it gets interesting. He told me that he shared the images of some of the intruders with his government colleagues, and they ran them through their databases. It seems that the guy with the beard, their apparent leader, is a potential person of interest with the FBI.

Even though they have yet to get a clear image of his face, the beard, body type and, fact that he and his group are after *you*, leads them to believe that he is the leader of a militia group with connections to Delray. I had also shared the license plate number I had memorized during my escape. They ran the plates and learned that the truck was registered in Delray, but couldn't trace the owners.

"So ... a militia group," I said. "Our hunch was right then. Do they know the name of the psycho who leads this group, whatever they call themselves?"

"There are many militia groups across the country, but they think this one goes by the name of the Big River Volunteer Militia, or BRVM for short. It is quite large, with compounds and operatives not only in Arkansas near Delray, but also several other states that border the Mississippi River. They are very secretive and smart, however, and the FBI has yet to identify the specific locations of their compounds. The authorities also don't have a good photo or likeness of their leader."

"Does the leader have a name," I asked?

"It is surely an alias, but the FBI knows that he goes by the name of Leroy Jones."

"Wow," I said. "It sounds like he has quite an extensive operation. What else do they have going on, besides trying to murder me, and what agencies are involved in catching them?"

"My brother didn't say a lot," said Amanda, "just that they were involved in a variety of criminal enterprises. I didn't ask about the agencies, but it is understandable that, given they are engaged in a multi-state criminal enterprise, the FBI would be involved."

Amanda, looking at me directly and speaking slowly and clearly, then said, "Noah, my brother did say that you will have some decisions to make. He spoke to some folks up the chain of command with the FBI and learned that taking down this militia group is a key priority of the agency. You are currently their best hope of finding and capturing the leader and helping them take down the organization. I shared your suspicion that the trouble with your crooked colleagues and the university, and the militia coming after you, is all tied together somehow. He agreed that it made sense."

That comes back to my earlier thought of me being the bait, I thought. "OK," I said, "will they be using a carrot or a stick to get me to help?"

"It looks like both actually," said Amanda, sounding somewhat apologetic. "From his conversation with the higher-ups, he said they will likely threaten you with prosecution, given that you broke the law by evading arrest back in Delray, but be willing to forgive your actions if you help them. They would also provide witness protection services for you, as well as the standard protective services while you help them. He didn't provide any more details, because that is all the information he could gather from his conversation. He did say, however, that the FBI would be contacting us very soon."

I turned to look out the window at the gray dusk of the day, as night approached and the revelers would soon be flooding the streets of the French Quarter, enjoying all that New Orleans had to offer. I felt a mix of comfort and happiness being with Amanda in the luxury hotel room, but I was also filled with uncertainty and anxiety, as my instincts told me that the path ahead would hold more danger and difficulty.

Amanda grabbed my hands from across the table and asked, "Are you OK Noah?"

I replied, "Sure, I'm fine. It would seem the best option — and perhaps the only reasonable option — is to cooperate with the FBI. As they say, 'in for a penny, in for a pound.'"

"Yes," replied Amanda, "In for a penny, in for a pound. I'm with you all the way."

With her words still sweetly ringing in my ears, I walked over to the bed, laid down, and fell fast asleep.

As I was drifting off to sleep, somewhere between a dream-state and consciousness, I could hear Amanda on the phone with her brother say "Bro, tell your FBI folks that we're in."

"Great," was his unheard reply. "That will make things much easier for everyone."

Chapter 20

Turning the Tide

I WOKE THE next morning to find Amanda lying next to me in bed. Her eyes fluttered open, and we gazed at each other while time stood still. She took my hand, and as our fingers intertwined, an electricity coursed through that simple connection that made the next hour something inevitable. The feel of her warm body against mine, the soft scent of her perfume, and the rhythm of our bodies as we moved in perfect sync, was purely magical. Being with her was like entering another realm, where all my troubles were far, far away — to be replaced with a feeling of love, warmth and comfort that was beyond compare. I think we both knew that this time it was more than temporary, and that we were meant to be together.

Afterwards, Amanda said, "Why don't you get a shower while I make some calls."

I agreed, and after a nice relaxing shower, we had a light breakfast of steel cut oatmeal with fresh blueberries, warm croissants with butter and strawberry jam, and a bowl of fruit. We washed it down with fresh squeezed orange juice and some of New Orleans' finest chicory coffee.

After we had eaten, I said, "There seem to be a lot of moving pieces, but I feel certain that many of them belong to the same puzzle. One piece involves my colleagues and the university going to extreme measures to get me out and silence me. The other piece involves this militia group and their efforts to silence me for good. The common thread is that no-one wants me to share what I know. There *must* be a connection."

"I would agree," said Amanda. "It might be helpful to be a bit introspective. What are your objectives at this point?"

The obvious came to mind. "First," I said, "I want to stay alive."

"That is an excellent objective," said Amanda playfully.

"Second, even if I don't want to stay at Delray University, I certainly don't want to be fired. That would be a fatal mark on my record. Third, I want justice in the form of criminal convictions and civil liability for those involved in wrongdoing — no matter how far up the chain it goes."

"Go big or go home is what I always say," said Amanda.

God, I loved this girl. "It appears as though we will have two main allies in the battles going forward — the FBI and my lawyer, Gary Easterling."

Amanda said, "I took the liberty of calling my brother last night after you fell asleep and told him that you were willing to work with the FBI. He was pleased to hear that."

"I thought I heard you talking as I was falling asleep but couldn't be sure."

"You weren't dreaming. I called him back this morning while you were in the shower to find out if he had heard anything else. During our conversation, my phone beeped with a call coming in from the New Orleans FBI Field Office. I spoke with Special Agents Carina Petrova and Matthew Steele. They are the lead agents on a case investigating the BRVM, and would like to meet with you at their offices the day after tomorrow. The agents said that they would look forward to working with us."

Noticing that she had caught my attention when she said the word "us," Amanda explained. "Given that I am neck deep in all of this, they allowed me to assist. I hope that is OK with you, even though I'm going to do it anyway."

I chuckled and said, "That sounds great, Amanda. I think that we will also need to get back in touch with Gary. His involvement is particularly important. I'll call him and see if he can meet us somewhere halfway between here and Delray for lunch so that we can discuss matters."

Amanda let me use her cell phone and I dialed Gary's private number. Gary answered and immediately asked, "Noah, are you OK? I've been very concerned since the last call. What happened?"

"Amanda and I are both OK. It was close, but I have a guardian angel — and I do mean angel — who helped me escape." I went on to tell him the story of our harrowing escape, and that we were now in New Orleans."

"That is amazing," said Gary. "I have no words."

"We also learned the FBI suspects that the people who burned down Amanda's cabin and made the attempt on our lives in Baton Rouge belong to a group called the Big River Volunteer Militia — BRVM for short — a multi-state organization involved in various criminal enterprises. Their leader goes by the name of Leroy Jones, though this is most certainly an alias."

"That is interesting," said Gary, "and adds a few important pieces to this puzzle."

Switching gears, Gary said, "So what is the plan for you now?"

"I was hoping that you could help me with that. I was wondering if you would be able to meet with me and Amanda in person. Are you free tomorrow, and do you remember that great little riverside restaurant in Natchez, Mississippi?"

"I am — and I do," said Gary.

"We can drive up from where we are staying in New Orleans and meet you there. It is a bit of a drive for each of us, but a good halfway point."

Gary replied, "I'll clear my schedule and make a day of it. I could meet you there at noon."

"Perfect," I said.

"Noah, there are a few things you need to know before we meet, not all of them pleasant. First, as you might have suspected, the university has circled the wagons and basically shut down all communication regarding the computer incident. They want to put this behind them quickly and for good. As for the media, they finally got tired of not getting more scoop and went home. I'm sure they went searching for the newest story that would capture the public's short attention span and decided to move on, so all is quiet on that front now. I have tried to reach Ronald Turpin — the one they pinned the blame on — but he has disappeared and is no longer in the area."

The phone went silent for a moment before Gary continued. "I hesitate to tell you this because I don't want to disturb you, but I have several pieces of bad news. First, your house has been broken into and ransacked. The police are investigating, but haven't made much progress."

My blood pressure spiked as I hoped that they hadn't damaged any of my artwork or prized personal belongings.

Gary continued, "All I could gather after speaking with a friend on the force was that a neighbor, an older woman named Melba, had seen what she described as 'militia boys' pull out of your driveway in a dirty pickup truck. She noticed them because, as she put it, 'they burned rubber,' heading out of your driveway. She didn't get a good look at any of their faces, and neither did she get a license plate number. She said that she went over to the house to check on it after they left and found that the front door was broken, and the house had been ransacked. My friend on the force said privately that it appeared as though they were looking for something."

"If I had to guess," I said, "they were probably looking for any incriminating information I might have left behind that was tied to Finch or the BRVM. It makes me wonder...."

"Wonder what? asked Gary, as I paused to think.

"It makes me wonder if Finch has a family connection to the BRVM. In other words, does he have family members who are in the BRVM, or any ties to this Leroy Jones guy? Would your paralegal be able to research this angle?"

Gary replied, "Brittany is very sharp. I'll put her on it after we hang up."

Thinking of how crazy our lives had been recently, and how important the memo and recording were to how things might play out, I asked, "Gary, since we still have the originals of the memo and recording, and given how important they seem to be, would you mind if we turned them over to you for safekeeping when we meet tomorrow? Given the lengths that the bad guys are going to keep us from going public with the information, I would rather keep it safe with you."

"I would be happy to hold onto it," said Gary. "We will keep it in what we call, 'The Vault.' It is a high security, fireproof safe, where we keep only the most important client documents and other evidence."

"Thanks, Gary," I said.

"Stay safe and I'll see you tomorrow. And by the way, I look forward to meeting Amanda. I gather that she is a lovely person."

"She is all that and more," I said, before ending the call.

Amanda and I decided to throw caution to the wind and spent the afternoon strolling through the French Quarter, shopping, and people-watching, followed by a fabulous dinner at Antoine's, and capped by an even more enjoyable time back at the room.

Chapter 21

Brainstorm

THE DRIVE UP to Mississippi in the Porsche Cayman was exhilarating, and thankfully without incident. We arrived in Natchez shortly before noon, where we easily found a parking spot outside of the restaurant. The rustic, nautical-themed building, situated on a bluff overlooking the Mississippi river, was a favorite of both locals and tourists, with a cozy interior punctuated by a wood burning fireplace.

We had arrived before Gary, so we went in and found a table near the window that would afford as much privacy as possible. It was the off-season, so only a few tables were occupied, likely all by locals. From our table we could see the river rushing by below. The hypnotic rush of the water carried me back to the unpleasant memories of the past few weeks. I thought about the close calls, the constant worry of being pursued, and the uncertainty of what lay ahead.

Amanda must have sensed my thoughts. She took my hand — this simple act bringing me back to the moment. She said, in a voice that gave me strength and hope, "Noah, we will get through this, and you will succeed in bringing those cowards to justice. We just need to keep our heads together and emotions at bay as much as possible. I have complete faith that you will prevail."

"No," I corrected her. "*We* will prevail," and with heartfelt appreciation, I said, "Thanks Amanda. I needed to hear that."

We ordered iced teas and only had to wait about five minutes before Gary entered the restaurant. We waved him over, and he strode to our table with that air of confidence that seemed to constantly surround him. He was dressed, as usual, in a nicely tailored business suit, and was easy to identify with his signature well-manicured salt and pepper goatee and horned rim glasses.

I said, "Gary, I'd like to introduce you to Amanda Strauss."

"Amanda, it is truly a pleasure to finally meet you. I understand that you all have been through some difficulties, and that you pulled Noah out of the fire, so to speak."

Amanda grinned and said, "With some help from my brother and the contingency plans he keeps in place. It is nice to meet you as well. Noah speaks very highly of you."

"He exaggerates, but I'll take any compliments that come my way."

The waitress, who seemed to treat everyone as an old friend, calling them *Honey* or *Sweetie*, came over and took our order. Gary asked how we were doing, and how we liked our hotel in New Orleans. He told us a story about one of his more colorful experiences in the Big Easy while in college, and we all had a good, long, genuine laugh. It felt good to be with people that I felt so comfortable with, and for a moment I forgot my worries and actually felt normal.

After some small talk about fishing and the weather, we moved on to talking business and reality came charging back. Handing him the envelope, I said, "Gary, this envelope contains the memo along with other documents we feel are important, a copy of the recording on a thumb drive, as well as a written transcript of the recording that Amanda helped me type."

"Thanks," said Gary. I've read the photo-copied documents that were left in my care, but oddly, the memo wasn't included. It will be helpful to read the memo again to put it all into context."

He put on his reading glasses, then opened the envelope and removed the memo and transcript of the recording. He read the memo several times, then moved on to the transcript and read, and re-read the text of the recording. When he was finished, he sat back, looked over at us, and said, "This now gives me better perspective from the standpoint of litigation. There are also pros and cons associated with it. So, starting with the age old question, I have some good news and some bad news. Which would you like to hear first?"

"The bad news," Amanda and I said in unison.

"Good choice," said Gary. "It is always best to get the bad news out of the way. And it's not so much bad news, but more of a challenge that we will have to overcome. As you probably know, the secretly taped video recording would likely not be admissible in court. Even though Patricia practically admitted that they were damaging your career in retaliation for bringing a legitimate ethics complaint in your capacity as a faculty and administrator, if we were unable to use this evidence in a lawsuit, it would weaken our ability to succeed on a retaliation claim. As for the memo, the fact that it was technically stolen would not only raise some serious concerns with a judge, but also would present a difficult lift in terms of arguing admissibility, as it could be argued that the document was obtained illegally and should therefore not be admissible as evidence in the case."

"We suspected that would be the case," I admitted.

"It clearly isn't worthless though," said Gary. "In fact, it could be quite valuable if the information can be used to help demonstrate culpability — or, guilt — as it relates to a possible larger criminal enterprise connected with the militia. We will need to see how that plays out. I'll keep the original, and a copy of the recording, but I think that it would be wise to share a copy of the memo with the FBI. I will handle any civil proceedings where we sue for monetary damages, but I think that all criminal matters, at least at this point, would be in the FBI's orbit. This information will be valuable to them."

"That makes sense," I replied.

"So, do you want to hear the good news?" asked Gary.

"Absolutely," I said, while Amanda nodded yes.

Gary brightened and said, "Well, as you might have also suspected, the university and your colleagues made a major mistake.

"What was that?" I asked.

"The university," said Gary, "made both a rare — and major — error. Universities are typically slow to act and usually take the high road out of concern for liability, so the actions they took in response to what they believed you had done were highly unusual and aggressive. The university was overconfident in relying on the IT report that you had incriminating files on your computer. They also wanted to get the issue behind them as quickly as possible."

"Excuse me, Gary," I interrupted, "but the university communications team and the lawyers don't act alone. They have to get their orders from someone."

"That is correct," said Gary, "and that someone — or some people — would have to be high up the chain *and* be incredibly nervous to pull the trigger on this so quickly. I'm certain that knowing the who and the why would get us the answers we need."

"Should I break into the provost's office next?" I asked jokingly.

"No!" replied Amanda and Gary as one voice.

I raised my hands and said, "Hey, just kidding."

Gary laughed and continued, "Thanks for the comic interlude. Now where was I?"

"Oh yes, I spoke with the university's top attorney, Jim Sanford, who came as close to an apology as I have ever seen someone in that position make. When we spoke, I think they already had hatched a plan to deflect blame onto Turpin and claim ignorance, which would help them mitigate public relations damage. Though it remained unsaid, both Jim and I knew, however, that the university would have a tough time defending a defamation claim. The fact remains that they publicly announced something about you that was untrue — regardless of what they believed at the time — and which was highly damaging to your reputation and career."

"You can say that again," I said. "My career in academia may be over."

"Let's not get ahead of ourselves, Noah," said Gary. "This is a marathon, and the race isn't nearly over."

"They really didn't ever apologize or publicly say that I *wasn't* to blame in any direct way," I said.

"That is true and may also work in our favor," said Gary. "They were stuck between a rock and a hard place on that one, trying to wash their hands of the whole thing, while also wanting to keep you implicitly at fault in the public eye in hopes of tainting a future jury pool if we were to bring a lawsuit for defamation at some point."

"The university plays dirty, doesn't it?" I said bitterly.

Gary nodded once and continued, "If we choose to bring suit, I think we can name defendants starting with Dr. Finch, all the way up the chain to the university itself. We are talking millions in potential damages. If this is a claim that you would like to bring, I'll start working on it right away."

"What is the potential downside?" I asked.

"Well, it definitely won't put you in the university's good graces, and they have many ways to make your life miserable or run you out, despite the fact that you have tenure and every reason in the world to bring a lawsuit against them. However, given all that has transpired, it probably would not be wise to go back to work there anyway."

I looked over to Amanda, and she nodded slightly. "All right then," I said, "Let's go full steam ahead with the defamation lawsuit."

"OK," said Gary, "I think that is a good idea."

"And now for the really good news," said Gary.

"There's more?" asked Amanda, mirroring my thoughts.

"Yes," said Gary, "and this will be information that will be helpful to the FBI."

Brimming with anticipation, I asked, "What is it, Gary?"

Gary took a sip of sweet tea and said excitedly, "My brilliant paralegal, Brittany, has done it again. After a long afternoon and night of research, and following leads through some of my local connections, she made several important discoveries. The information that she uncovered could change the playing field considerably."

Amanda said, "We need all the good news we can get. Please tell us what Brittany found."

Gary cleared his throat, took a gulp of tea, and said, "Using some of our proprietary databases, plus some that we use by agreement with law enforcement, Brittany was able to make valuable progress toward learning the true identity of Leroy Jones and connections he might have to your colleagues, Howard Finch in particular.

"I'll attempt to summarize her search methods and findings. Based on what you told us, Brittany began her search, learning as much as she could about the BRVM — and their leader, Leroy Jones. They are so secretive, however, there wasn't much

to learn. We know that Leroy Jones, whose name we understand to be an alias, is very reclusive. There are no public videos
or photos of him as leader of the BRVM. He only makes public
statements through recordings that use some type of voice-
altering computerized device. As you know, the group appears
to have ties to the Delray area and operates in a broader multi-
state area that borders the Mississippi River, hence the use of
'Big River' in the name. Also, from what you told me from your
conversation with the FBI, Leroy Jones and the BRVM were the
ones they suspect have made attempts on your life."

Gary continued, "Given what you requested, Brittany set
out to determine the true identity of Leroy Jones, and what
connection he might have to Dr. Finch. She began her search
with Finch, and luck was on her side. She found a public
ancestry page with the Finch family tree. She looked at the
tree and followed along the branches until she saw a name
that caught her attention. The name was Roy Johnson, a first
cousin of Finch, and a name that sounded similar to Leroy
Jones – Leroy-Roy, and Jones-Johnson. She thought it possible
that Leroy Jones was an alias for Roy Johnson, so she followed
this line of reasoning."

"A bit of a reach, but I guess that makes sense," I said. "You
have to start somewhere."

Gary merely smiled in response to my comment.

"Brittany searched state and local police records for Roy
Johnson but reached a dead end. Next, she conducted a search
on one of our proprietary archival databases using the terms
'Delray' and 'Roy Johnson' and found a news story that gave an
account of a domestic violence dispute between a Mrs. Elvira
Johnson and Mr. Roy Johnson. Elvira claimed to have been
beaten by her husband within an inch of her life in a dispute
involving a TV remote, of all things. She pressed charges that
were later dropped. The article went on to discuss the unfortunate plight of many women who live with abusive husbands."

"This man is a monster," said Amanda.

"Yes, he is," said Gary, "and Brittany set out to discover more about him. She found, to her surprise and satisfaction, that the article provided a photo of Roy Johnson from his high school yearbook. The article also listed the address for Roy and Elvira. This isn't typical for a news article of this type. The reporter must have added the photo and address to let people know who this monster was, and where he lived."

My heart was pounding as I realized we might be getting closer to finding answers to some particularly important questions.

"Amazing," I said. "But wait, didn't you say that you searched the police records and couldn't find a record of Roy Johnson?"

"That is true, and we wondered about that as well. Our best guess is that he was released shortly after he was booked, and it looks like a record of his arrest was either never made, or just removed. We suspect that if Roy Johnson is who we think he is, then he had powerful connections in Delray — enough to keep his name out of any official records. Anonymity would have been particularly important to both him and his allies."

Gary continued. "Brittany then searched the county tax records from back then using Roy and Elvira's address and discovered that they were living in a rental property about a mile out of town on a small farm, owned by ... drum roll please ... a Dr. Howard Finch."

"So, there *is* a connection," said Amanda. "I wish we knew more."

Gary said, "Hang with me, there *is* more."

"Brittany continued her search looking for subsequent news about Roy and Elvira Johnson. Elvira is a unique name, and she soon came upon her obituary. Her obituary made reference to the cause of Elvira's death, noting that she had died tragically and unexpectedly from a fall from a horse."

"Sure," said Amanda, the anger rising in her voice. "Just like her bruises and injuries came from running into a door, or from some other *accident*."

"I guess this suggests that he is capable of murder, which would make for at least one thing that Roy Johnson has in common with his supposed alias, Leroy Jones" I said.

"Like I said, there is more to the story, so just be patient," said Gary.

"Brittany searched further and oddly, there was no reference to a Roy Johnson living near Delray after Elvira's death. She even conducted a real estate and public records search and found nothing. He had literally disappeared."

"So, he could have either just moved far away, or had his name changed and gone into hiding," said Amanda.

"As you will see," said Gary, "it is most likely the latter."

"Brittany had reached a dead end on Roy Johnson, so she changed course and decided to work the Finch angle again. An idea came to her, and she decided to check out Finch's Facebook page. Fortunately for her, Finch had the privacy settings for his page set to public view. She was able to access all his photos that way. After scouring a sizable number of them, she came across a family photo taken in the past that was labeled 'family reunion.' While scanning the faces, she came across a person in the group that caught her eye. She looked back at the high school yearbook photo of Roy Johnson, and noticed that even considering the age difference, the facial features seemed a match."

"Wait a minute," I said, barely able to contain my excitement. Roy Johnson, the man who brutally assaulted his wife, is the same person in Finch's family photo?"

"We believe so," said Gary. "And the genealogy records would put the Roy Johnson, first cousin of Howard Finch that Brittany found, in the same age category as the Roy Johnson from the news article."

"Let me get this straight," said Amanda, her sharp mind working it through. We know that Finch has a first cousin named Roy Johnson. We have a photo of a family member whose image matches that of a Roy Johnson who rented a house from Dr. Finch. We also know that Roy Johnson brutally assaulted his wife, and is therefore a violent and dangerous man."

"So, if the two photos are indeed of the same person, then Finch and Roy Johnson," I said, putting two and two together, "are related. They are also most likely first cousins. It would be too much of a coincidence to believe otherwise. Did you bring copies or screenshots of the photos that Brittany found?"

There are at least a few moments in everyone's life when a change in life's direction hangs in the balance. *This was one of those times.*

"I did," said Gary, "Brittany took a screenshot and printed out the picture of the family photo on our high resolution printer. She did the same with the yearbook photo. In the family photo, Roy Johnson is third from the left on the back row. Note that you will also see Finch, front and center.

"I had Brittany focus on his image from the family photo and enlarge it without losing too much resolution. You will see this in the second photo. The third photo is a copy of the black and white yearbook picture from the news article."

Gary slid the photos over as time stood still.

I looked at the photos closely, then looked over at Amanda, with recognition showing in my eyes, and said, "That is him! I'm certain that is the same man I saw on the river who tried to kill me — same beady eyes and facial features. Even though the man in these earlier pictures doesn't have a beard, I am certain it is him."

"So," said Gary, his analytical mind summarizing what we now knew. "Roy Johnson is very likely Leroy Jones, which means ..."

"Howard Finch is very likely related to Leroy Jones, the leader of the BRVM.," Amanda and I said as one. "They are probably even first cousins," I added. "And we now know that Howard Finch is — for certain — related to someone who attempted to murder both me and Amanda."

We all sat in silence, processing what we had just learned.

Gary, ever the pragmatist, broke the silence, saying, "We have taken a step in the right direction, and now have some valuable information to provide the FBI. Amanda, if you will let me know where to send it, I'll share a copy of our findings, as well as a summary of our conclusions with them."

"I'll ask my brother. Since Noah is meeting with the FBI agents tomorrow, we will need to get this information to them soon."

"OK," said Gary, "I'll type up a summary after we are done here, and have Brittany put it together and get it ready to send over."

"Great," said Amanda. "I'll call my brother on the drive home and provide you with an email or text address."

"This should make my meeting with them go more smoothly tomorrow," I added, feeling hopeful. "I want to sincerely thank you both. If not for you all, I would probably still be floating with the current somewhere, heading toward Mexico."

They both chuckled, and we said our goodbyes, each of us knowing that we had a long road ahead of us.

"Good luck," said Gary as we headed out the door. "If you need anything, I'm just a phone call away."

"Thanks," I said, as we walked to the car, slid into the comfortable, form fitting leather seats, and sped away — back towards the Big Easy.

Chapter 22

Powerful Allies

AFTER AN ENJOYABLE drive filled with lengthy discussions, we arrived back in New Orleans. Returning to our hotel, we changed and went down to the gym for a long workout. Later, feeling happy and relaxed from the physical exertion, and a hot shower, we decided to order takeout from Commander's Palace. The meal came straight from one of the best restaurants in the French Quarter, and paired with a nice wine, we feasted on corn fried oysters, fresh bread and artisanal cheeses, and pecan-crusted fish. We followed the delicious dinner with a fantastic dessert of beignets and Creole bread pudding. After finishing every bite of our meal, we laid on the bed, holding each other close, and watched reruns of old movies until we fell asleep in each other's arms.

The next day came too fast, and in what seemed like the blink of an eye, I found myself sitting in the FBI New Orleans Field Office waiting to be interviewed. When I arrived at the FBI offices, it was not at all what I had expected. Contrary to television shows where there was constant drama and some level of chaos, the place was almost peaceful, and the people I encountered on my way in were professional, courteous, and friendly.

After checking in and giving my name and reason for coming, I was greeted by an agent and taken to an interview room. Unlike the interrogation rooms that I had seen on TV and in the movies, this room felt more like the waiting room for a doctor's office, with comfortable chairs and furnishings that made me feel at ease. I was even given a cup of coffee while I was waiting that was not half bad.

Five minutes later, two agents — a stern looking man, and a woman with a no-nonsense demeanor — entered the room.

"Hello," said the female agent, "we are sorry to make you wait. I am Special Agent Carina Petrova, and this is my partner, Special Agent Matthew Steele."

We shook hands, and since they obviously knew who I was, I simply said, "It's nice to meet you." I could tell immediately that they were professionals.

Agent Steele turned to me and said, "Dr. Banks, we know that your time is valuable, so we will get straight to the heart of the matter. Your attorney, Mr. Gary Easterling, contacted us late yesterday afternoon and was kind enough to share some information that his office had uncovered regarding one of your faculty colleagues and a person of interest to us — a Mr. Leroy Jones. He also shared a summary of his findings which included revelations that were made at his meeting with you yesterday. He told us that you recognized a person — one believed to be a Mr. Roy Johnson — in a family photo of your colleague at Delray University — a Dr. Howard Finch. We understand that this person you identified, Roy Johnson, was the same person you believe was responsible for the attempts on your life. We also have reason to believe that he was the person responsible for the attack on the Strauss residence.

Like a well-choreographed dance, Agent Petrova took over and said, "You have helped us find an important piece of the puzzle in our attempt to apprehend members of a militia group called the Big River Volunteer Militia, or BRVM. Up until now, we have known truly little about the suspected leader who goes by the name Leroy Jones, one of his many ever-changing aliases. He never shows his face, and on the rare occasion that he makes a public announcement, it is done either through a voice-altered recording, or in writing and provided anonymously to the press. All we have are a few grainy images taken from a distance at a location that we believe once belonged to his militia group, and more recently, a few stills from video surveillance footage taken at the house you were occupying at the time he and his militia operatives stormed the Strauss residence. It must have been extremely important to him, *and personal*, to come after you himself and risk exposure. He was obviously overconfident as well, thinking that you would be easy prey. As they say, 'dead men tell no tales.'"

Taking back the baton, and giving a stern look to his partner, Agent Steele said, "Our techs ran facial recognition analyses and compared the fractional facial images caught by cameras outside the Strauss' home, the yearbook photo of Roy Johnson, the picture from the Finch family reunion, and the low-grade images that we had, and found that all matched key features to a high degree of probability. Our techs then generated a digital photo utilizing matching facial features, adding a beard, and accounting for his suspected current age."

"We were also able to confirm," interjected agent Steele, "through our intelligence gathering capabilities, that Roy Johnson is, in fact, Howard Finch's first cousin."

Petrova continued. "We need to confirm that the man in the computer-generated photo created by our tech team is the same man you observed in your encounters with him."

Agent Steele slid the image toward me. "Please, take your time," said Steele.

I didn't need time. I nearly gasped when I saw the computer-generated image of the man with beady eyes and a full gray beard, staring back at me from the photo.

Catching my breath, I said firmly, "That's him. I'm sure of it."

Agents Steele and Petrova shared a glance, the hardness in their eyes replaced with something that looked like, perhaps, relief.

"You have just confirmed for us that this man," said Agent Steele, clearing his throat, "is Leroy Jones, leader of the BRVM, and the first cousin of your colleague, Dr. Howard Finch."

"So, my colleague Howard Finch's cousin is a murderous scum who is the leader of a group of murderous scum," I said disgustedly.

"That is one way to put it," said Agent Petrova, with a tight smile on her lips.

"Discovering Leroy Jones' true identity is a huge step in the right direction for our investigation, but we still don't know where to find him. He has probably gone to ground since he would not want to risk further exposure. This doesn't mean that you are safe though. His goons are likely still out there and on the hunt for you."

"That is reassuring," I said with obvious sarcasm.

"We will be offering 24/7 protection for both you and Amanda, so you don't need to worry," said Agent Steele. "I also doubt that they will find you in New Orleans, but you can't be too careful."

Getting the conversation back on track, Agent Petrova said, "Like I said, you have helped us immensely, Dr. Banks. Discovering Leroy Jones' true identity is very important to our investigation. We are still faced with the challenge, though, of finding him and the location of his compounds. We believe that his militia group may be one of the largest in the nation, funded by the illegal manufacture and sale of drugs, as well as other criminal enterprises such as prostitution and human trafficking, gambling, and black market weapons sales. As you might suspect, it is important that we take them down. In fact, it is an Agency priority."

"What can I do to help?" I asked, throwing myself into the deep end without a float.

"First," said Agent Petrova, "it is important for you to know that we are now working under an agreement of strict confidence. With this meeting being taped, do you agree to keep everything that is said and done between you and the FBI in the strictest confidence."

"Almost," I replied, and could immediately tell that this answer was not going down well with them.

"What do you mean by that?" asked Agent Steele in a serious tone.

"I mean," I replied, "that I am sharing everything with my partner in all of this, Amanda Strauss. She knows everything that I know, and I wish to continue keeping her informed as we go forward. I am also sharing information with my attorney, Gary Easterling."

Agent Petrova, seeming to relax a bit, smiled, and said, "Mr. Easterling has signed a confidentiality agreement, so you are free to speak with him on matters relevant to our investigation. As for Amanda, we have already been informed by our superiors that she has clearance on all matters related to this case."

That was easy, I thought. Who the heck was her brother, anyway, to have this much influence? I let it go since I was sure they wouldn't tell me.

Agent Petrova then said, "OK, Noah, now that we know you will keep matters related to this case only between yourself, your attorney and Amanda, we can proceed. Like I said, we don't know where Leroy and his militia are located, and therefore have not been able to make arrests, and bring them to justice. We need you to help us find them. Now that we know the connection between Leroy Jones (aka Roy Johnson) and Dr. Finch, and have you on our side, we can make progress. We will need for you to go undercover to help us learn where Leroy and his militia are hiding. In return, we'll make every effort to ensure that the risk to you is minimal and can even put you in the Witness Protection Program once this is over. What do you think?"

"Why not?" I said, "I'm in."

"Good," said Agent Steele. "Perhaps you could tell us a little about Dr. Finch. Thinking back, do you recall ever having any suspicions that he was connected to a fringe group or was engaged in anything illegal?"

I told Steele about his use of recreational drugs and recounted some of my experiences while on his sailboat on Lake Summit, a large lake near Delray.

I said, "Thinking back, at one point earlier in my career I recall that he would brag and tell tall tales. One story that stuck with me was one he told when I was on his sailboat with some junior faculty colleagues. He had a few beers and told this story about how his sailboat had once been becalmed — was dead in the water due to a lack of wind — on the lake some years ago, and how he had made his graduate student pull his boat to his cousin's dock while swimming and holding the bow rope between his teeth so they could get some gas for his trolling motor. He seemed to take great joy in recalling how he had exerted his control over this poor student. He has an abusive personality, so the mistreatment of his student was probably true, but I didn't think more about his cousin having a dock on the lake. There was no reason to."

"Did he give any specifics about his cousin" asked Petrova.

"Not much but I seem to recall that he referred to his cousin as *he*, or *him*. Wait a minute! Now that I think about it, I remember him saying it was his cousin *Roy's* dock. How could I have forgotten that?"

"This might be the break we've been looking for," said Agent Steele. "Where was this dock located?"

"That is where it gets tricky," I said. "It is an exceptionally large lake that is bordered almost entirely with houses and boat docks, except for a few patches of low-lying shoreline that you couldn't build on due to occasional flooding. It would be challenging to find the right dock. Who knows, he also may have been just telling me a load of crap, which was always a possibility with him."

Agent Petrova said, "This is a good lead, and frankly the *only* lead relevant to their whereabouts we presently have. Dr. Banks, we will need more information to help us find the specific location of the dock. Would you be willing to go undercover to help us find it? We can map out a plan for you to meet with Finch and coax more information out of him."

"I would be more than happy to do this," I said. "He has a huge ego and loves to tell stories, so it might be possible to tease it out of him."

Petrova and Steele shared a glance, and Petrova said, "Dr. Banks, you have no idea how helpful you have been already to our investigation. With this new angle to pursue — through the connection with your colleagues, who appear to be up to their necks in some highly questionable behavior — we have renewed momentum in our investigation of the BRVM and Leroy Jones. We want to stress that we will make every attempt to keep you out of harm's way, but given what we know about this group, and the past attempts on your life, the path forward is likely not to be without danger. I just want to be fully transparent about this. We will put together a plan and be back in touch with you to finalize it and hear your input. In the meantime, we will have agents providing protective services for you. You may also want to give serious thought to entering our witness protection program once your role in all of this has concluded. The meeting is over, unless you have anything else to add, so you are free to leave. Our agents will escort you out."

"Thank you," I replied, unable to think of anything more to share.

We shook hands and I headed out the door and back to the hotel with two agents, my newly acquired bodyguards, in tow.

While I was walking, I thought about their offer of witness protection. On the surface it sounded reasonable. I didn't know how long the group's tentacles were, or those of others who might also be involved. The implications of going into hiding, and most likely losing my career and all I had worked so hard for, however, was not all that appealing.

Another big question concerned Amanda, and what would happen to her. *Would we go into hiding together?* I was sure that a life in hiding would not hold a great deal of appeal to her either. We would need to talk about it.

I was happy to help the FBI agents, and desperately wanted to bring these criminals to justice. It made sense that, since we now knew that Finch and Leroy Jones (aka Roy Johnson) were related, connections between the militia, Finch, and my other crooked university colleagues would start to materialize.

We were heading out to the deep waters to catch the big fish now. I knew enough about this fishing expedition, though, to realize that I would be little more than the bait. Hopefully when they reeled me back in, I would still have my skin intact, while also bringing them the big fish. I knew that the FBI would be supportive — but were only using me to meet their own goals.

I would need luck, Amanda by my side, some serious cunning, and a little planning of my own to survive this dangerous game.

Chapter 23

The Bait

WHEN I RETURNED to the hotel, I found Amanda sitting on the edge of the bed, eager to hear about my meeting and learn what had happened.

"Basically, Amanda," I said, "They want to use me as bait to help them find the BRVM compounds and apprehend Leroy and his followers."

"Is that all?" Amanda said with playful sarcasm. "Pray tell, Noah, how do they intend to *use* you?"

"I'm not quite sure yet," I replied, "but I think it will involve trying to draw more information out of Finch that would be useful to them."

"So, they are going on a big fishing expedition," said Amanda. "It sounds like you are now a critical player in their investigation. You do realize that if Leroy and his gang — and whoever else is involved — are eventually apprehended, there will be a trial, and you will probably be called to testify. From what I know about these things, criminals usually don't take too kindly to those who help put them behind bars."

"It gets better," I said, my voice laced with irony. "No-one knows for certain whether this goes up the university chain of command, and if so, how far it goes. The higher this might go, and the more deeply this is connected to this mysterious militia group, the more challenging it is likely to become — and perhaps the more dangerous it could become. It certainly wouldn't put me in the good graces of the university."

"You can say that again," said Amanda.

"You need to know," I said, "The FBI has offered to put me in a witness protection program after this is all said and done, and this offer would be extended to you as well."

Amanda looked back at me blankly with a far-off look for a few seconds, before her eyes flashed back to the present, and looked as if they had been ignited and reflected a raging fire within.

"Hell no!" she finally said. "I'm not going into witness protection, and neither should you! I won't run from these Assholes, and I would rather die than back down from any of them. I say we help put those jerks behind bars for the rest of their miserable lives. I would especially like to see Leroy Jones, or whatever name the coward hides behind, rot in jail after what we learned about him beating, and most likely murdering, his poor wife Elvira. I can only imagine the hell that poor woman went through."

Amanda took a few deep breaths and composed herself. "You know, they all must pay for their deeds, and I think that the only real way out of this for both of us is to take them to the mat, in the sense that you follow through with your civil lawsuits, press criminal charges if that becomes necessary, and support the FBI in their investigation to the very end. Once that is done, we take our chances and trust that justice will be served."

"Who knows, if the lawsuits are successful, maybe we can move to Tahiti," she said half-jokingly.

Man, I loved this woman. She was utterly amazing. Instead of responding, I pulled her to me, and we let our emotions run between and through us, in a way that led to a single-minded purpose over the next hour. As we lay naked and sweating in the twisted sheets, I said, "You know what Amanda, I agree. With you around, who needs witness protection anyway? I bet you could take every one of them down all by yourself."

She smiled and said, "Thanks Noah, but I'll have to admit, I am human, and do harbor some fear, but I really think that with you and me working as a team, and with the FBI behind us, everything will turn out fine in the long run."

The following day, we received the much anticipated call from the FBI. The plan they had produced was simple, but would take some coordination and advance planning to make it work.

Amanda and I would head back to Delray, where the FBI had a safehouse for us to live in. No-one would know that the FBI was involved, and my cover story, for anyone who asked, would be that I was renting a place until my house was fixed up, and the local authorities believed that it would be safe for me to return after the break-in. I would also tell them that I had chosen the place where I would be living because it was a *safe* neighborhood — with houses tightly spaced, good lighting and plenty of neighbors to watch what was going on. This would be believable — particularly given the incident at the cabin. I knew how the rumor mill worked at the university.

Undercover FBI agents would occupy rooms in a fully equipped basement, while Amanda and I would occupy the main floor. The agents would only come and go on rare occasions, from a well concealed back entrance in the very early morning hours.

I was to go back to work and be a model citizen. Since I was still technically a faculty on the payroll, they would have to accept my return. I was sure that going back would be uncomfortable, but that really didn't matter. It only mattered that I would be there for the opportunity to covertly record something that would be helpful to the FBI. They wanted me to set up a private meeting with Finch, and would wire me with an electronic audio device concealed in the button of my shirt. They had permission from the court so that anything revealed by the device would be admissible in court.

I called Gary and told him the FBI's plan, and he, after listening carefully and asking several questions, seemed satisfied enough that I should follow through with it.

Next, I emailed Finch and Dean Winston and told them that I had returned. They emailed back right away with the typical falsely sympathetic statements that I would have anticipated. They also reminded me that, now that I was back, termination proceedings would resume due to my earlier indiscretions — my unauthorized intrusion on the private affairs of the Institute — and they would be providing me with more information in the coming days.

These people sure knew how to make a guy feel good, I thought sarcastically. The email also said that there would be a faculty meeting tomorrow, and that it was required that I be there. I fired back an email asking Finch if we could meet after the meeting, and to my surprise, he emailed right back and said that he would be happy to meet.

Amanda and I made the drive back to Delray, Amanda in her brother's Porsche, and me in a nondescript car, compliments of the FBI. With the undercover agents assigned to protect us following at a discrete distance, we finally arrived at our new home, a plain house in a cookie-cutter neighborhood where every house looked the same. The closer we came to Delray, the more my stomach tightened into knots. Our arrival at the house did nothing to improve my condition. After a restless night of sleep, morning finally arrived, and following my typical morning rituals, I headed back to my place of work — *the lion's den*.

The faculty meeting was held in the downstairs conference room, which doubled as a classroom for small graduate classes.

The room was cramped with mismatched chairs, and a conference table that was badly scratched, with patches of dark patina left there by the many hands, arms and elbows that had deposited oil and dirt over the years.

As the faculty rolled in — typically late, which seemed like an unwritten rule for faculty meetings — I was greeted and offered concerns, some sincere and some clearly fake. I had to focus to relax the tenseness in my muscles, given that I was seriously uncomfortable but didn't want to show it.

Anansi, in her characteristically politically correct and disingenuous manner, said, "Noah, we were so *very* concerned after hearing about the incident at the cabin, where we were told you had been staying. We didn't know whether you were dead or alive, and you were gone for so long that it caused all of us a great deal of worry. You should have trusted that we would find the jerk who planted those horrible files on your computer."

I bristled at these comments, not only because they were insincere, but also because she was subtly shifting fault to me, making it look like I was to blame for making them worry, and for lacking trust in *them*. How dare she say this, as her closest colleagues were the ones who planted the files on my computer, forced me to run and stay hidden and risk my very life. *Hell, she was probably in on it,* I thought. I could also guess that she had already measured my office to see if it would be suitable for her needs.

It took an extreme amount of self-control to present a calm outward demeanor, but knowing that I was now the hunter instead of the hunted helped immensely. I thought about the times I had been deer hunting with my father back home, and how he had taught me to control my breathing and have patience when stalking prey.

I now visualized Patricia, Howard, and Anansi as my prey, which allowed me to moderate my breathing and heart rate, focus on my reason for attending this meeting, and the plan that the FBI had put into place. It seemed almost like Anansi, who was excellent at judging people, sensed this change in my bearing and may have even seen a certain look in my eye that put her on alert. She suddenly went quiet and looked away. I decided not to respond, and to let her imagination run with whatever she thought I was thinking.

I looked directly over at Patricia, who refused to make eye contact and looked away as well. Dr. Larry Pickering, another of my undesirable colleagues, sat brooding in the corner, refusing to look up from his phone. It is funny how people who can be so intimidating in their outward words and actions, are really just cowards who subconsciously live in fear of being exposed for their misdeeds. I sincerely hoped that I could bring them to justice, and watch their arrogant facades melt away.

After a brief period of small talk with several colleagues whom I liked and respected — responding to their sincere concerns about my well-being, and thanking those who had covered my classes — Dr. Finch called the meeting to order, and everyone settled down.

The meeting began with Dr. Finch recognizing my presence and saying, "I'm sure you all join me in welcoming back our colleague, Dr. Noah Banks, who has been through quite an ordeal. As I'm sure Noah knows, I am here to help in any way possible, even if it is to just provide a listening ear. I'm sure that all of you feel the same way."

With that, he looked away, ending any further attention on me, and continued the meeting on a few superficial and meaningless issues.

I knew that Finch's sole interest was to draw a paycheck and cover his ass, while raking in the big money from his unethical and illegal dealings. He would ensure that nothing was ever ac-complished, as the open-ended questions and opportunity for debate among faculty about issues of the day led to circular arguments and reasoning that wore people out long before the threat of any decision of substance could be made. This insulated him from any push-back by either faculty or administration, while still allowing him to maintain the appearance of transparency and faculty governance. It was a win-win for Finch, and furthered the chaos and confusion in which he and his colleagues thrived, but in which the department withered.

At the conclusion of the meeting, I caught Finch and asked him if our meeting was still on. He said, "Why, yes, Noah. I'm looking forward to chatting. We will meet in my office with Dr. Marshall and Dr. Jackson in attendance. As you may have missed during your little trip, I have named Dr. Jackson as the associate department head to assist me with personnel matters. They will both be attending, given their supervisory roles over faculty."

The "my little trip" jab and the inference that it would be three against one, and that I would be powerless, raised my ire some, but I let it go. I needed to keep my focus.

I responded to his arrogant remarks with a simple, "Thanks Howard. I look forward to the meeting and am glad that Patricia and Anansi will be joining us."

Howard merely grunted and headed toward his office.

Since the covert listening device provided by the FBI was concealed in the button of my shirt, I had no worries about being caught spying. Also, the transmitter, despite its incredibly small size, was super strong and could transmit a long-distance — well within range of the FBI undercover van located in the next parking lot over from our building.

I was going to do this mostly ad lib, even though the FBI had given me a rough script to follow. They wanted to see if I could get Howard or his colleagues to say anything that might lead to more information about the militia or their connection to the university. That was the general idea. What they wanted most of all, though, was information on the whereabouts of

Leroy Jones and the BRVM compounds. Finding the location of the dock was an important first step.

The FBI hoped that if they could locate the dock, this would lead them to their hideout where they could capture and interrogate members of the militia and, if they were lucky, Leroy Jones himself. The FBI then hoped to learn enough through interrogation to take down the entire operation, including those associated with the university to the extent that it might be involved.

The FBI had conducted an extensive database search but hadn't found any property belonging to a Mr. Roy Johnson or Leroy Jones, much less a dock on property belonging to him. Given that this was a large lake, and there were a great many docks on it, they needed something to help narrow down the location. The BRVM could be hiding right under everyone's noses at a house, or houses, along the lake, or they could be back in the woods away from the lake accessible by only a dock. It was anyone's guess without more information.

The FBI was cautiously optimistic that I could learn something at the meeting that would be useful to them. It was my intention to give it my best shot — walking the thin line between gathering information and showing my hand.

Chapter 24

Game of Deception

OUR MEETING WOULD take place in Howard's office around a small conference table. The powerful faculty were always in competition for the best offices, and Finch had laid claim to the second largest office on the floor, only 5 square feet smaller than Dr. Marshall's office. I knew about this because I had seen her measuring the offices to ensure that she had the largest one. I was uncertain which term best described her, but narcissist or egoist would probably work. I had a few other of the more colorful variety, but this was not the time to let my mind go in that direction.

I forced myself to focus on the reason that I was here, in a den of vipers, with only my wits and composure to assure any chance of success in gathering information that would be useful to the FBI — and which might be my only hope for salvation.

I might only get one chance at this, I thought to myself, *so I had better make it good.*

Controlling my breathing and heart rate, I put on my poker face, and walked into the room. Finch's office was adorned with all sorts of accolades for his many academic accomplishments, with a *trophy wall* sporting diplomas, pictures with dignitaries and awards that was second to none. I wondered how, with such a big ego, he could even fit his big head through the door frame. It was all too obvious from the way he decorated his office that he sincerely believed that the world revolved around him. All faculty have egos, and I would be the first to admit it, but his went *way* beyond the norm.

Around the small conference table sat Patricia, Howard, and Anansi, each carrying their most serious expressions, and each with a smugness that made my stomach churn. To be in such close proximity to them for the second time today was almost more than I could handle.

After taking a seat at the table, we made our usual polite greetings, while all the while thinking the most heinous of thoughts of each other behind our masks of professionalism. This was standard for these types of meetings between these types of people across campus. Very few faculty liked their supervisors, and very few supervisors respected the faculty whom they supervised. Perhaps it was because they had poor self-esteem, but most of my supervisors over the years would make fun of their faculty by assigning unflattering nicknames to them, which they thought were cute and funny, but which the faculty often didn't. The faculty would just play along and accept the abusive behavior of their supervisors, because they either wanted to gain favor with them, or were afraid of negative consequences if they dared to speak up and bring a complaint. Faculty also knew that administrators came and went, and keeping quiet was often the most effective and safest way to conduct your affairs as a faculty member.

My plan going in was to play the role of the compliant professor to the hilt, but here at the last minute, another strategy, one that was a bit reckless, began to take form in my mind.

Howard asked me the proforma question upon entering, "Noah, would you like a bottled water or coffee?"

"No, thank you," I politely responded, even though I would have enjoyed a cup of coffee from his personal supply under different circumstances, as Howard was something of a coffee connoisseur. Though I appreciated quality java, this would not be the kind of meeting where I could enjoy it.

Howard began our little meeting by saying, "Noah, we thank you for coming, and I want to say up front how sorry we were to hear about your *unfortunate circumstances*."

I had about fifty snarky replies running through my head, but knowing that this was as close to an apology for intentionally trying to ruin my reputation and life as I would get, I simply nodded and said, "Thank you."

Wasting no time, and assuredly loving every minute of this, he next said, "Despite the difficulties you have faced, I regret that I have to remind you of this Noah, but the administration has decided to continue the case against you for termination of employment *for cause*. Your prior indiscretions — breaking and entering and theft, if you recall — were just too important to ignore, and the university has decided that it would set bad precedent if you were not held accountable for your actions."

Anansi and Patricia, sitting there rigid and stone-faced, simply gave slight nods that I suspected were meant to show their support for the verdict that Howard had announced. Their facial expressions were both disapproving and condescending. Brushing aside my anger, and staying focused, I saw a small opening and took it.

Sounding as hurt, scared and indignant as possible, I said, "So, Dr. Finch, where is *your* accountability for screwing your graduate student in your office when I came to tell you about the big grant I scored when I was a junior faculty, or when you abused your graduate student by having him pull your sailboat with the bow line in his *teeth* to that dock which you said your cousin owned?"

I looked around the table to see reactions and was satisfied to see Patricia part her lips briefly in what appeared to be an expression of amusement, whereas Anansi looked absolutely astounded that I had made those accusations to the *great* Dr. Howard Finch. For his part, the only "tell" that Howard gave was a reddening of his face, which I knew from experience was an indication that he was hiding some emotion, the nature of which was difficult to ascertain.

Anansi, looking indignant, quickly rebuked me, saying, "Noah, that is uncalled for. You may not understand just *how* serious this is. Your words and actions here will not help your case in the slightest. I'm sorry, but I will have to file a report for insubordination."

Not wanting to lose the moment or momentum, I dug deeper. I looked Howard straight in the eye and said, "I bet all of your tall tales — like when you told us that you had won a marathon, or that you were a high school football champion — were just that, 'big lies.' And come to think of it, your story about having some poor kid swim your boat to some imaginary dock with a rope in his teeth was probably a load of crap as well."

I had pushed it just far enough, so I held my breath waiting to see if he had taken the bait. Howard turned away from me for a brief few seconds, I assumed in an attempt to compose himself, and said with poorly concealed constraint, "Are you calling me a liar, Noah? That means a lot coming from a pedophile."

Howard hesitated ever so briefly, and then continued. "For what it's worth, the story about my student swimming my boat to shore was true. He wanted *so much* to serve me that he even did it with the setting sun blinding him and swimming to that old, red dock that my cousin owned, because the water leading up to it was too deep to stand. He was that devoted to me! Now let's get back to your situation, and just so you know, I will be filing an additional report for insubordination and to document your inappropriate behavior. This will be put into your personnel file and used in the termination for cause proceedings, as if we didn't already have enough in that file. Your file is getting quite full now, Noah."

This was going better than I could have ever imagined and seemed almost too easy. I was OK with easy, though, as I needed the break, one that had been handed to me and my friends at the FBI on a silver platter. I knew that I had just scored big by drawing out information from Howard that would help the FBI in finding the dock that would hopefully lead them to a militia hideout or compound. I also hoped that Leroy would be there when the FBI initiated their raid.

A common mistake that many make is to keep pushing when you have already achieved your goal. I knew that it was best at this point to leave and make it look like they had me where they wanted me, so I lowered my head, and with my most apologetic look, said, "I'm very sorry you all. I guess that with all the stress I've been under, I lost my composure. I beg you to forget what I've said and show mercy on me."

They all just looked at me with outward sympathy that held not a scintilla of actual sympathy. Dr. Finch, appearing to have regained his composure said, "Noah, this will end our meeting, but you must know that, despite your mental state and various life challenges, we will proceed with the termination for cause proceedings. Dr. Jackson will be sending you an email outlining your rights with a timeline for the case and hearing. It will move rather quickly now, so I would suggest that you read the email and begin preparations for your defense immediately. We want to give you every opportunity to prepare a proper defense, so if you have questions about the process, we would be more than happy to help. However, we will not field questions about the substance of the matter.

"Also, after your behavior today, it is clear that our communications should be more formal. Dean Winston has said that he is willing to assist with procedural matters related to the proceeding but, like us, will not address substantive issues of relevance to the facts or circumstances surrounding your case. Also, as this is most likely your final semester here, you may wish to start cleaning out your office so that it will be ready for another faculty to occupy. Please excuse us while we discuss other matters of importance to the department, and please shut the door on your way out."

Under normal circumstances, I would have been livid, and a good bit depressed. But, given that I had just been handed information that was critical to the FBI's investigation, I was feeling great. The pedophile comment might also help score us a few extra points in the defamation lawsuit. I felt good as I left the building and headed for my car, and the debriefing with the FBI that was coming up.

I also felt good about the hidden ace that I had up my sleeve, one that not even the FBI knew about.

Chapter 25

Pit of Vipers

BACK IN FINCH'S office, the group was debriefing.

"Well," said Finch, "I think that we learned *a lot* from this meeting. Noah's amateurish attempt at deception — attempting to have me reveal the location of my cousin Leroy and their militia group — was more than I could have hoped."

"Do you think that he is working with the FBI and was wired during our meeting?" asked Anansi.

"I'm sure of it," replied Howard. "Leroy and some members of his group quickly discovered where Noah was staying when he came back into town last night. It was what they didn't find that first put me on alert. There was no indication that a realtor had been involved in the rental or purchase of the home that he was staying in, and everything about the house and location was unremarkable. Leroy had tracked down a few of his adversaries in the past who were in witness protection, the operative phrase being 'were in witness protection,' and had told me what to look for. This situation seemed to check all the boxes.

"I asked Leroy to put the house under surveillance and, keeping a safe distance, one of his boys, through his night vision scope, saw two men enter the back of the house around

4:30 in the morning. It was obvious that these weren't Noah's two long lost uncles coming to visit. The obvious conclusion is that Noah is working with the Feds, and the FBI has provided them with a protection detail.

"Leroy told me that Noah had a good look at his face when he thought he had him cornered on the river. He never would have revealed himself if he thought there was any chance that Noah would escape. It was a rare mistake for Leroy. He said that the guy must have nine lives, given how he has escaped three of his attempts so far. When given the chance, Leroy said that he wasn't going to wait for six more. He will finish him off at the next opportunity."

Patricia, who normally held her composure, looked a bit ashen. The reality of being an accomplice to attempted murder, and the involvement of the FBI, was starting to sink in. "So, what do we do now, Howard? This has become quite serious with the involvement of the FBI."

Howard said, "Don't worry Patricia, we are still untouchable. While the FBI may suspect that we are involved, they are merely going on a fishing expedition. They may have discovered that I am related to Leroy Jones, who we know from the past as Roy Johnson, but there is no law against that. I'm sure that the trail ends there for them. Also, the property that the FBI will now find, given the breadcrumbs I threw out for Noah and the FBI to follow, can't be linked in any way to Leroy or the BRVM. It is held by a friend of 'the cause,' who himself has hidden the true ownership of the property through shell corporations and other legal maneuverings. It is totally untraceable back to us, Leroy, or anyone else associated with our dealings.

"They also know nothing about the drugs that we buy from the BRVM that turn us a big profit through our *venture* here at the university."

"Wait," said Anansi, with a look of trepidation. "You always said to never talk openly about the *venture*, as you call it. Why are we doing it now, and on campus?"

"I had the office swept before the meeting today, and it is clean," said Howard. "No listening devices were found other than those that we control and possess. We can feel confident that this conversation is safe."

"OK," said Anansi. "I just wanted to be sure. I could lose *everything* if this ever leaked."

"We all could," said Patricia, with malice in her voice.

Anansi turned to Patricia and said, "You know that I appreciate the *bonuses* that you deposit in my account every month, as a reward for being such a good 'team player,' as you call it, — not asking questions and looking the other way — but since we are talking about it, and the stakes are so high, can share more of the details with me?"

Patricia looked over to Howard for approval, who simply nodded.

Patricia said, "I guess it is safe to tell you, Anansi. Up to this point, we have kept the details from you, but you are correct in that you know enough to be found complicit. And you are correct. The stakes are indeed very high. The thought of spending time in a federal prison should be enough to keep your lips sealed. So, to answer your question, and bring you deeper into our little joint venture, I'll tell you more."

Anansi listened intently as small beads of sweat formed on her forehead.

For the next 15 minutes, Patricia described the scheme in detail – from the purchase of LSD and cocaine from the BRVM, to delivering it to Snow, and his role in vetting and grooming hand-selected faculty to serve as dealers, ultimately selling the product to students."

Patricia, however, like a good card player, didn't show her entire hand – omitting the part about how the cash for drug exchanges with the BRVM were made. The fewer people who knew that information, the better.

"When she was finished, Anansi, always putting self-preservation above everything else, asked, "But how do we keep this operation, and our involvement, hidden?"

"Excellent question," remarked Patricia. "Amos uses the age old tactic of bullying and intimidation to keep everyone in line. Also, the enterprise is highly compartmentalized, with campus dealers and distributors unaware of the involvement of others, or the campus-wide scope of the operation. The only direct link is between Amos and me. I'm not worried, though, because we are well insulated through our *personal* relationship, one based on trust — or at least honor among thieves."

"That is quite an ingenious plan," said Anansi, blindly stroking Patricia's ego in the face of such horrendous dishonesty and corruption. "I was wondering though, how Dr. Snow can orchestrate this without being caught. Wouldn't his high-profile position put him in the spotlight and make him vulnerable?"

"Actually," replied Patricia, "it is just the opposite. His high-profile position as head of personnel for the university helps to conceal his transactions. No-one would ever suspect a drug deal to be taking place in the office of the associate provost. It is one of the most secure and private places on campus. The bottom line is that we are well insulated from harm and the possibility of having our involvement become known — and we are getting rich from it.

Howard, barely able to contain his excitement, said, "And Anansi, Patricia is right, these transactions supplement our faculty salaries quite nicely indeed. And now that you have been fully briefed, you can help us grow our enterprise — and share a bigger cut of the profits."

"Howard is right," said Patricia. "The markup is so high that we all do quite well financially. I have personally quadrupled what I made from our nifty profits by way of the corporation and manipulation of state and grant funds in just a few years. Another year and I'll be able to buy that home in Aspen that I've been eyeing."

Patricia concluded, in her most self-righteous tone, with a final comment. "I do feel a *little* bad about the students who have become addicted and are going down the proverbial rabbit hole, but it really is *their* fault, if anything. They just lack *discipline.*"

Ignoring this last comment and in a monotone voice, Howard said, "Yes, it has been quite profitable and should stay that way if we maintain *our* discipline and keep a close eye on things. It might also be helpful to our cause if we slow down the Feds a bit."

"What are you thinking, Howard?" Patricia asked, with a hint of apprehension in her voice.

Anansi, feeling as if she were on a runaway train, stared blankly ahead.

"Here is what I'm thinking," said Finch, pulling Anansi further into their evil orbit. "Given the information that I quite brilliantly provided the snooping FBI through our hapless colleague Noah, I feel certain they will soon discover the location of the dock and plan a raid on the property. Given that the property has no roads leading to it, and is surrounded by other privately held properties, their best point of entry will be by water and dock access.

"I will have Leroy and the boys tie up one of their old boats to the dock, load the main tanks and two spares to the brim with gasoline, and set a motion detection detonation trigger on them. When the Feds and, hopefully, our friend Noah, get within ten feet of the boat, either by land or water, the trigger will cause the boat to explode and incinerate everything within range of the blast. Leroy and the boys would love to eliminate some Feds, and I would love to get Noah out of the picture for good. The best part is that they would be left scratching their heads and mourning their losses, while there would be no-one to connect with the deed."

Anansi, looking aghast, said, "Look, Howard, I'm OK going along with our arrangement here on campus to distribute the product and see a nice profit, but being an accomplice to the murder of federal agents is *not* something that I am comfortable with."

This comment was met with silence and a somber and menacing look from both Howard and Patricia.

"Look, Anansi," said Howard, with a look of pure cruelty in his eyes, "In case you want to suffer the same fate as Noah and the unfortunate Feds who go near that dock, or would like to spend some serious time in a federal penitentiary, I would suggest that you just keep quiet and turn your back to this. You do not have to agree, but you do have to at least look the other way. We all know you are good at that. Leroy and the boys mean business, as well as the Feds, so either way you are screwed if you decide to get cold feet and back out of this."

With prison or death as her only options, Anansi just nodded her head and, with downcast eyes and in a solemn voice, said, "OK, I guess I see your point. I'll keep quiet. You have my word."

Patricia, for her part, remained silent and expressionless.

"Good girl," said Howard. "I thought that you would see it our way." He then smiled and said, "It may not be the 4th of July, but I'm ready for a good fireworks show."

He was still chuckling to himself as Patricia and Anansi left his office.

Chapter 26

Cat and Mouse

WHOEVER SAID THAT waiting was the hardest part, was absolutely right. I had been sitting in my truck for the past hour, giving Finch, Patricia and Anansi plenty of time to conclude their private meeting. Thirty minutes would probably have been enough, but I wanted to err on the side of caution.

I picked up my cell phone, and with trembling hands, opened the app.

Back when Amanda and I had some free time in New Orleans, on the day before our meeting with Gary, we had gone out and wandered through shops in and around the French Quarter. As we were browsing the shops, she stopped me in front of an electronics store with all the latest gadgets, and led me in. When inside, she took my hand and walked me over to a section of the store which had covert surveillance devices. The section was wholly devoted to audio listening devices. Some were quite clever, with recording devices disguised as alarm clocks, thumb drives, and even a pen that looked very much like the one that Ted had given me. Next to them, in a glass case were more sophisticated monitoring devices. These were the types that could be attached to the underside of a car by a magnet or, if inside, under a table or chair by an adhesive.

As we examined the various devices, Amanda turned to me and said, "You know, Noah, you could use a little insurance. When you get back to the university, even if the FBI has you wired for sound, so to speak, with a hidden microphone, it would be good to have your own. You never know when it might come in handy."

We looked them over and found a miniature listening device that had an adhesive backing, allowing it to be stuck beneath a table or chair. We also learned, after speaking with a knowledgeable sales staff, that it could transmit a signal to a cell phone within 200 yards of where it was placed. I thought to myself that, if needed, I could place it under a table, desk or chair and it would transmit a conversation to my cell phone to be recorded, whether located in my car, office, or other location within range.

Unknown to both the FBI and my *low-life* colleagues, was that while I was in the meeting with them earlier, and when they were paying me the least amount of attention, I had stuck the bug on the underside of the table. My hope was that they were so confident in themselves and thought so little of me, they would never suspect that I would be putting *them* under surveillance. It was a stroke of luck that the three of them had stayed in the office to have their debriefing.

I suspected their meeting would be a debrief of the one that I had with them, as I was sure they would want to gloat. I also hoped they would say things that they had bottled up during our meeting. Maybe they would say something that I could use in my defense at the termination proceedings, or that may be helpful in a civil lawsuit. I also hoped that they might speak further about the location of the dock and reveal more information that would be helpful to the FBI. I would soon know.

I put in my four-digit password, opened my phone, and found the app that I had uploaded. I had tested it before and had a good idea of how it worked, and most importantly, *that* it worked.

As I sat in the comfort and relative safety of my truck, I opened my phone, then the app, and with a sigh of relief, found the recorded message. I hit *play* and listened. This was the moment of truth. Either they were just talking about mundane departmental matters, and I had no additional information that would be of help to me or the FBI, or I would hit paydirt, and finally be a step ahead of them for the first time.

As it turned out, I hit paydirt, big time! After playing through the recording three or four times, I committed the substance of their conversation to memory and prayed a word of thanks for my good fortune. Actually, *good fortune* did not even come close to describing how good this information was for both me and the FBI.

I had known for some time the lengths they would go to keep me quiet and remove me from the university. Now I knew the larger purpose behind their actions, and it shook me to the core. It also angered me that they would be responsible for selling drugs to students. From what Patricia said in the recording, they didn't seem to understand that their actions were despicable. She even had the nerve to blame the students that bought the drugs for being weak and lacking discipline. That was some seriously twisted and sick thinking.

In addition to being angry, I felt simply overwhelmed and beyond disappointed that this would be happening in the upper administration of a well-respected university. Even though it was my place of employment and one that I associated with work, I had grown attached to the university, was an ardent fan of the sports teams, particularly football, and knew every word of the school song. I really enjoyed the feel and excitement of being associated with a big university where the opportunities for academic growth seemed boundless. The sexual misconduct, unethical behavior, backstabbing, and all that I had seen during the course of my employment was, of course, terrible, but this took things to a whole other level.

I drove a few miles from campus and parked at a fast-food restaurant where I felt that I wouldn't arouse attention. It was time to call my friends at the FBI.

I decided to dial up Petrova, who I hoped would be with her partner. She answered on the second ring.

I breathlessly blurted out, "Hi, Agent Petrova, this is Noah. I have vital information to share with you."

She said, "Just calm down, Noah. Let me put you on speaker phone so you can communicate with Agent Steele as well. He is right here."

Once she had me on speaker, she said, "Here is Agent Steele. Before you get started, he has something to say."

Steele said, "Hi, Noah. I have some good news. It looks like we now know where that dock is located. It didn't take long for our techs to locate it once the audio came through to us from your conversation with your colleagues. This is extremely valuable information. You did great. We are already assembling an assault team and putting a plan in place. We will approach the property by way of the dock, as the property is surrounded by privately owned lands. Unfortunately, we don't have an aerial drone at the ready, but surveillance photos show what looks like a compound, or at least a group of buildings, a few hundred yards inland from the dock on higher ground. We should be ready to go before dawn tomorrow morning."

"Wait," I said, with urgency. "Agent Steele, you may want to re-think those plans."

"What?" he asked, sounding a bit annoyed that a college professor would be telling him, a seasoned FBI agent, how to plan an operation of this type. He must have thought that I was overstepping and wanted to tell them how to do their job.

Sensing his agitation, I quickly let him know why. I said, "Agent Steel, you need to know that after I left the meeting, Drs. Finch, Marshall and Jackson stayed behind to meet privately."

"Wow," he said, "I wish we knew what was said in that meeting. That could have been important. I should have thought to have you place a bug in the room."

Feeling a bit full of myself, I said, "Actually, I didn't tell you, and I have to apologize for that, but I took it upon myself to place a listening device under their desk while I was meeting with them." As these words left my mouth, I could feel their anticipation building.

I took a deep breath, knowing that what I told them would change the trajectory of everything going forward, and gave them a synopsis of what my colleagues had talked about after I had left. After about 10 seconds of silence on the other end of the phone, I asked, "Hello, is everything OK?"

I didn't know that I could stun two seasoned FBI agents into silence, but apparently, I had. Petrova was the first to respond.

She said, "That is incredible Noah. There is no need to apologize for not telling us about the bug. There will likely be some challenges getting the recording admitted into evidence if we get to court eventually, but this is incredibly valuable information. We first have to say thanks. You most likely saved not only our lives, but also those of our fellow agents."

Steele was the next to speak. He said, "Thank you Noah, and I mean that with all sincerity. This will change our plans entirely. It looks as though Dr. Finch is much cleverer, or should I say, conniving, than we gave him credit for. Instead of us luring him into a trap, he was doing it to us, and with dire consequences. He intentionally fed you and us enough information, without looking suspicious, to help us locate the dock. We would have fallen right into their trap if you hadn't secretly recorded their conversation.

"I will need to run this up the chain, but anticipate that we will still conduct the raid, though in a safe manner. I suspect that Leroy will be far away from the property on the lake when we make the raid, but would not be surprised, however, if they have someone watching, through binoculars or a scope, to observe and report back on the action to their leader."

To Petrova, he said, "If we have the go-ahead on the operation, we'll send some agents out there ahead of time to check out the more obvious observation points. Maybe we can get lucky and apprehend one of them."

I knew that it was naïve of me to ask, but I couldn't help but interrupt. I quickly asked, "How could you ever approach and land on the dock safely knowing that it is armed to explode?"

Steele responded, as calmly and with as much patience as his partner, saying, "As for the operation, if we proceed, we will likely now have an unmanned craft make the approach to the dock. Though we don't have an aerial drone, we do have a submersible drone that can give us a visual. If it triggers the device and everything blows to kingdom come, we'll have evidence to support a conviction of those responsible for attempted murder. I will also put in a call to the big boys and girls in DC to get the ball rolling on an undercover operation at the university to bring those involved in the 'drug ring' to justice.

"Noah, we will need for you to keep acting as if you don't know anything about their operations and to just go with the flow at work for now. It would probably arouse less suspicion if you went back to your office for the remainder of the day. This should put them at ease, as it would be normal behavior under the circumstances, even though they are on to you. They know that you are working with us, but what they don't know is that you, and we, are now aware of their entire operation. This knowledge gives us a huge advantage, but we'll need to work quickly and with great care to keep it."

"Couldn't you all just arrest them now?" I asked.

"We could," replied Petrova, "but then Leroy and his militia group would go underground, and we would lose our opportunity to apprehend them and bring them to justice. You must remember that they are involved in a whole host of bad things. This is certainly a big piece, and an awfully bad one, but if we could net them all, then it would mean that we could cure the disease, rather than just treat the symptoms."

That's an interesting way to put it, I thought. But it made sense. *They were very much like a disease, spreading their sickness far and wide.*

Chapter 27

Boom

IT WAS A clear, chilly morning, a few days after my meeting with Finch and company and the events that had led us to this point. First light was at least an hour away, as we sat in the FBI operations van parked in a secluded pullout area on the side of the lake, opposite and some distance from the dock that Finch had meant for us to find. There were five of us in the van: me, of course, and Amanda; Steele and Petrova; and a drone tech. The tech looked perfectly at home behind the controls of what looked like a fancy video game device.

Looking out the darkened windows of the van, at this early hour, we could faintly see the outline of the lake, but not much more. We wouldn't be able to see with the naked eye, the dock, or the boat moored to it until the sun, still below the horizon, came up enough to light things up. Our eyes for now were focused on the extensive panel of monitors inside the van that would give us a front row view of the action as seen through the submersible's night vision optics. It promised to be quite the show.

We had arrived several hours earlier to prepare, so we were all working on little to no sleep, but with my travel mug filled to the brim with hot black coffee, and adrenaline pumping through my veins, sleep was the last thing on my mind.

It was reported that no observers had been spotted by the advance team through their night vision goggles as we had hoped. No-one had been seen perched in a tree, and all that had been seen on land were a few deer and small animals scurrying about. All was quiet out there.

The dock was empty except for a single boat tied to it. I couldn't make out the type of boat from the drone feedback, as it was still a good distance away, but it looked old and worn. The submersible drone had been launched and was about half-way across the lake at this point, heading in a straight line for the dock and what might be its own *drone funeral.*

LITTLE DID WE know that on the same side of the lake, and not far away, sitting in the darkness behind a dormer window in one of the many houses that lined this side of the lake, was Dr. Larry Pickering. Howard had arranged for Larry to be on lookout to watch and record the events he hoped would unfold across the lake in the early morning hours. Leroy and Finch had been tipped off the day before, when Leroy's advance scouts had seen some unusual activity on the lake. Even though the men and women they observed, casually walking or jogging along the lake trail, or bird-watching through binoculars, were not wearing the colors or lettering of the FBI on their clothing, their appearance and practiced movements practically screamed *Federal Agent.* They were also a bit too focused on the old red dock across the lake with a boat that had been moored there only two days earlier. Based on the report, Leroy and Finch decided to recall Leroy's boys, and put Larry in place to observe. With the recent activity, they felt certain that the FBI would strike soon.

Finch knew that Larry was impulsive, and didn't always trust his judgment, but with instructions to stay hidden, and from his position on the far side of the lake, he believed that even Larry couldn't screw this up. At least, that was what he hoped. Also, he and Leroy felt that something this big needed to be recorded for posterity, and it was just too risky for Leroy to be there in person. Howard also didn't want to put himself personally at risk, and neither did Patricia. They felt that spying was somehow beneath them. Anansi, who was getting cold feet anyway, would neither want to do it, nor would she be a desirable choice.

Patricia would have a hand in it, though. The house was owned by a close colleague of Dr. Marshall, whose daughter had a key and would check on the house once a week while the owners were gone on sabbatical. It was the perfect observation point, as it was highly unlikely the Feds would suspect anything happening there, and it was practically invisible, nestled among so many other high value properties along the lake.

Larry had jumped at the chance to serve as the lookout, even though it meant getting up at such an ungodly hour. He had enjoyed the beautiful lakefront home, arriving in the late afternoon only yesterday after receiving a last-minute call and request from his friend and colleague Howard. He had dinner and a few glasses of wine shortly after arriving and went to bed early, waking at 3 a.m. to get in position. He felt a bit sluggish, but with his adrenaline pumping over the excitement of what he expected would be a fantastic "fireworks display," he was more than up to the task.

Larry, sitting a few feet back from the window in the dark, felt that he would likely be invisible to anyone outside. The only downside was that he didn't have night vision equipment, and was only able to retrieve a set of binoculars with average magnifying power to watch the show. He rubbed the sleep from his eyes and waited.

IT WAS STILL dark outside, made even darker by a low cloud cover that foreshadowed another gray winter day. The submersible drone was equipped with a night vision scope with heat sensing capabilities on a periscope-like structure. It rose from the drone to just slightly above the surface as it made its way across the lake.

The submersible powered silently through the water on lithium batteries through a high-tech propulsion system. If visible to anyone, it would resemble Nessie gliding silently across the darkened waters of Loch Ness.

All of us were watching the monitor in the van as the drone approached within 250 yards of the dock. We could now clearly see the old rickety dock with peeling red paint, and the faded lettering on the side of the boat indicating that it was an old Sea Ray cabin cruiser. The information relayed to us from the night-vision optics and thermal sensors on the drone didn't indicate that there was anyone in the vicinity of the dock, or on the dock or boat itself. We didn't know, however, whether anyone was inside the boat. The submersible's heat sensing capabilities couldn't penetrate the hull, but we assumed that there were no people on the boat for the obvious reason that it was supposed to be rigged to explode.

Steele turned to the technician manning the drone and said, "Stop forward progress, and rotate the scope to give us a 360 degree view." The tech did as he was asked and the scope scanned the bank nearest the dock that was grassy and flat, further out to the side where a tree line appeared, and beyond to some houses lining the lake. As the scope turned further, the view swept across the open lake and scanned the houses lining the lake on the side we were on.

He then said, "Move the scope slowly as it scans the houses along this side of the lake."

As the row of houses came into view, we could see the occasional bloom of a heat signature from various vents and pipes, but no heat signatures or images of any people near a window, on the docks, or anywhere outside. All the houses appeared dark and vacant.

Suddenly, Petrova, in an excited voice shouted, "Stop! I think that I saw something." In a calmer tone, she continued, "Please scan back to the house that the scope just passed."

When the tech had done what she asked, Petrova said, "Freeze it there." We all peered intently at the screen, trying desperately to see what she had seen.

"Look," she said, "there appears to be movement and a slight heat signature in that upper dormer window. It could just be a house cat, or the night vision optics playing tricks on my mind, but I swear that I saw movement in that window."

I could see what looked like a faint heat signature, but it could have been my mind just wanting to believe it was there.

Steele, having complete trust in his partner and her instincts, said "I'll send an agent over there. We don't have a warrant to enter the house, but we can have someone outside the house watch from a concealed location."

After scanning the rest of the area and seeing no more movement in the dormer window of the lake house, Steele said to the tech, "Now, please focus on the target once again, and continue forward until you reach a distance of 100 yards from the target.

What happened next was unexpected and changed my expectation as to the fate of the drone that I had suspected was on a suicide mission.

Steele turned to the tech and said, "Flood the tube and fire the torpedo."

I would soon learn that the "torpedo" was a battery powered rubber object about the size and shape of an elongated football. The tech said, "Roger that. The torpedo will reach the boat in approximately 1 minute."

As the timer counted down, we all sat in silent anticipation of what would happen when the torpedo neared the boat. Even though we were all mentally anticipating an explosion, it was still quite startling when it happened.

The torpedo was within ten feet of the boat when our world was literally rocked. We could hear and see the explosion simultaneously through the drone's periscope and the darkened window of the van as a blinding flash of light lit the dark, early-morning sky, followed briefly by a loud "boom." The image quickly vanished as the submersible was tossed and turned in the water by the concussive force of the explosion.

SITTING BEHIND THE dormer window with his binoculars focused on the boat, and with his phone wedged in the window frame filming the event, Larry was temporarily blinded by the brightness of the explosion. The sound trailed the light by a few beats before thudding into the walls of the house, sounding like the bass from an amped up stereo system.

Larry muttered a few colorful expletives and withdrew the binoculars from his eyes, temporarily blinded by the brilliant light. As his eyes adjusted, he raised the binoculars again and looked across the lake. He saw flaming embers that had taken flight, and a large plume of gray smoke that rose against the backdrop of the ink black sky.

It was exhilarating to watch, and extremely satisfying, with thoughts of removing Noah from their worries and keeping the Feds off their trail spiking his endorphins to a high more pleasurable than any amount of wine could. He was after all, a silent partner in his colleague's evil scheme, and happily shared the spoils. As the final flames began to die from the spectacular explosion across the lake, Larry picked up his cell phone and dialed Howard.

Larry had no way to know that Howard's phone had been tapped by the Feds, subsequent to a legal warrant, or that they would be listening to their every word, as Steele had intercepted the call and was playing it over the van's speaker system in real time.

When Howard answered the call, we heard Larry say, breathlessly, "Howard, it was spectacular! It was better than planned, or anything you could have imagined. I wish you could have seen it. It was quite the show. The boat was blown sky high! No-one anywhere close to that dock could have survived the blast. It was that powerful."

Howard, sounding pleased and anxious to know more, asked, "Larry, were you able to see the Feds or Noah on the dock, or anywhere within the blast radius?"

Larry, clearly not wanting to disappoint, replied, "Well, I didn't have eyes on them specifically, but I did think that I saw the outline of a boat approaching without running lights. It was probably an inflatable with an electric motor for stealth."

We knew that Larry had not actually seen such a thing, but the mind is a funny thing. It often fills in the blanks from the real world with that which we want to see.

"Great," said Howard, "We may have solved several of our problems in one fell swoop. Now get out of there and back to town once the sun comes up. You don't want to draw attention to yourself by leaving now, so soon after the blast and in the dark. Also, Larry, be aware of your surroundings, as you never know what the Feds may have up their sleeves. They will probably be shocked by what just happened and will want to converge on the scene to see if any of their fellow Feds are still alive, but don't let your guard down. We don't want any evidence that we are connected to this in any way."

"I understand, Howard. I'll make myself invisible," Larry replied.

Later, Larry left the house and hurried back to his car, oblivious to the fact that his every move was being observed.

WITH THE MISSION concluded, I said, "Agents Petrova and Steele, thank you for the opportunity to sit in on the operation. Is there anything more that I can do to help?"

Petrova replied, "Noah, I think that you have done enough for now. We will process what we know and come up with a plan. We'll be back in touch in a few days with more information and to let you know what we want to do going forward. They won't know whether you were killed in the blast, and we can use their uncertainty to our advantage."

"OK," I said. "Since we want to keep them guessing, I understand that I can't just roll on back to the safehouse, since we know they have the place under surveillance."

"You are right," she said. "How would you like to go back to New Orleans for another visit? You would have to stay in the hotel room and not wander about the city this time, though."

"OK," I said, "on two conditions: one, Amanda comes with me; and two, Amanda gets to choose the hotel."

"I know she has expensive tastes," Petrova said, grinning widely, "but yeah, sure. I think I could have this approved, given that you two just saved the lives of some of our finest FBI agents, including yours truly. Amanda, since they will need to believe that you are still living at the safehouse, we will need to bring in one of our agents who closely resembles you to play the role of *Amanda Strauss*."

"That makes sense," said Amanda, "and I think I know what you will ask me next."

"Yes," said Petrova, "can we have the keys to your brother's car?"

Amanda, sounding reluctant, said, "OK. But *not a scratch*."

"Not a *scratch*," replied Petrova. "Agent Cross will have your ride here in 15 minutes. Our agents have already grabbed some of your clothes and toiletries for what we hope will be a short stay in New Orleans."

"Thanks," I said, on behalf of both myself and Amanda, still amped from the explosion and, realization that my colleagues wanted me dead.

Steele, sensing my anxiety, calmly laid out what we knew, along with some forward thinking. He said, "given that Dr. Finch would believe in the possibility of your death, Noah, we'll feed his imagination with a story that local law enforcement will provide to the media that the blast on the lake, which some had likely awoken to in the early morning hours, was the result of an explosion on a boat caused by faulty wiring and subsequent arcing that ignited the fuel tanks. The police will only report that an investigation into the incident is ongoing and that there is no word yet on any injuries or fatalities."

"That will keep them guessing, I suppose," I responded.

"We won't have much time before they figure out what really happened though," replied Steele, "so we will need to move fast."

The SUV that would take us on our trip to New Orleans arrived a few minutes later. I slid into the backseat of the surprisingly comfortable vehicle, and we began our journey.

Amanda kissed me on the cheek and squeezed my hand to remind me that she was right there beside me, and then we debriefed informally, comparing notes, and reliving the past few hours — some of the most surreal of our lives.

"I think," I told Amanda, "that this turned out better than anyone could have anticipated. The boat exploded in spectacular fashion, and it was so dark that no-one could know whether I, or any FBI agents, had been blown to smithereens."

"The best part," Amanda exclaimed, "is they found that Dr. Pickering had been watching the show from the window of a house across the lake. Petrova is amazing isn't she, with her ability to spot something that no-one else saw."

"I know," I said. "Even knowing where to look, I couldn't have been certain that I had seen anything. I'm impressed as well that they thought to tap Finch's phone."

Amanda said, "It looks as though they would have enough evidence to bring in Howard, Patricia, and their inner circle now, but I know they want to achieve their original and larger goal of taking down the militia group. They now have the additional purpose of prosecuting those involved in the university drug ring. Once they find the crucial, physical link between the militia and your colleagues, they will all fall like a house of cards."

"You're right," I said. "What we know of their conversations is certainly damning evidence, but to truly take them down, we need direct evidence of their involvement."

Returning to the present, I said, "It looks like our destination is New Orleans once again. If their promise holds true, they won't be putting us up at some fleabag hotel on government budget terms. I saw you say something to Steele before we got in the car. Were you telling him where you wanted to stay?"

"You are quite observant, Dr. Banks," she said. "I requested a suite at the Ritz Carlton, with an unlimited expense account for food and drinks."

"Wow," I said, "and he went for it?"

"Yep," said Amanda. "I told him that he could trust us to keep our expenses within reason."

"Yeah," I said with a laugh, "*Within reason.*"

Chapter 28

Floating a Plan

THE DRIVE TO New Orleans was uneventful, spent with us both falling fast asleep, Amanda with her head on my shoulder. When we arrived at the hotel, the first word that came to mind was *elegant*. If the quality of the hotel itself wasn't enough, this time we had a suite with club level access. It had a sitting room, study, and separate bedroom, punctuated with a spectacular view. With complimentary culinary offerings provided throughout the day, we wouldn't be breaking the bank purchasing food. I was sure that the FBI would want to make our stay as brief as possible, though, given the cost they would incur.

Since I didn't have anything pressing, and Amanda, while nearing the end of her vacation leave, was free for the time being, there wasn't much for us to do. Also, the FBI was handling everything at this point so all we really had to do was wait and enjoy the city. Even though Steele had instructed us not to leave the hotel, Amanda, putting on her most sad and doleful expression, was able to convince the agents on protective detail to let us sneak out.

We were only allowed to leave the hotel, however, on several conditions, one being that we went out in disguise. I chose to wear a blonde wig under an old Hornets baseball cap, while Amanda wore a floppy hat and applied so much make-up that I hardly recognized her. The agents were always within ten feet of us, another condition of our outings. It was better than nothing, though, and did little to lessen the fun we had on those occasions. When it was all said and done, we greatly overindulged on the incredible food and beverages the city had to offer.

We were brought back to reality only two days after we had arrived by a phone call from Steele. He did not sound happy.

I knew that it was inconceivable that he could be angry with me, and it turned out that I was right. He was unhappy with how the undercover operation at the university was progressing. He told me that the FBI had brought in undercover agents to learn more about the drug operation by asking around about where to purchase drugs on campus.

Steele said, "We brought in some undercover agents to investigate, but their operation is so compartmentalized and secretive that it is impossible to crack. Even if we were to take down one of the student dealers and identify and apprehend the faculty member who was supplying them, this would only serve to alert those up the chain. Once that happened, they would shut down the whole operation and go to ground. It stands to reason that your colleagues would in turn alert Leroy and the BRVM, who would go to ground as well. It is like a game of Jenga where we have a limited number of moves. If we make a mistake, the whole thing collapses."

"Have Finch or his inner circle done or said anything that might be useful to your investigation," I asked.

Steele said, "Not yet. We have them under surveillance but so far, they haven't demonstrated any suspicious activity or behavior. His phone calls are benign, and we can't bug his office as we know he is very careful on that front. Also, it seems that the bug you placed under his table has gone silent."

224 ~ J.O. SPENGLER

"I'm sorry," I replied, "but I'm not very sophisticated when it comes to these types of things."

"Actually," replied Steele, "it worked perfectly in our favor. Since it only transmitted for a brief period of time, any subsequent sweeps wouldn't pick it up. They probably just wave the wand around instead of looking under every object in the room."

"Glad that I could be of service through my naivete," I said, tongue in cheek.

Steele laughed and said, "Agent Petrova and I have been talking and feel that we need to take a different approach, and we will need your help."

Petrova, providing the perfect segway, said, "We wanted to give the bottom-up approach a shot first, seeing if we could trace the campus drug operation, quietly, from the student buyers back up the chain since going higher up would only serve to put them on notice that we are on to them. This approach, as agent Steele mentioned, has not met with success. I believe that the only move that we have remaining is to find a way to apprehend members of the BRVM when they make the exchange of drugs for money."

"That would make sense," said Amanda, "but seems like a tall order."

"It is," replied Petrova. "Our research and quiet inquiries from undercover agents have come up empty on any sightings of militia members on campus."

"In all the years I've worked on campus as a faculty and administrator," I said, "I've never heard of any of my colleagues having a connection to that group. In fact, as I mentioned before, I had never heard of the BRVM until recently."

"Yes," said Petrova, "they have an uncanny ability to fly below the radar. Sometimes it feels like we are chasing ghosts. From an operational standpoint, though, it would be too risky for them to make the exchange on campus. My feeling is that none of the BRVM, including Leroy, have ever stepped foot on campus."

"So, what is your plan?" asked Amanda, getting back to the heart of the matter.

Steele answered, saying simply, "We don't have one. Well, we don't have one yet, at least. It looks like we will need your help once again."

"Agents Steele and Petrova," I said, as an idea began to take form, "let us give this some thought and we will get back with you — tomorrow noon at the latest."

"Thanks," said Steele, "Please remember that our window is short."

"Make it 9 a.m., then," I said, hoping that my idea wasn't too half-baked.

After they had hung up, Amanda looked at me and said, "So, Noah, you must have an idea rolling around in that big brain of yours. Let me hear it."

"OK," I said. "This is what I'm thinking. If they are making an exchange, as Steele suggests, it would be too risky to conduct on campus. It would make sense that it would also be too risky to make the exchanges in Delray."

"So, it would have to happen somewhere outside of Delray, but most likely within the BRVM's territory," said Amanda.

"It is a large territory," I said. "Can you pull up a map on your computer?

Amanda pulled up a map, and we examined it.

"We learned from Petrova that they believe their territory includes the states of Arkansas, Mississippi, Tennessee, Kentucky, and Missouri. Since they are the *Big River* Volunteer Militia, it would make sense they are located, or at least conduct their business, somewhere near the Mississippi river in each state."

"Still, with this kind of territory to cover, and with some fairly remote areas, in addition to larger cities, I can see why the FBI has had trouble catching them," said Amanda.

"We have an advantage though," I said. "We can use the university as a center point and make some assumptions. One assumption is that our colleagues wouldn't want to travel too far to make the exchanges."

"So somewhere in the neighborhood of a three or four hour drive — I would wager at least no more than five — each way," reasoned Amanda.

"And they would have a choice," I said. "They could either make the exchanges in a remote location ..."

"Or in a place that no-one would ever suspect, perhaps right under the noses of everyone," said Amanda.

"I think that is a good point," I said. "They wouldn't want anyone to know the location of their hideouts, so it very well could be done in a public place — but in a *way* that no-one would suspect."

"Speaking of maintaining secrecy, we know that Finch, Patricia and company are pretty good at this as well," said Amanda. She went on to talk about the Institute and recount the stories I had told her of their secretive nature and forbidden areas.

As I listened, something she said earlier was nagging me. It was just at the edge of my brain. *If only* ... Then it hit me.

"Amanda," I said excitedly, "do you recall what you said about how they might carry out the exchange?"

"You mean," she said, "that it might be done in a public place under everyone's noses?"

"Exactly," I said. "*Under everyone's noses.* I think this is the key to everything."

"For that to happen," Amanda thought out loud, "they would need to do it during the regular course of their business. Something related to their university work. You had told me that teaching, research, and service were your job duties."

"That is correct," I said. "You can rule out teaching since that is done on campus. As for service, they sometimes serve on university committees and provide various forms of support on campus, but again, that occurs on university grounds."

"So that leaves research," said Amanda.

"Yes," I replied. "It is also the primary function of the Institute."

"Let's take this a step further," I said. "Research enterprises utilize students, ideally to learn the research process while pursuing their undergraduate or graduate studies to later become academics themselves. What if ... Patricia and Howard were using students, through intimidation or monetary incentives, to act as runners, delivering packages of money to BRVM members, while picking up packages containing cocaine and LSD from them in exchange? It would be the perfect cover, making exchanges under the guise of university research."

"Maybe the students don't need to be coerced," said Amanda hopefully. "They may not know the packages contain contraband and believe that they are making the exchanges for a legitimate purpose related to the research."

"That is possible," I agreed, "And I hope that would be the case."

Thinking further, I said, "Also, it is well known that Patricia's research is mainly community based, often requiring travel within a four state region. She has access to a fleet of university vehicles that students use to reach the communities where they collect data, often through door-to-door interviews of households."

"This would narrow down the search radius then," said Amanda. "Wait a minute, I think I have an old map." Amanda pulled out a map, found the town of Delray and, estimating an outermost distance of 300 miles from Delray, used her fingers like a crude protractor to demonstrate the area in which the transactions might occur using this logic.

"Whew," I said. "That is a lot of ground to cover. We have no idea how or where specifically the exchanges would be made. Would they be made at a house, on the side of the road, at a truck stop ...? And by hand-to-hand exchange, drop-offs or by some other method? There are still too many unknowns."

Amanda thought for a moment and asked, "Don't you still know some of the students who currently work as Institute staff? Perhaps you could help us find answers by speaking to one of them. Are there any students you could trust?"

"Yes," I replied without hesitation. "There is someone."

Amanda and I spent the next few hours hatching a plan, and then punching holes in it until we were satisfied that it was solid enough to float to Steele and Petrova. Satisfied that our plan was sound, and with no more to do, we enjoyed the hotel amenities with a satisfying workout, a dip in the pool and some relaxing time in the hot tub. Another amazing dinner and some quality alone-time was followed by a restful night's sleep.

At 9 o'clock sharp the next day, our phone rang. Steele, with barely concealed anticipation in his voice, asked, "Dr. Banks, do we have a plan?"

"Yes," I replied, and I told him about our theory on how the drugs and money were exchanged, and how I could find out more through my connection with a student employee of the Institute — Kelly Barton.

Agent Steele listened intently and said, "So, you trust this person? You do realize the implications if she betrays your trust, don't you?"

"I do," I said, "but I think she can be trusted. There is risk in everything, but I believe that this is the best chance we have."

There was silence on the other end of the line.

After a moment, Steele said simply, "Let's do it then."

It was the answer that I wanted to hear. Boy, I sure hoped that our assumptions were correct.

Chapter 29

Matter of Trust

KELLY BARTON, THE woman in whom I was putting my trust, was a doctoral student in the Sociology Department, nearing completion of her dissertation. I served on her doctoral committee and had known her for several years. She was smart and intuitive, telling me on more than one occasion that she suspected foul play within the Institute. As a student carrying a lot of debt, however, she only worked for the Institute to keep afloat financially. We would meet on a regular basis to discuss her progress in the doctoral program, and talk about her career ideas and aspirations.

I called Kelly on her cell phone, as landline calls to anyone in the Institute could not be trusted. I had learned long ago that calls to Institute personnel were monitored. When she answered, I said, "Kelly, it's me. I need to talk with you privately."

Kelly, sensing the need for discretion, didn't use my name, and simply said, "Hang on."

I could hear heels clicking on pavement in the background and, a few minutes later, the *thump* of a car door shutting. A few minutes later, sounding slightly winded from her walk, she said, "I'm in the privacy of my car now."

Then, with relief in her voice, she blurted out, "It is so great to hear from you. How are you doing? Is everything OK? I mean, well, Dr. Banks, we all thought you were dead. There was a rumor going around the college that you were out drinking with some friends at a wild party on the lake and your boat caught on fire and exploded. We couldn't get any more information on it, and when you didn't return to campus and no-one had heard from you, we thought the worst. I'm so relieved and happy to know that you are all right."

I thought, *Wow, they are still trying to smear my reputation, even after they think that I died in the explosion.*

"I'm so sorry that you all were worried," I said genuinely. "I especially didn't mean to put you through that, but there is a need for discretion. I would like to talk with you in private. Would you be able to meet with me for a walk at Riverside Park tomorrow — let's say, around 10 a.m.?" I knew that Riverside Park was in a small town on the way to Pine Bluff, and the odds of being spotted by someone I knew were practically zero.

"And Kelly," I said hesitantly, "I'm laying low these days with all that has been going on, so I would appreciate it if you wouldn't tell anyone that you had heard from me."

"Sure," said Kelly, putting me at ease. "That sounds great. I'll see you then."

Kelly was smart and knew better than to ask questions. I was relieved that she hadn't. There would be time for that when we met tomorrow.

With the meeting arranged, Amanda and I enjoyed breakfast, compliments of room service, then packed our bags and reluctantly checked out of our luxury hotel to head north toward Delray and back to face my troubles head on. Agent Steele had put us on a strict timeline, and wanted to have an actionable plan in place by the first of next week.

As we hit the road, we both wondered if the FBI would find us a decent place to stay. I lived in a college town, so nothing comparable to our most recent digs would even come close. What they found for us, however, was a very pleasant surprise.

The FBI drove us to a state park a few miles south of where Amanda' cabin, when it was still standing, had been located. I knew about this place, but rarely visited, given that I never saw the need, since the cabin that Amanda let me use had everything that I could want — and it was free.

The state park was genuinely nice. I made a mental note that I would need to visit this place more often in the future. The park had their own cabins that, while not having the same feel of home, were comfortable and well appointed. The cabin we were provided even had its own fireplace and jacuzzi tub.

After the long drive, we unpacked and freshened up. Despite the trauma that I had endured when Amanda's cabin had been torched, the smell of a wood cabin always made me feel safe and comfortable. In this instance, it helped as well to know that two federal agents were staying in the cabin next to ours.

Amanda uncorked a bottle of wine while I opened boxes of Chinese takeout we had picked up along the way. We arranged them on the table with some napkins and utensils. After taking a sip of wine, Amanda said to me, "Noah, let's take stock of where we are and what will be happening from here."

"OK," I said. "You know that I spoke with Kelly, and I will be meeting her at Riverside Park tomorrow. She doesn't know anything yet, but I'm sure she suspects that I will have something interesting to share. I think the fact that she is trustworthy," I said, "works in our favor. She is not only trusted by me, but also, at least to some extent, by my colleagues at the Institute."

"How so?" replied Amanda. "It makes me nervous that she would have earned their trust. Is there any chance she has a secret loyalty to them?"

"I think that at one point she may have held some form of loyalty to them," I said. "They *did* employ her when she needed the income, and at least gave her the impression that she would be learning on the job while earning her doctorate. I understand that it changed, however, when after four years, she had not made any progress toward her doctoral degree. She came to understand that they were just using her to do their work and generate income for both them and the Institute. Patricia is a master at using intimidation tactics and vulnerable students to work like slaves to line her pockets. Patricia represents everything that I find wrong with higher education. It should always be about the students first, not solely the personal interests of the faculty."

"I see," said Amanda. "So, Kelly is both a disgruntled employee *and* student."

"You could say that," I said. "Not long after I first came to know her, she met with me to discuss her progress in the doctoral program. She had been so brainwashed to think that her role was to meet every need of her advisor, Patricia, that she had lost track of her own needs, desires, and opportunities. It opened my eyes to the problems posed by powerful faculty who generate large sums of money for themselves and the university on the backs of their students."

"I bet that not many people know that this kind of abuse happens in higher education," said Amanda. "I sure didn't."

"Probably not," I said. "And to make matters worse, look what happened to me when I tried to address what I perceived to be unethical behavior — what we now know to be *illegal* behavior. I'm not just fighting to save my career. I'm fighting to save my life."

Amanda looked at me with an endless well of sympathy in her eyes and said, "Noah, we will right this ship. Together, I genuinely believe that we can help the FBI bring these people to justice. Then, maybe, just maybe, Delray University and others like it, will start putting students ahead of monetary gain, and address fairness and ethics in ways that will result in real and lasting positive change."

"Now, getting back to your meeting with Kelly. What are your thoughts on how she might be able to help?"

"Given that she had gained a decent amount of trust at the Institute," I replied, "she should have access to some of their research and personnel databases. I'm thinking that if she could print or download files that contain details of their current research projects, it could help us determine where they are making the exchanges."

"See if she can find information on the times and dates of any off-campus research activities as well," said Amanda.

"Good idea," I said. "I'll be straight with her on what is happening, and what is needed. I trust that she will find the right files for us."

"Once we have them in hand," said Amanda, "I can help piece the puzzle together."

"Thanks, Amanda," I said. "I mean it."

At 9:00 a.m. the following morning, the agents on protective detail knocked on our cabin door and asked if I was ready to go. Agent Cross, who I remembered from his surveillance of Dr. Pickering at the lake said, "We have a car waiting that you can use to drive to your meeting this morning. I'll follow behind and keep watch to make sure that no-one is following or watching you."

"Thanks," I said.

The scenic drive to Riverside Park went by way too fast. I never grew tired of this part of the country, with its natural beauty. Entering the park, I pulled into the parking lot and saw only two other cars, one of which belonged to Kelly. I got out of my car and walked over to the trail entrance where she was standing, looking at a map behind a sheet of plexiglass placed under a wooden awning at the trailhead. She immediately recognized me and gave me a brief hug.

"It is good to see you, Dr. Banks," she said. "I love this park. The walkway along the river is one of the best walking trails I've encountered. It is just beautiful."

"I agree," I said. "It is one of my favorites too." I had to admit, it was the perfect day to be outside. The air was crystal clear and the sky a deep blue, with refreshing temperatures in the mid-60s. I almost forgot about the huge implications of this meeting and how it might shape the future lives of quite a few people.

After walking for about five minutes, and making small talk, Kelly stopped and looked over at me expectantly. She said, "Dr. Banks, what is it that you want to talk about?"

"OK, Kelly," I replied. "We have known each other for a few years now and I have absolute trust in you, so I'm going to tell you some things that you *must* keep in total confidence."

She merely nodded and said, "Of course." Knowing her so well, that was all the confirmation that I needed.

Over the next ten minutes, as we walked the scenic trail along the river, I provided her with a synopsis of my experiences, including the computer issues, my escape downriver, meeting up with Amanda, the attacks by the BRVM, and our return to Delray. I purposefully omitted the university's involvement in the drug ring. I was saving that for later. She asked a few questions but knew to avoid those which were obviously off limits.

I took a deep breath, and a leap of faith, and said, "Kelly, you told me before that you suspected something seriously bad was happening at the Institute and that you felt that Dr. Finch and Dr. Marshall were involved. I'm going to be straight with you on what I believe they are actually doing, and this will involve a level of trust beyond —"

Before I could finish the sentence, Kelly said firmly, "Of course."

I looked her in the eyes, nodded and proceeded to tell her about the conversation that took place between Howard, Patricia, and Anansi that was secretly recorded with the bug that I had placed under their table. I gave particular attention to their discussion of the campus-wide drug operation, and their participation in it.

When I had finished, Kelly looked back at me with a look of pure astonishment. A mischievous smile quickly took its place, and she said, "You bugged their office? That is fantastic! I'm so glad that you gave them a taste of their own medicine."

"What goes around, comes around," I said.

Kelly continued, "After what you just told me, I know one thing for sure. I won't be working there much longer. I think I'll put in my resignation today."

"Kelly," I said, "hear me out. We may need you to stay on just a bit longer if you are willing to help. Knowing they participate in a campus-wide drug ring, and make drug for money exchanges with a militia group, we need to know how this is occurring. My hypothesis is that the exchanges are being made through students working as researchers in the field, likely doing in person interviews, perhaps door to door in rural communities."

"That makes sense," said Kelly, "but I still can't believe this is happening. It's like a bad dream or watching an action thriller movie. I would love to see them come to justice, and it is just horrible that they would be involved in selling drugs to students and working with a criminal organization. What can I do to help?"

"We need a list of their current grants, who is involved, their roles, and the settings and populations of their studies, travel records, and any other records you can get without putting yourself in harm's way. This will hopefully provide us with some useful personnel and locational data."

"No problem," said Kelly. "I can pull it off the shared drive."

"Don't email it to me though," I said, "since we both know that our emails aren't private. I may have told you that, when I was doing equipment checks while serving as department head, I had seen where Dr. Marshall had her personal server connected to the college's server. I believe to this day that she is able to hook into both the hard drives and email accounts of anyone in the college."

Kelly replied, "I know what you mean. I highly suspect that is the case too. I'll get over there today and go into my office, close the door, and print out all the information. That way I won't leave an electronic trail. I can put the information in several envelopes and give them to you. Where are you staying? I can drop it by."

"Well," I said, "due to several attempts on my life, I am currently in hiding." Just then, a thought occurred to me. "You know Ted quite well, right? Just leave it in his home mailbox, and I'll pick it up there. I can't thank you enough."

"Sure," she said, "I should be able to copy the files when I get back to the office and will drop them in Ted's mailbox on my way home after work shortly after five."

We finished our hike and, after saying our goodbyes, I went to my car and called Ted. He answered and, as expected, expressed his concern, followed by smart questions that cut to the chase on what was happening. I answered his questions, at least those that I could, and told him about my meeting with Kelly. I also asked him for a favor — to call my parents and let them know that I was OK and would be in touch soon.

Later that day, around 5:30 p.m., I drove by Ted's mailbox and retrieved four sealed, very thick envelopes. I hoped the information contained in them would help us find the answers we needed to solve this riddle.

When I arrived back at the cabin, Amanda met me at the door with a look of unbridled anticipation. I smiled, handed her the folders, and said, "OK, Sherlock, let's make this mystery, history." A shake of her head and tight-lipped smile was her only response.

I put a pot of Japanese green tea on the stove and, a few minutes later, poured us each a cup, adding a touch of milk and honey. With Steele and Petrova busy running down their own leads, we would, for our part, begin analyzing the information that Kelly had provided.

Without looking up from the papers now spread across the large wooden table in the center of the room, Amanda said, "OK, now for some serious sleuthing."

Chapter 30

Sherlock

AMANDA MOVED a stack of papers aside to make room for her laptop, then fired it up and began her work in earnest. She loved this type of thing.

I left her alone as she worked non-stop, arranging papers, punching keys on her laptop, and looking back and forth between the printed copies and electronic information on her computer. She only stopped for a brief bite of dinner — one that our protection detail had kindly brought us.

Wanting to help, but knowing it was best to leave her alone, I stretched out on the couch as the evening wore on and unintentionally found myself entering a long, dreamless sleep. When I woke around 6 a.m. the next morning, I looked over to find Amanda asleep with her head on the desk.

Gently moving her to the couch, I covered her with a quilt, put a pillow beneath her head and kissed her on the forehead. During all of this, she never woke. I could only guess how long she had been up working on an answer to this riddle. I let her sleep while I made a cup of dark roast coffee and sat across from her in a comfortable chair. As I watched her sleep, I once again realized how beautiful she truly was, both inside and out.

She awoke about an hour later, wiping the sleep from her eyes and doing much as I had done earlier — trying to make sense of where she was, and why she was lying on the couch.

I said, "Hey, Sherlock, are you going to sleep all day?"

This earned me a dirty look, before she broke into a wide grin, and replied, "Some of us were up all night *working*, Mr. Rip Van Winkle."

I poured her a cup of the strong, black brew and brought over a plate of blueberry scones. As we munched on the scones and drank coffee, I asked, "So, what did you find?"

Amanda responded, "Patience, my good Watson. Let's move over to the table, and I'll tell you." I wanted her to get straight to the punchline, but I knew that she was methodical and would want to tell me the process. I also knew that understanding how she reached her conclusions would be important to the FBI. I sat back and listened.

"OK, Noah," she said with a beaming smile, which I took to be a good sign. "Let me start by explaining my methodology. First, I identified the Institute's current grant projects, as some were completed, while others haven't started yet. They are running quite the operation, and I can see how the university would be quite pleased with their productivity and funding success.

"Once I had identified the ongoing research projects, I looked for those that might meet our criteria of being suitable for a covert 'drug for money' exchange. As you know, most research work in the social sciences involves either primary or secondary data collection. As you also know, secondary data collection and analysis would involve work like analyzing websites or existing data sets. Since this type of work typically does not require travel to distant sites, I eliminated these projects from consideration. I believe there were six or seven of them.

"Next, and easy to eliminate, were the projects where surveys were conducted using online platforms. These can also be done without leaving the office, as the surveys are administered electronically to people who fill them out online. From there, data is collected and analyzed without the researcher having to leave the office. There were about a dozen of these types of projects.

"Since we are looking for projects that require researchers to work in the field, and travel to a remote location, what remained were two types of projects that fit the bill for projects in which the Institute was currently engaged.

"One type of project in their portfolio required travel to off-site locations to conduct intercept interviews. This, as you know, is where researchers go to a specific location in a public space and select people to interview at random or based on some predetermined criteria such as age, or gender. For projects in which the Institute was engaged, the setting was municipal parks and schools.

"We could rule out k-12 schools since that setting would be too risky for an exchange. I also ruled out parks for the same reason. While there might be some opportunity to make an exchange in a park if the right location was found, I believe that it would still offer too much exposure. These days, there are cameras everywhere in public spaces."

"That is a good point," I said. It did seem that one could go very few places without being observed. That was one reason I liked the river so much.

Amanda continued, "The other type of project in their portfolio, and one that would result in less exposure, required conducting interviews, door-to-door, of households in lower-income communities. They were surveying people about their perceptions of fairness in the provision of social services. What really caught my eye was that research staff were conducting interviews in communities across a four-state region

— Mississippi, Missouri, Kentucky, and Tennessee. It was also a longitudinal study, meaning that it would be conducted over a number of years."

"I would wager that we are on the right track then," I added, saying out loud what Amanda already knew. "And each state borders the Mississippi River *and* is within the BRVM's territory."

"Yes," said Amanda, adding, "and no-one would ever suspect them of wrongdoing or give the student researchers or their project a second thought."

"Right," I interjected again, "if the exchanges are associated with this project, it would literally be right under everyone's noses."

"Exactly," said Amanda. "A university sanctioned research project allows the perfect opportunity to move the money and drugs, as the police seldom pull over a government vehicle for random inspections, and even more rarely a university vehicle. Even if one of the Institute staff were pulled over for something like speeding, or running a red light, the odds that the authorities would search a university vehicle are slight."

Satisfied that we had likely identified the research project they were using as a cover for their illegal activities, I asked, "So, do we have any idea who they are most likely using as runners, and where they are most likely making the exchanges?"

Amanda smiled and replied, "Your former student Kelly was extremely helpful. She had printed off a spreadsheet with the names of the student workers and staff on all the Institute projects, with the name of the project, their role on the project, and the number of hours they worked per week. She also had travel records that I used for cross referencing."

"She is really good, isn't she," I said rhetorically.

"There seem to be four students that stand out. According to the timesheet records, it appears that Gary Young, a third-year doctoral student, Margaret Lewis, a second year doctoral student, and Fran Spencer and Rachel Rhodes, both master's students, work beyond the 20 hours per week they have recorded. I say this because even though they are on record — the official forms they submit and use in the event they are audited — for only working 20 hours per week as per university policy, cross referencing travel records shows that they would have to be working more than 20 hours, given the time and distance they would travel, in addition to the *unofficial* hours logged for field research activities."

"That is splendid work," I said, "but how does this help us understand where they are making the exchanges?"

"I'm glad you asked," said Amanda, again flashing me that amazing smile. "It doesn't show up unless you look across several documents. I don't think they ever expected anyone to look at them all together, nor all that closely."

"They probably wouldn't," I agreed.

"As I just mentioned, from the records, we know that these four students work the most hours and travel the most. Another spreadsheet gives a breakdown of specifically where each of them travel for this project. Their destinations are coded by zip code. When you look at the trips they take to certain zip codes, and then cross reference the time they spend there, something remarkable stands out. There are four separate zip codes that each of these students visit every other week, where they are logged for having stopped to conduct 'research activities' within the zip code area for approximately 30 minutes — *every* time they visit these locations."

"This isn't enough time to conduct their research," I said. "They would typically be spending multiple hours at each location collecting data. The time spent in those locations would likely vary some as well. Thirty minutes is enough time to make an exchange, if you include time allotted for waiting, and entering and exiting the place where the exchange is made. This *must* be it."

"I think we are on the right track," said Amanda. "Also, the time sheets indicate *when* they visit these locations. They each appear to make visits to one of the zip codes they are associated with every other week. If the pattern holds, they will make their next visits later this week."

"What time do they make these visits?" I asked.

"Again, according to the records, it appears as though the visits mostly last somewhere around 30 minutes and are logged as starting at 11:00 am."

"And the day?" I asked.

"Thursday," responded Amanda, "and if the pattern holds, their next visits will occur this week."

"That is awesome work!" Amanda," I said with admiration. "Now all we have to do is find out where these zip codes are located, and where *within* those zip codes the visits are taking place. If we look at the zip codes, perhaps something will stand out."

"I thought that I would save the fun part for both of us," said Amanda.

"OK then, let the sleuthing begin," I said as we both waited in anticipation to find out where these clandestine researchers were likely making the exchanges.

While I watched expectantly over her shoulder, Amanda performed a quick Google search by typing in each of the zip codes. Matching what Amanda had said earlier, the search results indicated that the zip codes were in four separate states — Mississippi, Missouri, Kentucky and Tennessee.

"They are really covering a lot of ground," I said.

"And their tracks," replied Amanda.

Amanda then pulled up each zip code separately, and we took a closer look using the map feature to see if they had any distinguishing characteristics or anything in common that might help us narrow down the location of the possible exchanges.

Peering at the computer screen like a psychic would a crystal ball, I said, "At first glance, it looks as though higher, middle and lower-income areas would all lie within the boundaries of these zip codes. These zip codes also encompass both rural and urban areas. This would make it easy for the Institute to cover its tracks, as there are lower-income communities — the population they are studying — within each of these zip codes."

"Notice," said Amanda, "that these zip codes all border, or are near the Mississippi River. This would put them in what should be the territory of the BRVM."

"Good point," I said.

"These are areas that are reasonably large, though," said Amanda. "I don't know how we could ever narrow down the location of a possible exchange well enough to be of assistance to the FBI."

"Maybe we could go there," I suggested, "and look for where they are conducting the interviews."

I knew this was a poor suggestion as soon as it left my mouth. Amanda seemed to know this too and remained silent. It would be like finding a needle in a haystack. We could also just give this information to the FBI and let them take it from here. They could put tracking devices on the vehicles and follow them to their destinations on Thursday, but the FBI would need to be in place at the destination before the exchanges occurred to properly execute a plan and make arrests with minimal resistance.

It looked like we had made substantial progress but had ultimately reached a dead end. We sat back from the computer screen in silence, our minds searching for some clue — any clue — that would lead us forward, but we came up empty.

After a few minutes, Amanda said, "Well Noah, at least we gave it the good ole' college try. We *have* made satisfactory progress though and provided the FBI with some valuable information that they didn't have before."

I decided to sit down, so I pulled up a chair next to Amanda. I kissed her on the cheek and said, "To get us this far was truly brilliant. You are one of a kind. There is something …"

I suddenly stopped talking and stared off into space, with Amanda shooting me a look of curiosity.

"Wait a minute," I finally said. "What did you just say a few minutes ago?"

She replied, "I said that at least we had made satisfactory progress."

"No," I said, as my instincts told me that something important was sitting at the outside edge of my consciousness.

"Well," replied Amanda, "I said that at least we gave it the good ole' college try."

With those words, the mists parted and the thought that had resided just outside my conscious mind suddenly emerged. "Amanda," I said excitedly, "I think you might have just given us the answer. Would you please pull up the maps of the areas where those zip codes are located again, this time with features and places labeled?"

When we pulled up the first zip code, I looked for the feature that would confirm my theory, and bingo, it was there. We pulled up the second and I found it again. My heart started to race as we pulled up the third. I found it again. The final zip code had one within its borders as well and confirmed my theory.

"Amanda," I said, "barely able to contain my excitement, each of these zip codes has a …"

"A college or university within the boundaries of the zip code," she said, before I could get it out.

Amanda was always one step ahead of me, but I was in no way jealous. I was elated.

"I just cannot believe that this is a coincidence," I said. "If I had to guess, the exchange is taking place on the campus of one of these universities in each of the four zip codes."

"And I would bet this is another way for them to cover their tracks," replied Amanda. "Given that there are peer institutions within these zip codes, they probably have colleagues at universities there who the students visit for legitimate reasons, like dropping off books, or research materials. They could even have colleagues who mentored their students, or who served on their thesis committees. It would be easy to make it look like legitimate business was conducted in the event they were ever audited, or anyone got nosey."

I added, "the faculty or other contacts there probably don't even know what is going on, but would be willing to say that, yes, they did meet with the students for legitimate reasons. And you are right, they may even be serving as members of the students' thesis committees, and perhaps even hold regular meetings with them after the exchanges are made. Faculty are usually blissfully unaware of the misdeeds of their colleagues and would rarely think that a student engaged in something unethical or illegal. It would provide the *perfect* cover."

"Still," I said, with a few unanswered questions remaining, "there are several universities in some of these zip codes. It may not be the largest one. Let me make a quick call."

I dialed Kelly's number, hoping that she was away from the office. When she answered and said that she was walking alone on the trail at Riverside Park, I felt relieved. I asked her if she knew the students we identified as most likely making the exchanges, and whether any of them had ties to universities out of state. Much to my delight, she told me that each of them had outside committee members at other universities, and they were all out of state. As luck would have it, each of the students had an advisor at a university in each of the four zip codes we had identified. I thanked her profusely and hung up. We now knew with a high degree of certainty where the exchanges were taking place.

Feeling on top of the world, I dialed Petrova's number. She answered immediately, and as before, put us on speaker so that Steele could join the call. Amanda told them what we had discovered, providing the suspected locations and times, and that the next visits were expected to occur this Thursday. She also explained the process we used in reaching our conclusions. Both agents agreed that the reasoning was sound and expressed their gratitude.

Steele said, "This is magnificent work. The FBI could use people like you. With this information, I think we have a good chance of finally making some real headway on this case. We have entered a critical phase of the operation and anticipate moving quickly. Dr. Banks, we have given this some thought, and would like for you to return to the office on Monday. Your unanticipated return will provide a distraction, and hopefully hold their attention, while we set up and execute our operation. Amanda, you can come and go as you please, but I would suggest waiting until Noah's colleagues know he is back. As always, Agent Cross, who is heading up the protection detail, will be close at hand. We'll be back in touch."

Amanda and I gave each other *high fives*, feeling both anxious and excited about what might happen next.

Chapter 31

Gotcha

ON MONDAY, I headed to campus and my office. Even though I was on leave and not teaching, I still had projects, papers, and work with students that needed attention. The FBI had provided me a laptop with enough security features to keep out even the most intrepid of hackers, even though the work that I was doing on it was entirely benign. They said that it was a necessary precaution.

I inserted myself at least partially back into my life of academia, having been met upon my return with about as much insincerity as I could stand. Believing that I had perished during the explosion at the dock, Finch, Patricia, and their cronies were all barely able to conceal their surprise, and disappointment, upon seeing me.

Finch was the first to come see me, walking up to the open door of my now spartan office with few personal items left to adorn it. He said, with a laughable attempt at candor, "So glad to see you. We heard about the little party on the lake and the terrible explosion. Rumor had it that you had been severely injured or killed in the blast. I am so glad that you are OK."

I had no words, so I just sat there dumbly, and looked at him. I then decided that I should feed him a lie for a lie and gave him my cover story. "Thanks," I said. "My father had been ill, and I went to visit him. Since I'm on leave, I didn't think that I needed to give notice."

"No, no, you didn't," replied Fitch. "I hope that your father has a full and speedy recovery." With that, he turned and walked away. I guess we had both had our fill of BS.

Keeping with my cover, I told the same story to others who asked. I felt bad about lying to my trusted colleagues, but I didn't have a choice. When asked where I was staying, I simply said that I was staying outside of town, which was true, until I found a new place to live, which was not true. I had no intention of living here once this was all over. The remainder of the day was uneventful, and I returned to the cabin and the welcome embrace of the woman I loved.

The earth turned and Tuesday morning came, and with it, a feeling of anxious dread. It made me sick to my stomach to return to campus. When Finch strolled up to my office door at 9 a.m., anger was added to the noxious brew of emotions flowing through me. Without knocking, Finch walked into my office and stood where he could see what I was doing on my computer. He lacked any semblance of tact or respect for others, so this minor invasion of my privacy would be expected of him.

I swiveled my chair around to face him and saw the smug look on his face. He said, "Would you have a few minutes to chat?"

"Sure," was my only reply.

He said, "We'll meet in my office." He waited for me to save what I was working on, and together we took the short trip down the hall.

We sat at the same table where I had placed the bug, affording me the opportunity to sit where I had planted it. I hoped to remove it if the opportunity arose.

Once we were seated, Finch asked, "Noah, would you like a cup of coffee or a bottle of water?"

"Sure," I replied. "I would like a cup of coffee."

Finch responded by getting up and leaving the room, giving me the opportunity to instantly search and find the bug that I had planted under the table during my last meeting here. I pulled it free and jammed it in my pocket just as Finch returned.

He said, "My doctoral student is getting it for you." We made small talk while we waited, and very soon, the student arrived with a cup of coffee in a Styrofoam cup. I could tell right away that it wasn't the good stuff that Finch usually had on hand for himself and guests he wished to impress. This had come directly from the student work area. It was lukewarm and black as pitch, with a stale, bitter and burnt taste. Tipping the cup and pretending to take a sip of the vile liquid, I thanked the student and set the cup aside.

Without preamble, Finch started our meeting by saying in his most solemn tone, "As one of my faculty, you know that I am highly sympathetic to your hardships, but we are all enduring some form of difficulty in one way or another. I'll say again, though as I'm sure you are aware, while we remain sympathetic to your circumstances, your earlier actions have left us with no choice but to continue the action against you for termination of employment *for cause*."

I noticed that he put additional emphasis on the words *for cause. How many times would he tell me this?* I thought to myself. It seemed to now be his mantra. I remained silent.

"How have things been going with drawing up your defense?" he asked with an evil glint in his eye. He was really enjoying this, believing that I didn't stand a chance.

I simply responded, "I've been working on it."

"Good, good," he replied. "The hearing has been set for three weeks from today in the Administration Building on the first floor. I really *am* pulling for you Noah. I know you are a good person, though a bit misguided, and I'm sure you will land on your feet when this is all over. I would recommend, however, that you take what you have learned from your experience here and apply it to your next job. Termination for *cause* is a serious offense, and will stay on your record, but given your past accomplishments, you should at least be able to find a part time teaching position at a community college, or maybe even some work assisting faculty on various projects. There are always options for someone with your abilities."

This was too much. I wanted to yank off his necktie and slowly strangle him with it while he begged for mercy, but thought better of it. I also knew something that he didn't. Once the FBI had completed their operation and come after him, *he* might be using that tie to strangle *himself.*

With our meeting adjourned, the obvious intent of which was to belittle and intimidate me, I went back to my office and sat down to think about something more pleasurable than defending myself against these idiots. My thoughts wandered back to the FBI undercover operation.

It was with great anticipation that I waited for the results. Steele had called yesterday and provided me with the basic outline of their plan. They would place undercover agents at the four universities — and on-campus locations — we had identified, and wait for the next exchanges.

I had met with Kelly again and asked her for the names of the student's advisors at these universities. She conducted a quick search and discovered their identities. Once we knew who they were, we went online and found the location of their offices. We then identified the visitor parking lot nearest to their offices. This helped narrow down the most likely locations on each campus where the exchanges would be made. To help pinpoint exactly where on campus the students would go, the FBI asked for — and were granted — permission by the court to covertly place tracking devices on the vehicles used by the Institute's project team.

Kelly had been helpful in this aspect of the operation as well. I had asked her to find out which vehicles were driven by the student staff members that we had identified. She knew each of them, at least by name, and with some discreet inquiries, was able to determine the vehicles they used.

I was ready to see them all come to justice, and Thursday came quickly.

At first light on Thursday morning, sitting in the loaner car at the far end of the parking lot, and wearing a hat and sunglasses to conceal my identity, I waited. It wasn't long before I saw the student researchers march to their respective vehicles carrying what I presumed to be legitimate research supplies and personal belongings, along with bags that I was certain contained wads of cash inside sealed envelopes.

I watched them leave the parking lot and called Steele. "They just loaded up the vehicles and left," I said.

"Good," was the one word reply.

Backing out of my parking space, I turned and, with a feeling of immense satisfaction, drove back to the cabin to wait with Amanda.

She had resumed her job at the accounting firm, but was working remotely. Given that her job in accounting allowed her to work from any location, she was able to work from the safety and comfort of the cabin. I had to admit that, although we both were taking it in stride, we were developing a bit of cabin fever — quite literally. Luckily, the cure for cabin fever would be coming soon.

Later that afternoon, my phone chimed with a call from Steele. When he answered, I could immediately tell by the tone of his voice that he had good news. I hit the button to put the call on speaker and laid the phone on the table in front of us. Steele got immediately to the point.

He said, "I have good news. Our undercover agents have been successful in apprehending the students and suspected militia members during an exchange of drugs for money. Fortunately, our agents were able to catch them in the act. It has all been done by the book, and we feel that the evidence obtained will hold up in court."

The tension in my body that had been there for so long, finally eased. It was funny how you often couldn't feel stress until it was gone. It was a good sensation but left me feeling numb. Amanda and I exchanged a brief smile.

Steele went on to say, "Please sit tight and do not leave the cabin or communicate with *anyone* electronically or otherwise until we give you the 'all clear.'"

"We understand," I said.

I thought he would hang up but instead he said, "Noah and Amanda, the FBI sincerely thanks you."

When the connection had ended, Amanda jumped in the air, pumped her fists, and shouted for joy. We embraced, and then danced around the cabin acting like we had just won the lottery.

Once we had finished our little celebration, Amanda shut down her computer and we turned our phones off. We decided to hand over all our electronics to the two agents protecting us, since we didn't trust ourselves to not go back online. It was just too ingrained in our psyches.

It turned out to be three days later, Sunday afternoon to be exact, before we heard back from Agents Steele and Petrova, but the wait, hiking, playing board games and reading books, had been well worth it.

Petrova took the lead on the conversation, saying, "Noah and Amanda, we hope you are doing well. We apologize for keeping you cooped up in that cabin, but we now have some news for you that we think you will want to hear."

"Thanks," I said, with anticipation building, "we are all ears."

"Let me start by saying that the recipients of the money for drugs, who we apprehended during the exchanges, were verified as members of the Big River Volunteer Militia. They are referred to as 'foot soldiers' for 'the cause.' Once apprehended, they were brought to an FBI field office where they were interviewed by our agents. Given their low rank in the organization, they told us, and we suspect they were being truthful, that they had never personally met Leroy Jones. They had only seen him speak at BRVM gatherings, and he was always surrounded by his security team. They also said that the word among the members was that he only spoke personally with his inner circle and top operatives.

"After some *convincing*, that included an offer to reduce their sentences in exchange for information, they finally gave up the location of two of the militia's compounds. Our agents raided them, fortunately with no casualties, and were successful in apprehending a number of BRVM members. Among those captured were a few of his top mission operatives, those hand-selected to carry out missions requiring absolute trust and certain military skills."

"Is it fair to say, then," I said, with a measure of disappointment in my voice, "that Leroy and most of his inner circle escaped?"

"That is a fair assessment," said Petrova. "There is good news though. Our agents were able to get one of his top mission operatives to flip in exchange for protection. Apparently, this guy had been to prison before and made some serious enemies. He was released before they put a shiv in his side. Obviously, he didn't want to go back."

"I would guess not," I said.

"He told us that he had served as a bodyguard for Leroy, and on one occasion had accompanied him to a private off-campus meeting with a 'Dr. Finch' from the university. He learned from that meeting about the 'drug ring' at the university and recalled hearing that a person named 'Dr. Marshall,' and another named 'Dr. Snow' were involved in the operation. He said that he remembered them saying something that made him believe that Dr. Snow was high up in the university administration. He is willing to testify to this at trial in exchange for his freedom and the opportunity to enter the witness protection program."

"Do you think that this will be enough, in addition to the recording that we have, to convict Drs. Finch, Marshall, and Snow, and their partners in crime?" asked Amanda.

Petrova responded, "The lawyers will know best, but they will assuredly use all the evidence that we can provide to our advantage. We also found, during our raids on the compounds, a cache of accounting documents that provide the times and dates of the transfers, as well as the amounts of money and drugs exchanged. There are notations in some of the documents that reference a 'Dr. Finch.' With evidence obtained from the raid, witness testimony, and other admissible evidence, we should have enough to convict. We also believe it to be highly likely that Finch and his crooked colleagues will flip on each other in exchange for leniency."

"So, what now?" I asked.

At this point, Steele took over and said, "We feel that we have enough evidence to arrest Dr. Finch, Dr. Snow, Dr. Marshall, Dr. Pickering, and Dr. Jackson. These are the big fish. There will likely be some smaller ones, but we'll start at or near the top. Would you like to help?"

"Sure" I said, feeling like I had just been asked if I would like to play a down in the Super Bowl. "What would you like for me to do?"

"This is not typical FBI protocol, but our superiors felt that, given all you have done for the agency, they would like to repay you in some way. I suggested that you may wish to be present for the arrest of your colleagues."

"You couldn't be more correct," I said, as a wave of eagerness coursed through me.

"Here is the plan. We don't believe that your colleagues know that we have apprehended the four students who work for the Institute, as well as the militia members, or that we have raided the compounds yet. Given the tap we have on his phone, we know that Dr. Finch is still in the dark on all of this. It looks like Leroy has gone to ground and left his cousin Howard hanging in the breeze. Also, the students told us that their supervisors didn't expect them back until tomorrow afternoon, and they weren't required to check in with them while they were out on their 'research assignments.'"

"The students," I asked, hoping they were innocent, "were they complicit in this?"

"From what we know so far," said Petrova, "unfortunately, we think so. We also think that it falls into a gray area, as they were certainly coerced. This should work in their favor during sentencing. They probably won't go to jail, but there still must be consequences for their actions."

"That makes sense, I guess," I said. Still, I had a heart for students, and it hurt me to know that their careers would be damaged.

"Anyway," said Steele, "we need to move fast for all the obvious reasons. We would also like to arrest your colleagues while they are all in one place. It is more efficient that way and ensures that no-one avoids capture. We will make the arrest of Dr. Snow in his office around the same time as we apprehend your colleagues. We need to do this tomorrow before noon, but the earlier, the better."

"It would make sense to try to get my colleagues together for a meeting, if you want them in the same place," I said. "Do you have any suggestions on how we can do that on such short notice?"

"We suggest that you bait them with something they can't resist, like telling them that you have information you would like to turn over in exchange for leniency in your termination proceedings. This should draw them in like bees to honey. See if they can make a meeting at 9 a.m. If this works, let us know, and our agents will coordinate this with the arrest of Associate Provost Snow."

"OK," I said. "I'll email them right now."

"Share their response with me as soon as you get it," said Steele before ending the call.

Chapter 32

Redemption

FORTUNATELY, MY EMAIL, sent on a Sunday, was received and read by Finch, and communicated to his colleagues. My hunch that he never fully stopped working, even on the week-end, was correct. I had baited the hook nicely, saying that I had in my possession, information that would be enlightening — not only to him, but also to Patricia, Anansi, and even Larry. With great satisfaction, he emailed back just 30 minutes later, saying that he had pulled the team together and they would expect me at his office at 9 a.m.

So, at 9 sharp, the following morning, I approached the office of Dr. Howard Finch with a mix of apprehension and anticipation. I hesitated, stole myself to what lay ahead, and knocked forcefully on the door. There was no response, even though our meeting was scheduled to begin right at nine. I could hear voices from within and knocked again, this time more forcefully. A few seconds later, the door was yanked open by a man who stood looking at me with a mixture of annoyance and disdain.

"Noah," said Finch, condescendingly, "can't you see that we are having a *private* conversation. I looked past him and, to both my pleasure and disgust, saw that all the ducks were in a row. Patricia, Anansi, Larry, and Finch were all there. It was a home run.

"I thought that we had a nine o'clock meeting," I said with as much authority as I could muster.

"Well," said Finch, our plans have changed. "We are meeting with Dean Winston, who is giving us advice on how to proceed on matters involving you."

Seated in a far corner of the table that was not visible to me when I first approached the door was Dean Winston. He looked my way with a blank stare.

"Even though you told us that you have information to share, the dean has recommended that we not speak with you regarding the termination proceedings, or any other matters related to your employment. He is arranging a meeting between you, him and the university attorney, Mr. Jim Sanford, for next Monday, and you can turn in whatever documents or other information you want to share at that time."

Little does he know, I thought to myself, *that by then, everything will look much different.*

"So, if you don't mind, please run along, and be considerate enough next time to respect our need for privacy while we are doing important university work."

Dr. Marshall looked up from her papers on the table and glared at me. With no attempt to be tactful, and in an glacial tone, she simply said, "Get out of here! Can't you see that we are busy."

"Actually," I replied, "I would like to say a few words to all of you."

"You can say a few words at the upcoming hearing," said Finch. "For now, you can leave before we call campus security."

With the confidence of knowing that I had serious backup, I pushed my way past Howard and into the room. Howard looked as if he was ready to try and push me out the door, but composed himself and said, "OK, let's hear what you have to say. But be quick about it. We need to get back to dealing with *important* matters in *private*."

I looked across the room, making eye contact with each of them, before posing a question. "What's more important than doing the right thing?" I asked.

They all looked at me with confusion on their faces.

"What do you mean?" asked Patricia. "We all want to do the right thing. That is why we are in higher education. I would hope that you have learned your lesson about knowing right from wrong after *your* indiscretions."

Howard stopped her. "Patricia, remember that we were instructed not to talk about issues related to Noah's hearing. There will be time for that soon enough."

"Actually," I said, regaining their attention, "I am not talking about me. I'm asking that question to *you*. I'll answer it for you though. *Nothing* is more important than doing that which is right. What is not right is being vindictive or hurting other people for the purpose of revenge, or to do these things to help oneself climb further up the ladder of success."

"Well, this is a nice lecture Noah, and of course we agree," said Finch, "but we have better things to do with our ..."

"But wait," I interjected, "I have more to say. And this will be a short lesson in knowing the difference between right and wrong. Let's start with the *wrong*. It is wrong to put incriminating information on a colleague's computer to frame them."

"You have no proof of that," said Howard, raising his voice. "We have already determined that it was the IT staff who did it, independently and without our knowledge. We —"

"Shut up!" were the next words that flew across the room, this time from Dean Winston. "Don't say a word, Howard. This advice comes straight from the university legal counsel."

Ignoring Dean Winston, I carried on, "It is wrong, I continued, and maybe you all will agree, to support and fund a criminal extremist militia group." I looked at each of my colleagues sitting at the table and said, slowly and deliberately, "Wouldn't you agree?"

At this comment, the looks on my colleague's faces turned from one of arrogance, to fear and suspicion. I also saw a hint of something sinister in their eyes. They were probably scripting multiple ways to end my life in the most painful way possible. Only Dean Winston held a different expression — as a look of confusion played across his face.

Playing his role to the end, Howard said, "What in the world are you talking about, Noah? I think that I'll need to call Campus Security now. You seem to be acting a bit unhinged." He made the comment with confidence, but made no move to go for his phone.

I forged ahead, speaking over Howard, and continued by saying, "It is wrong, and maybe you will agree with this Howard, to buy drugs from the Big River Volunteer Militia, run by your cousin Leroy Jones, aka Roy Johnson, and create a scheme within the university to sell these drugs to students whom you should be protecting, not hurting — and all of this to turn a profit."

At this comment, Howard's face turned from red to a purplish hue, and losing all control, he rushed toward me in a fit of rage. As he charged forward in the confined space, he tripped over Patricia's leg and fell face-first to the floor.

In the next instant, Steele and Petrova had burst into the room and were pulling his hands behind his back, securing them with zip ties. They did the same for Patricia, Larry, and Anansi. Larry was the only one to put up a fight, cursing and trying to push the agents away while proclaiming his innocence. His resistance only earned him a bloody nose, as he was slammed against the office wall. Dean Winston, his face ashen, and with his normal composure melted away, sat perfectly still with a look of unbridled fear on his face.

After reading them their rights, the agents led Howard, Patricia, Larry, and Anansi from the room and out the door, as if leading a parade, passing colleagues standing with mouths agape. On the way out the door, Steele said to them, "We are also putting your friend and accomplice, Dr. Amos Snow, in custody as we speak."

This was my moment, so I took advantage of it, looking each in the eye and saying in my most sarcastic voice, "I know that you all are just *misguided*. Please know that I am here to help. Even if it is just to have a shoulder to cry on. I'm sure you'll need it. Your cellmates might not be the compassionate types."

With that, I turned and followed them out, feeling better than I had in what seemed like ages.

After they had been put into FBI vehicles and driven away, Steele, Petrova, and I stood in the parking lot for a few moments, silently collecting our thoughts.

Steele broke the silence. "Noah, we still have some road left to travel. There will be a trial in due course, and the FBI will need you to testify. Do you think you will be up to it?"

"Of course," I said. "I wouldn't have it any other way."

"Protection for you and Amanda will be doubled," said Steele, "and the offer to put you both in witness protection when this is all over is still on the table."

"We'll play the 'witness protection offer' by ear," I said, "but we *will* take you up on the extra protection from now through the trial."

"That sounds reasonable," said Steele. "The trial will most likely take place in Federal District Court in Little Rock, so in addition to the protection detail, we will find a safe place for you and Amanda to stay during the trial. Until then, the world is your oyster. We have authority to provide you with the choice of location and hotel."

Be careful, I thought, *Amanda has expensive tastes.*

"And Noah," he said, "the trial will pass, and this will all eventually settle down. Just be patient and give it time to play out."

Chapter 33

Closure

STEELE WAS RIGHT. The trial did eventually end, and the matter did eventually die down. Amanda and I received additional protection from the FBI and had to move around some, but with Amanda calling the shots on accommodations, we never suffered. In fact, we never *even came close* to suffering.

The trial turned out to be everything that we had hoped, with Finch, Patricia, Larry, Anansi, and Associate Provost Snow each found guilty on various counts that included drug trafficking and conspiracy to commit murder. They would all be serving time in the penal system. Given plea deals, and their cooperation with the FBI, several of my crooked colleagues received reduced, or lighter sentences.

Finch, however, who had conspired with his cousin Leroy — or whatever name he was currently using — to have me removed from the face of the earth, would spend the most time in prison, as conspiracy to murder charges stuck most effectively to him. If he ever left prison, it wouldn't be until he reached a very old age. Acting arrogant and indignant throughout the trial, it was likely that, in his mind, as a true sociopathic, he never fully comprehended the fact that he had done anything wrong. Time housed with federal inmates would surely soften him up enough for a reality check, but one just never knew.

While the sentence might not have been strict enough, in my opinion, for Patricia, the humiliation and loss of power was an even greater punishment, as it was enough to drive her over the edge. This was evident throughout the trial, as she had to leave the courtroom often due to bouts of hysteria and acting out in fits of rage. After a thorough psychiatric evaluation, she was sentenced to serve her time confined to a psychiatric hospital surrounded by a fifteen-foot-high unclimbable fence. If her psychiatric condition during the trial and sentencing was any indication, it appeared that she would remain institutionalized longer term until her condition improved, if ever.

Dr. Snow had sat quietly throughout the proceedings, no doubt internalizing his fear and grief, and seeing not only an abrupt end to a once promising career in university administration, but a stint in a federal penitentiary ahead of him. His lawyers had bargained for, and were granted, a reduced sentence, along with the guarantee that he would be removed from the general prison population. His lawyers argued, with good reason, that since he had flipped on virtually everyone involved in the campus drug operation, he would not be safe if mixed with the other prisoners, where connections to the BRVM surely existed.

As for Dr. Pickering, he had a stress induced stroke and would also be serving his time in a psychiatric facility. With only his cognition affected, he shuffled past me after sentencing, repeating the words, as if a mantra, 'me tenured,' 'me tenured,' 'me tenured.' He would doubtless spend many years institutionalized, and who knows, maybe even in the same psychiatric facility as his colleague Patricia.

Anansi, true to form, turned on her colleagues to save herself, and was spared from serving time in prison. She had assisted the prosecution by providing records that demonstrated a direct link between the criminal activities of her colleagues and the militia. Under a favorable plea deal, she was sentenced to house arrest, put on probation, and required to provide community service and attend meetings on the dangers of drugs and addiction. She was also immediately fired from the university. It was likely that she would never work in higher education again. One less back-stabbing academic, I supposed, was a good thing.

I was not a vengeful person, but I had to admit that it was such sweet Karma to see my colleagues sentenced to time in prison after they had tried so hard to put *me* there. It was also great to see my crooked colleagues, after the jury read the verdict and later when sentencing was announced, shuffle past me with heads bowed in their orange jumpsuits, hands secured with zip ties, and in leg irons.

The students, since it was proved that they were coerced into making the exchanges, would not serve jail time, but would be required to perform community service. They were immediately expelled from the university for their part in the criminal enterprise, and would now have a criminal record. This would certainly put a serious damper on their career plans.

The FBI, acting on information obtained from Dr. Snow during plea bargaining, would be following leads to round up the faculty and students involved in the campus drug ring. I was pleased to know that the drugs they were distributing and selling, and which ruined lives, would no longer find their way to our students.

The trial itself was in some ways more satisfying than the outcome. To see the arrogance wash from Patricia's face, replaced by fear and despair — and resulting in a complete nervous breakdown as she came to grips with the fact that she could not escape culpability for her criminal acts — was deeply satisfying. Also, the opportunity to tell my story on the stand and detail the parts that added a few nails to the coffins of Howard and Patricia was extremely rewarding.

The defense attorneys, including the university counsel, I had to admit, were particularly good. Their clients had basically been caught dead to rights, and they still put up good arguments, although most were procedural in nature. The attorneys for the prosecution, however, were not only well prepared and exceptionally good at their jobs, but they also held all the cards. The FBI had done everything by the book, which made their job much easier. As such, they were successful in defeating the claims brought by the defense team, which gave them a clear path to fully prosecute all those responsible.

The university, for its part, just wanted to put the whole public relations nightmare behind them as quickly as possible. They were also on their heels from a civil suit that Gary brought on my behalf for defamation and retaliation. Gary, negotiating with the university from a rare position of strength, threatened a long discovery process that would bring out every sordid detail and drag the university through the mud for years to come if they didn't agree to his request for a large monetary settlement.

The university rarely caved or relented but given the criminal convictions of my colleagues who were, of course, university employees, — including Dr. Amos Snow, an *upper-level* university administrator — the fight had been taken out of them. They agreed to an out of court settlement to the tune of $75 million dollars. After taxes and expenses, including Gary's payment, I came away with close to $45 million.

I gave back a portion of my windfall to student mental health counseling services and a few other charities that provided opportunities for people with addictions to get clean and back on their feet. I also used some of the money to rebuild the cabin in the manner to which the love of my life, Amanda, had grown accustomed. It wasn't much bigger than before, but the furnishings and appliances were all top notch, and the materials used in the reconstruction were of the highest grade. I also had a bathhouse built near the river so that I could store my new kayak and change clothes in style whenever we visited.

The remainder of the settlement money was managed by a financial professional and friend, Steve, who was more than happy to manage my millions.

I also took Steele and Petrova's advice and made myself scarce. Only, I didn't go into witness protection and live in a nondescript house on a nondescript street hidden away in suburbia. Neither Amanda nor I wanted to live like that.

Where Amanda and I lived for now was high on a ridge on the island of St. John in the Virgin Islands. The place had an amazing view and provided easy access to a secluded cove that was perfect for swimming and snorkeling, or just lying about in the warm sun. We were both developing nice tans and, with swimming, hiking, and jogging, were staying healthy and fit. There was also a tiki bar not far down the road, where we would meet mariners and tourists gathering for drinks in the waning light of day.

Our new home was as close to perfection as one could get. It was also a suitable place to hide, given that any of the *BRVM boys* who might discover our location and come for us would stand out like a sore thumb on the island. At any rate, it was about as safe a place, and as nice a place, as we could find to hide out and enjoy life.

The university had halted the termination proceedings against me, and had instead, in a complete reversal — and in an obvious effort to save face — offered me the opportunity to return to Delray as faculty, or even in an administrative role. Who knew, perhaps I could return as dean since Winston was on his way out.

Even though there was no direct evidence that he knew about, or had been involved in wrongdoing, Winston had stated his intention to resign under the premise that he wanted to spend more time with family. In truth, he was being forced out because, as dean, he was ultimately responsible for what happened under his watch. There was just too much noise in the system for him to stay. Ted had told me, though, that he heard through the grapevine that Winston might be coming back to oversee academic advising for student-athletes. Sometimes bad pennies just keep turning up, I suppose.

In response to the offer to return to Delray, I told the provost that I would need some time to consider it, throwing in a demand for a year of paid leave. I didn't really need the money, but what the heck, it felt good to make them pay, and the health benefits were nice.

Deep down, though, I was hesitant to go back to Delray University, or perhaps to academia at all. As it stood, I was just too jaded. Anyway, I would at least have to wait until they caught Leroy and we could return without fear of his vengeance. I knew that it would also be wise to wait until things settled down some, given that my reputation had been thoroughly smeared.

I had the luxury of time, though, to think things through and ponder my future as I looked out on the Sir Francis Drake Channel at the deep blue waters and magnificent beauty of the sunlight playing on the waters of the Caribbean.

To my side, was another beauty, Amanda, with the sunlight reflecting the colors of the rainbow off her large diamond engagement ring.

Man, life was good!

Dr. Spengler has achieved success as a bestselling nonfiction book author in higher education for over two decades. He is also a seasoned former university professor and administrator, having served at two large research universities - rising through the ranks from assistant to full professor, and on to serve in university administration. As an author of fiction, Dr. Spengler draws upon a perspective gained from working *behind the curtain* in academia to create thrillers set in higher education that are certain to entertain readers from all walks of life.

CPSIA information can be obtained
at www.ICGtesting.com
Printed in the USA
BVHW092115280622
640819BV00010B/672